A LACK OF
TEMPERANCE

A LACK OF
TEMPERANCE

ANNA LOAN-WILSEY

KENSINGTON BOOKS
www.kensingtonbooks.com

KENSINGTON BOOKS are published by

Kensington Publishing Corp.
119 West 40th Street
New York, NY 10018

All Kensington titles, imprints, and distributed lines are available at special quantity discounts for bulk purchases for sales promotion, premiums, fund-raising, educational, or institutional use.

Special book excerpts or customized printings can also be created to fit specific needs. For details, write or phone the office of the Kensington Special Sales Manager: Kensington Publishing Corp., 119 West 40th Street, New York, NY 10018. Attn. Special Sales Department. Phone: 1-800-221-2647.

Kensington and the K logo Reg. U.S. Pat. & TM Off.

ISBN-13: 978-0-7582-7634-6
ISBN-10: 0-7582-7634-6

First Kensington Trade Paperback Printing: October 2012
10 9 8 7 6 5 4 3 2 1

Printed in the United States of America

To Brian,

for everything

Temperance:
moderation in all things healthful;
total abstinence from all things harmful.

—XENOPHON, 400 B.C.

CHAPTER 1

It was chaos. Several whiskey barrels had been left smashed and blazing in the middle of the road. Stray dogs fought over a pile of refuse on the side of a building. Despite the late hour, I had to dodge crowds of spectators milling about on the sidewalks, all curious bystanders like me. Dozens of women with placards reading WE SERVE THE TYRANT ALCOHOL NO LONGER and 'TIS HERE WE PLEDGE ETERNAL HATE, TO ALL THAT CAN INTOXICATE marched in a loose configuration, shouting taunts. Several others actually brandished hammers and axes. Most wore sky blue sashes tied at their waist, and all were hatless. I plunged into the crowd of women. Could it be that some of the demonstrators had only a few hours ago waved and laughed at me from a tally-ho coach? They seemed frightening figures now as they began to sing in unison.

Who hath wounds without a cause?
He who breaks God's holy laws;
He who scorns the Lord divine,
While he tarries at the wine.

Who hath redness at the eyes?
Who brings poverty and sighs?
Unto homes almost divine,
While he tarries at the wine?

Touch not, taste not, handle not:
Drink will make the dark, dark blot,
Like an adder it will sting,
And at last to ruin bring,
They who tarry at the drink.

I fought my way through the marchers and settled against a pillar on the porch of a dry goods store. Several men, reeking of whiskey, leaned against the shuttered store window, the gaslight flickering on their shadowed faces. A gang of children, with their feet dangling over the side, lined up along the porch with their backs to me, as if ready to watch a circus parade. All eyes were directed at a squat, unpainted, wooden one-story building across the street, the Cavern Saloon. A small solitary female figure, as if on cue, appeared in a window, waving a hatchet above her head from *inside* the saloon. The barroom's sign, a yellow geyser of foaming ale, swung above the door in counterpoint to the woman's waving arm. My first impression of the scene had been right; the world had gone topsy-turvy.

"Home wrecker!" she screamed as she brought the hatchet down.

The windowpane exploded outward, raining glass in all directions. Instinctively I threw up my hands. The dogs scattered in opposite directions, one with two links of sausage dangling from its mouth. A bystander dropped into the dirt screaming, covering her face. A man in a top hat raced over to her aid.

What am I doing here? I wondered why I had ever left the comfort and luxury of my room. I never should've come down here when I heard that shout of "fire."

A shouting contest between the marching women and several bystanders began as the figure in the window was grabbed by other larger silhouettes and lifted from view. They reappeared moments later in the doorway. It was almost comical. Three men between them carried a nymph of a woman, and still she had an arm free with which she whacked her assailants with a cane.

"Get the police," one of the men shouted.

They made the mistake of setting her down. With a hard rap on one man's head and another on a second man's knee, the tiny woman freed herself and ran back into the saloon.

"Get out of here, you crazy woman!" someone shouted from within.

She reappeared moments later in the doorway, with a lighted lamp above her head.

"The righteous will prevail," she proclaimed. "Evil will burn eternal."

"She isn't really going to do it, is she?" I said out loud to no one in particular. Several worried faces nodded in reply.

There was a collective hush in the instant before the woman smashed the lamp to the floor and disappeared in a plume of smoke. As men streamed into the saloon to contain the rising flames, two women, dressed entirely in sky blue, emerged from inside. They looked appalling. Brown and yellow splotches covered their dresses. One woman's sleeve had been rent off at the shoulder; the other's hem dragged behind her. Each carried a hatchet in one hand and an arm of the tiny window-smashing arsonist in the other, dragging her from the burning building and across the street. A third woman in blue raced from the saloon and joined them.

Is that the woman I met this afternoon? It couldn't be.

For several minutes, my view was obscured by the temperance supporters who gathered around the women, shaking hands and patting each other on the back. *Who is this woman at the center of the chaos and destruction? What kind of person goes around vandalizing saloons at night?* I pressed into the crowd for a better look.

She wasn't what I expected. Guarded on all sides by her associates in blue, she loomed large for her petite frame, wearing a black dress and black turban hat with veil netting that had ripped in two places, and she was old, very old, with white hair and skin that was wrinkled and sun-spotted. Her high-necked collar accentuated a mark on her face, either a birthmark or smoke ashes, which extended from her right ear across her entire cheek. She gasped for breath, and her knuckles were white from clenching her cane. Her stooping shoulders gave the impression that her body was frail, but we were all witnesses to that deception. She looked up and caught me gaping at her. Her face was flushed and her eyes were piercing blue, but she seemed dazed and unable to look me in the eyes for long. She wasn't like any old woman I'd ever met before.

"It's the police," someone shouted.

Whistles blew as a police wagon parted the people milling about in the street. Two of the younger women immediately lifted the old woman easily to her feet. One of them grabbed my arm briefly for support. Only then did I realize, to my horror, that the brown splotches on the women's dresses were blood.

"We've got to get Mother Trevelyan to safety," one of the women in blue said to her companions.

Mother Trevelyan?

I nearly shouted after them that there must be some mistake. I watched, aghast, as three bedraggled figures in blue escorted my new employer down the street.

CHAPTER 2

I should've suspected something was amiss earlier that afternoon when I had arrived in town. A porter, his shoulder wedged against an overloaded cart, barely missed running over my hem as I stepped from the train. Two squealing children ran past me into the crowd. Countless invalids being pushed in chairs or leaning on crutches mingled seamlessly with the more mobile travelers about me. I stood on the platform, shielding my eyes from the late-afternoon glare, and stared at my fellow passengers. *What kind of place is this?*

I gazed up into the shadows towering above at the sweet gum and oak-covered hillsides, at the colorful leaves still tenaciously clinging to the branches, at rocky outcrops promising a few new specimens for my collection. I was already looking forward to my first hike. But that would have to wait. Brimming with the excitement and anticipation that always came with a new engagement, I adjusted my gloves, brushed my new suit for soot, straightened my new bonnet, and stepped off the platform.

Weaving through the flurry of one-horse gigs, buggies, and

buckboards loaded with crates and burlap sacks that crammed the depot yard, I made my way toward the public omnibus. As I waited in line for the bus, I pulled out my book, opening it to chapter 3: *Wild flowers and where they grow.* I'd read two pages on the family Compositae when a humped old woman in an old-fashioned black bonnet interrupted me.

"Are you here for the springs?"

"The springs? What springs?"

"What springs?" The old woman cackled, poking me with the walking stick she clutched between two knotted hands. "Oh, my, that's clever, miss, this being Eureka Springs and all. Yes, very funny." She stopped laughing when she realized I hadn't been joking. "Oh, you really aren't here for the springs, then, are you?"

"No, I'm sorry. I'm not. Are you?"

"Oh, my, yes."

She pointed to a man at the end of the line, leaning heavily on a crutch, and to the woman in line ahead of me, wearing a very fashionable small bonnet of blue felt with a green velvet bow tied under the chin. I fluffed the ostrich feathers on my straw hat self-consciously while staring at hers in envy.

"Most of us here are," the old woman said. "I've heard the waters can cure anything."

That explained the invalids I saw. They all thought they'd be cured by drinking water. The idea made me a bit uneasy.

"I've been plagued by the summer-complaint, and here it is November." The old woman stared at my face, then down at the book in my hands. "You should try it. The waters are also known for helping folks relax."

I closed my book. "Thank you, but like I said, I'm not here for the springs."

"Then maybe you're here for the temperance rally?" the old woman said.

"I'm here for the springs," a raspy voice behind me said.

We both turned toward the lady in the blue felt hat. I could now see she wore a patch over her left eye. Poor woman, I thought. And to think I was jealous of her hat.

"Oh yes, I'm blind in this eye. It's completely crusted over." She pointed to the patch.

Her hand trembled from the effort. "An uncle had the same condition, but worse. Both eyes were glued shut. He looked like a sea creature, as if his eyelashes were encrusted in rime and barnacles." She shivered slightly. "But he stayed three months, used Crescent, Johnson, and Oil water, and came back a cured man."

"Will you also be attending the ladies' temperance convention, then?" The old woman pointed to a button on the blinded lady's lapel. With a sky blue background, which I would later learn was the official color of the American Women's Temperance Coalition, representing purity and heaven, the button read *AWTC* in black capital letters. "I'm not a member, but I've timed my visit here in hopes of attending a few meetings and the Saturday-night rally."

"I am a member." Crimson rising in her cheeks, the blinded woman lowered her voice. "I'm ashamed to admit it, though, since I'd forgotten all about the temperance convention until I read about Mrs. Trevelyan in this morning's newspaper. They can slander her all they want, but that there's a God-fearing woman for you."

"Amen to that," the old woman exclaimed. "Someone on the train read me that article in the Cassville paper. That's the third saloon smashed in a month. I hope I catch a glimpse of her at the rally. You don't think the police will prevent her from attending, do you?"

Slander? Police? *And I thought working for Captain Amsterdam was a challenge.*

"You're not suggesting that Mrs. Trevelyan . . . ?" I said.

"Don't worry; the righteous . . . will . . . prevail."

The blinded lady faltered in her reply as her attention was drawn to a black man in a rumpled floppy felt hat who stomped in our direction. He deftly avoided the infirm as he navigated the crowd.

"You Hattie Davish?" he demanded.

"Yes, I'm Miss Davish."

"I've a wagon waiting."

"Thank you, but I'll ride the bus." As I turned toward the approaching omnibus, the man stepped in front of me, blocking my way. "Excuse me," I said, trying to keep the alarm out of my voice.

"No, I'm to take you to the Arcadia," the man said as he grabbed my suitcases and hatboxes.

"Not this," I exclaimed, clasping the handle as he attempted to yank my typewriter case away from me. People in line turned to see what the commotion was.

"Are you all right, miss?" the old woman asked.

"Mrs. Trevelyan arranged it," the man said. "Now, if you don't mind?" He motioned for me to follow him.

I nodded tentatively to the old woman. After a quick glance over my shoulder at the people boarding the omnibus, wishing I were among them, I followed the man to a four-passenger depot wagon, parked behind a tally-ho coach. Hitched to four horses, the tally-ho carried at least a dozen animated women. The driver flung my luggage onto the top of the wagon. He stood by as I clambered into the vacant passenger compartment, then climbed into the driver's seat in front of me, all the while scowling at the boisterous women in the overloaded tally-ho.

"Every year there's more of you anti-liquor ladies." He turned his head and spat. "Like a horde of deer flies, never leaving an honest fellow alone. Why do y'all have to come here, stirring up trouble, anyway?"

"You're mistaken," I said. "I'm not an 'anti-liquor lady.' "

"Yeah, well . . ." The driver spat again, and then sat quietly for a moment, a crease forming on his brow. "But, ah, if I'm picking you up for that Mrs. Trevelyan, I thought . . ."

"Mrs. Trevelyan is my new employer," I said, tapping on the case in my lap. "I've never even met her."

The wagon lurched forward and we started toward town. Unlike cities that have convenient downtown locations, the train depot in Eureka Springs was situated at the far northeast corner of town, the closest parcel of flat ground the Eureka Springs Railway Company could find. Several minutes of silence had passed when the driver, pointing with his thumb behind him, said, "Ah, sorry about that there, ma'am."

His reaction to Mrs. Trevelyan and the other temperance ladies had added to my rising anxiety, so I was grateful to clear the air. I leaned forward and extended my hand. "Apology accepted, Mr. . . . ?"

He switched the reins to return my handshake. "It's Thomas."

The wagon passed a cluster of people gathered near a curving rock wall. I craned my neck to look back. "Was that one of the springs, Thomas?"

He nodded but was distracted. I was still leaning out the window when the driver started shaking his head. "I hate to be the one to tell you this, ma'am. I mean, it's too bad you had to come all this way to learn the truth."

"What truth, Thomas? I don't understand." I pulled back from the window.

"Working folks can't expect a lot from the likes of them. Someone might've had the common decency to warn you." *Warn me? About what?* "They could've wired you so you didn't have to waste your time."

"But I did receive a telegram from Mrs. Trevelyan, two days ago. See? Here it is." I pulled it from my handbag and read its contents for the third time.

THE WESTERN UNION TELEGRAPH COMPANY
NUMBER *23*   SENT BY *HF*   REC'D BY *DC* CHECK *20 paid*
RECEIVED at *No. 14 Broadway, Kansas City, MO Nov 4* **1892**
Dated: *Eureka Springs, AR*   *11:14am*
To: *H Davish   Larson Boarding House Kansas City*

Your services required recommended by Windom-Greene
expect you Sunday on four ten all arranged
Mrs. E. Trevelyan

"So here I am, at the exact time and place that she re-quested." Thomas brought the depot wagon to a sudden halt. As I was thrown forward, I grabbed my typewriter case so it didn't fly off my lap.

"But don't you see, ma'am," he said, twisting back to face me. "The lady might not even be here anymore. And she sure ain't gonna need a secretary where she's going."

Thomas's comment brought back the conversation I was having at the depot before he arrived. I wished I'd had a chance to question the women in line about Mrs. Trevelyan. They seemed to know more than I did.

"Then why did she hire me and tell me to meet her here?" I asked.

Thomas spat over the side of the wagon, barely missing the flanks of the tally-ho's lead horse as it pulled abreast of our wagon. The tally-ho's driver scowled at Thomas, but the tem-perance women, oblivious to the incident, continued to sing and laugh and joke. Several women waved as the tally-ho took the hill before us. I waved back, some of my initial exhilaration returning.

"That's my point, ma'am," Thomas said. "You shouldn't have come in the first place."

CHAPTER 3

The Arcadia Hotel wasn't at all what I'd expected. After traveling on the train for hours through empty countryside, the grand scale of the hotel took me by surprise. Nestled on the top of a mountain, overlooking "the Springs," even from a great distance, it dominated the skyline of the town. I caught glimpses of it through the trees as we drove up the wide carriage road that wound toward the top of the mountain. It was a five-story limestone building with a gray slate roof, a lookout tower, and too many chimneys to count. Verandas surrounded the second and third floors. From what I could tell, the hotel afforded a spectacular view of the village and valley below.

"At least you get to stay at the Arcadia."

Thomas, who wouldn't say another word about Mrs. Trevelyan, didn't have the same reservation about describing the hotel he worked for. According to him, the dining room served the finest food, the baths were unsurpassed, the service was renowned. They included a daily supply of bottled water, from any spring in town, on demand.

". . . and there's no less than three different springs being pumped into the bathing rooms. Of course there's steam heat in every room. Even the servants' quarters have electric lighting and indoor plumbing; the whole works," he said. "There are dozens of hotels and boarding houses in town, ma'am, but the Arcadia is the best. And it's not just me saying so. I've heard it's as good as any of those fancy hotels out East."

As we crested the hill, the forest opened up to reveal the hotel, resplendent in its row of flags across the front, immense gold-leaf painted clock, and meticulously manicured parkland, complete with stables, lawns, and gardens, radiating out in all directions. It was breathtaking.

And I'm to be staying here?

I caught a glimpse of an arbor-covered staircase going down the hill. A large fountain with marble statues dominated the center of a circular drive and sparkled in the last rays of the setting sun. Two hatless women sat on a wall encircling the fountain, laughing and dipping drinking cups into its basin.

Thomas helped me out of the wagon. I stepped down onto a red carpet that led up a long flight of stairs, passing over a wide front portico filled with rocking chairs, and ended at tall double entrance doors. The front portico was empty except for a white-haired man smoking a pipe.

"Is there a servants' entrance, Thomas?" I asked.

"Not for you, ma'am. You're a guest here now."

"Oh, no, I couldn't. That wouldn't be proper."

A bellboy hovered around the entrance. He had flaming red hair that clashed with his uniform and brimless cap. He scurried over to collect my luggage as Thomas retrieved my typewriter case.

"Just so you know, Owen," the driver said, gesturing with his thumb toward the approaching tally-ho laden with women I'd seen at the depot, "she ain't one of them." Then he tipped his hat. "Enjoy your stay, ma'am." He was shaking his head as he mounted the wagon and drove away.

"Right this way," Owen said. His free arm directed me toward the front doors. I walked up the stairs, amazed at the sudden turn in events. Two days ago, I was in Kansas City at Mrs. Larson's Boarding House for Single Women, wondering what to do on my first day off in years. Today, I was at the Arcadia Hotel in Eureka Springs, Arkansas, the most luxurious hotel west of the Mississippi River.

Standing here, it was difficult to believe what they had said at the train station about my new employer. The woman as described wouldn't be welcome at such a highly respectable hotel. Besides, Sir Arthur wouldn't recommend me to someone of questionable character. Granted, I haven't enjoyed every assignment that he has generously provided for me, but such is the working life. I'm grateful for his patronage, and I know how fortunate I am. I have always been able to rely on his sound judgment. Otherwise I might never have accepted this assignment, sight unseen, no matter how marvelous the accommodations.

"After you, ma'am."

I hadn't realized I'd been blocking the entrance. The corner of my suitcase pressed into my back as the bellboy, a few steps behind me, guided me through the open doors into the opulent hotel lobby. The chandelier's crystal prisms in the high ceiling above were catching the setting sun, casting sparkling light across the expansive wooden inlay floors. The inside of the hotel was as impressive as the outside. I felt out of place and hastily tried in vain to contain the wisps of chestnut hair that hung loosely about my face.

A massive fireplace dominated the rotunda. Made of limestone brick, the hearth was six feet wide and loomed large enough for a person to stand in. Thick Persian rugs were laid out throughout the lobby. A cluster of plush-looking couches, armchairs, and rocking chairs spanned out in a wide semi-circle. Several men, all reading the evening newspaper, sat with their feet propped up, availing themselves of the small fire burning in the hearth.

"May I?" I asked one of the gentlemen, pointing to a copy of the *Cassville Democrat* next to him on the table.

"Be my guest, young lady."

Scanning the headlines and shifting through Cassville's society pages, I could find no mention of a temperance rally. Instead, news and commentary on the upcoming elections filled the pages. Nor did I find anything more enlightening than a mention of Mrs. Trevelyan in a snippet about broken windows at a local barroom. The owner had insinuated "that temperance woman" was "not all she claimed to be." This must be the "saloon smashing" the old woman at the depot had alluded to. Had I been needlessly anxious after all?

Beyond the fireplace, a series of French doors opened onto a smaller version of the front portico. Several women, with sashes of sky blue tied at their waist, emerged from the parlor on the right, singing.

> *Who hath sorrow? Who hath woe?*
> *They who dare not answer no;*
> *They whose feet to sin incline,*
> *While they tarry at the wine.*

> *Who hath babblings, who hath strife?*
> *He who leads a drunkard's life;*
> *He whose loved ones weep and pine,*
> *While he tarries at the wine.*

The men around the fireplace looked up and frowned as one when the women approached. Without a sideways glance at the stares directed their way, the women passed me and continued singing right out the front door.

The chime of an elevator bell to my right drew my attention away from the temperance women to an elegant couple gliding down the broad stairway. I brushed the front of my jacket and readjusted a cuff. They passed without acknowledging me and, following the aroma emanating from my left, disappeared down the hallway.

The bellboy dropped my luggage with a thud.

"You check in at the desk over there," he said. "Ring the bell when you're ready."

The office was tucked away in the corner of the room. The registration desk, extending a half a dozen feet and covered with swirls of intricate carvings, had a locked brass mailbox at one end and a bell at the other. Pigeonhole shelves lined the back wall. I walked over to the desk and lightly tapped the bell. A man with a stoic countenance and a bald pate appeared out of a back room and asked for my name.

"Miss Hattie Davish," the clerk repeated as he flipped through a registration book. "Ah, yes, here it is." Turning his back to me, he took a key and a packet of letters from one of the pigeonholes. He handed them both to me. "Welcome to the Arcadia, Miss Davish. You'll be staying in room 220."

"Excuse me, but I think there's been a mistake. I'm not here as a guest, as everyone seems to think, but as a secretary and personal assistant to Mrs. Trevelyan. A room in the servants' quarters will be quite adequate, I assure you."

"There's no mistake, Miss Davish. Mrs. Trevelyan left strict instructions. You're to stay in the room adjacent to her own; Mrs. Trevelyan is next door, in room 218. And you're to assume responsibility for her correspondences immediately upon arrival. She'll provide further instructions when she sees fit." He indicated the packet that he had just handed me with a tilt of his chin. "Seeing that there's no mail today, those are all telegrams and hand-delivered letters. Yesterday's mail is already in your room."

I looked back at the opulence of the lobby and the men around the fireplace. Was one of them staring at me? "I don't feel comfortable with these arrangements. Don't you think it's inappropriate for me to stay with the guests," I looked at the clerk's name tag, "Mr. Oxnard?"

"I'm sorry, miss, but these are your instructions. Mrs. Trevelyan won't have you mingling with the servants." The clerk snapped the registration book shut. "You're gonna have to stay in a guest room."

"May I ask if Mrs. Trevelyan is still staying at the hotel?"

The clerk squinted and knitted his brow. "Didn't I already say, Miss Davish, that she's staying in room 218?"

"Yes, of course. Thank you, Mr. Oxnard." Again some of my fears had been alleviated.

Then what was Thomas talking about?

"Mrs. Trevelyan?"

As the bellboy deposited my luggage in my room, I saw a woman go into room 218 down the hall. I knocked on the door. No reply. I knocked several times harder than was polite, and the door opened slightly.

"Mrs. Trevelyan?" I repeated as I peered inside. A small table lamp illuminated the cool yellows, blues, and reds infused throughout the lavish room, in the floral wallpaper that had flecks of gold leaf paint, in the wall-to-wall Belgian carpeting, in the velvet-cushioned chairs, in the brocade counterpane on the walnut four-poster bed, and in the inlay on the mahogany wardrobe, which stood eight feet tall against the wall. Machine-turned oak moldings surrounded the doors, windows, and ceiling, complementing the large oak desk. Only a large, well-worn steamer trunk in the middle of the room seemed out of place. A blond woman in her early thirties, only a few years older than me, was retrieving something from the back of the wardrobe. She was oddly attired in a completely sky blue dress and matching hooded cape, a faux pas for this time of day and so late in the season.

"Mrs. Trevelyan? I'm sorry. The door was ajar." The woman quickly hid something in her cape before turning around. Her curving hips and ample bosom swayed as she walked toward me standing in her open doorway. Despite her size, she glided across the room as if she were balancing a book on her head. Two scars, on her left cheek and chin, were all that marred her plump, round face. She held a Bible in her hand.

"I'm Hattie Davish, ma'am. I hope this isn't an inopportune time, but I've only just arrived."

"Oh, dear, no, I'm not Mother Trevelyan. You've missed her by a quarter of an hour. I am Mrs. Josephine Piers." She offered me her soft, manicured hand. "So you're the one Mother Trevelyan sent for? Well, Miss Davish, I've never met a professional lady typewriter before, though I hear you come highly recommended."

"I assure you that I'm more than a typist. As a trained private secretary, with extensive experience serving clients such as herself, I'd stake my reputation on exceeding Mrs. Trevelyan's expectations."

"Of course you would. Still, it's a shame. You came all this way for nothing. Mother Trevelyan doesn't require your services."

"Why do you say that, Mrs. Piers? The depot wagon driver said so as well, but the desk clerk assured me Mrs. Trevelyan is still staying at the hotel."

"Of course she's still staying at the hotel. Where would she go? No, no, you misunderstand me. I'm Mother Trevelyan's secretary now, and have been for almost two weeks. After that dreadful woman eloped, I humbly volunteered my services to the cause. I told Mother Trevelyan that she needn't send for you. Divine intervention brought me to her and the coalition, and I feel blessed to serve."

"I admire your charity, Mrs. Piers, but Mrs. Trevelyan has already paid me a week's wages in advance."

"That's all right. You keep the wages." She took my chin in her hand and turned my head one way and then another, scrutinizing my face. "Look at those dark circles, such a shame for one with such expressive hazel eyes." I glared at her in consternation. "And I'd stay out of the sun. You're getting freckles."

Releasing my chin, she inspected me from head to toe. "And you're so thin. You could obviously use a holiday. When was the last time you had a day off? Poor girl. Obviously God was at work bringing you here. Enjoy the spas. Attend our meetings. A drink from the springs will refresh your soul."

"Thank you, but I'm here to work."

She shrugged her shoulders. "I didn't mean to offend you. I only meant that I reap great joy from helping the cause. It's God's work. So take a much-needed vacation." She reached for the packet of letters under my arm. "I'll take care of that now." I took a step back.

"I'm sorry, Mrs. Piers. But my instructions are to assume responsibility of her correspondences. Until I hear otherwise from Mrs. Trevelyan herself, I'll do what I was paid to do. Now would you be kind enough to tell me where I can find Mrs. Trevelyan?"

Calm down.

I stood in the middle of my room with my eyes closed and took a few deep breaths.

"Un, deux, trois . . ." Counting in French to relax was a

trick I'd learned as a child. *"Trente-huit, trente-neuf, quarante."*
Reaching forty with no effect, I gave up.

In a burst of frustration, I flung my key, purse, gloves, and
jacket to the floor. I unpinned my hat from my hair, and then
tossed it on the bed. With her kindness, Mrs. Piers had touched
a nerve.

*I don't need a vacation. I don't need the spas. I need to get to
work.*

But Mrs. Piers had informed me that Mrs. Trevelyan was at
a sermon and would be indisposed until morning. I dropped
into a nearby chair, hung my head, and sighed. When I looked
up, the room had grown dark. Still feeling petulant, I tried to
remember what the bellboy told me to do. Fumbling, I felt for
the brass plate next to the door and pushed a button on the
wall. Brilliant electric light from the Edison lamps illuminated
every inch of the small, airy room, reaching into the corners of
the lofty ceilings and tiled fireplace.

Instead of the simple, white-walled room I had been expecting to stay in, this room was full of color and opulence. I
was suddenly humbled and ashamed of my outburst. It was the
nicest room I'd ever stayed in. Though smaller and decorated
in shades of warm burgundy, gold, and green, it was almost a
duplicate version of Mrs. Trevelyan's room, down to the large
oak desk and crystal vase on the tea table overflowing with ivy
and azalea blossoms. In this room, though, a mound of un-
opened correspondences marred the desk's polished surface.
No care had been taken. Telegrams, letters, and parcels had
been thrown haphazardly in a heap. A few letters had fallen to
the floor.

I picked up the letters, collected up my things from the
bed, and added the newest correspondences to the pile. I
arranged everything into neat stacks and set up my typewriter.
I opened the desk drawer and found ample supplies of sta-

tionery, pens, and ink. I unpacked my luggage and put every-thing away. In the bath assigned to me, two identical small ma-hogany washstands stood side by side. One, labeled *222,* was already covered with ladies' toilet articles. The other, labeled *220,* was empty except for a bottle of water marked *Basin Spring.* I opened the drawer; it was packed with thick, plush green towels. I pulled one out and held it to my cheek. I rel-ished the softness, a stark contrast to the rest of the room, the necessary porcelain features of modern plumbing, the hard, bright white tiles covering the walls, the black and white mosaic tile covering the floor. Only the sword fern on a stand rivaled the warmth of the towel.

At least Thomas was right about the baths. This is extravagance itself.

Next to the towel I tentatively set out the contents of my toilet case, a pitiful few items, on the right corner edge of the expansive washstand top, in case this space wasn't all meant for me. I aligned the bottles in a row and straightened my hair-brush.

There, I thought. *Now all's in order.*

With nothing left to do, I returned to my room to eat. De-spite my rushed departure, Mrs. Larson had packed me a lunch: sliced cold chicken, bread, butter, pickles, and several pieces of her specialty, ginger snaps. I'd only eaten half the meal on the train. A velvet burgundy drape, pulled back to one side, revealed a French door, which led to a second-story bal-cony I'd seen from the carriage earlier. I tried to open it. The door swung open, letting in a breeze that dispelled the stuffy air in the room. I took my dinner out on the balcony and, es-pying a bench, spread my meal out on my lap. I took a deep breath of the crisp, clean air. All around me, glowing in the last rays of the setting sun, was a wide expanse of mountains and valley and sky. The evening should've been lovely. But then that eerie glow had appeared down the hill toward town, in the darkest part of the valley, in the saloon district. I had risen to my feet, and leaning on the wrought-iron railing, I'd heard a shout. As soft as an echo, I'd heard it again: *"Fire."*

I hadn't known yet where my curiosity would lead me. I hadn't known yet that Mrs. Trevelyan was at the center of the bedlam below. But considering how extraordinary everything about this job had been so far, I shouldn't have been surprised.

CHAPTER 4

"Are you injured?"

His warm, gentle voice surprised me. I tore my focus away from Mrs. Trevelyan's retreating figure to see not one of the saloon men, covered in soot from the extinguished fire and smelling of beer, but a gentleman holding his top hat. He was handsome and sparkling clean from his shining, polished shoes, to his tidy mustache, to the glisten on his teeth as he smiled. My heart skipped a beat. But wasn't this the man who had come to the injured woman's aid when the window shattered? Shouldn't he be at least disheveled?

"No, I'm fine. Thank you," I said. "What's going on?"

"Blue laws don't mean much here," he said. He glanced back at the men stomping out the flames in the doorway. "It seems the temperance ladies took offense."

"I was told they were attending a sermon."

"That's one way of looking at it."

"Was the lady by the window badly injured?" I asked.

"Mrs. Turnbull? Luckily, no, though she did have several glass slivers in her face. Are you certain you're okay?" He lightly touched my sleeve at the point of two finger-shaped smears. "There's blood here."

"Oh, no." I pointed to Mrs. Trevelyan and her companions. "One of those women grasped my sleeve. It must've come from them." He looked in the direction of my gaze, absentmindedly dusting dirt from his shoulders and sleeves. Of course he was covered in dust from the road. How could I have ever thought otherwise? He smiled again, and I knew.

"I hope we meet again, lovely lady," he said, tipping his hat. "Now if you'll excuse me." I covered my burning cheeks and watched as he ran up the road.

Upon returning to my room, I was anxious to get to work. I was exhausted, befuddled, and reeling from the events of the day. The long climb up the hill had helped, but nothing cures mental pandemonium like work. So with my ivory-handled letter opener in hand, I tackled the mound on the desk, slicing open envelopes and wax seals with an unusual zest. Sorting through every piece of correspondence, I separated the telegrams from the letters, the personal from the business. I always felt a thrill the moment before I opened that first letter for a new employer or took that first dictation.

What will I find? I wondered.

The first letter I read was from Florence Hawkings, of Little Rock, explaining why she wouldn't be able to attend the Eureka Springs meetings. The second was from one of Mrs. Trevelyan's daughters. I started a new pile. From long practice, I sorted through all of the letters, heedful to read only enough to determine whether it was private or should be placed in the growing stack of business papers. I prided myself on being able to pick out key words or a form of address in order to sort the letters without consciously being aware of their contents. It's a skill past employers have appreciated.

And yet I still learned a great deal about Mrs. Trevelyan.

She had at least two daughters, was a resident of St. Louis, had visited four states and thirteen cities in the past three months, corresponded with pastors, politicians, and businessmen. Many of the correspondences mentioned issues that concerned the American Women's Temperance Coalition, often referred to as the AWTC, such as the promotion of temperance education in schools, the status of an upcoming prohibition vote, and the success of a recent membership drive. Mrs. Trevelyan was its president.

I also learned more than I wanted to. As I myself had witnessed, she was a vocal advocate of violence toward "housebreakers," her word for saloons, and tonight was not the first time she had used canes, bricks, axes, and the like to attack them. Although some praised her, one gentleman's letter calling her work "righteous, legal, and reasonable," most condemned her, calling her vile names and, on occasion, threatening her. One such letter was particularly disturbing. It must've been hand-delivered to the hotel, having *Give to Mrs. Trevelyan's secretary* scribbled on the outside. I'd opened it with high anticipation, having thought it was meant for me. But the hotel's notation was to direct the letter only. Addressed to *Mother Trevelyan* and signed *J.M.,* the entire message consisted of a few short sentences.

> *Aren't satisfied, you self-righteous hypocrite? You*
> *better be, I've paid your price and you've bled*
> *me dry. There isn't any more. I never meant for her*
> *to die. Leave me alone, or I won't be able to say the*
> *same for you.*

The previous letters had made my stomach churn. But blackmail? Death? My hand was shaking when I placed it in the appropriate stack.

With my mind spinning, my fingers took over automatically as I typed a list of correspondents and placed it next to the stacks of letters, telegrams, and envelopes (which often yield additional information not included in the letter) lined up in a row on the corner of the desk. I pushed myself away, the chair scraping against the grain of the carpet, and stood. I paced the room several times, wringing my hands, trying to catch my breath. This wasn't what I'd expected. The satisfaction I normally felt after a good day's work eluded me. But why should I be surprised? I'd answered an urgent telegram from an employer who only hours ago tried to burn down a saloon. Among her papers I'd found threats, repugnant language, and a cryptic note referring to murder and blackmail. Was this what the driver at the train depot was warning me about? Should I have heeded what I'd taken for hearsay and taken the 6:18 back to Kansas City? Chills went down my spine. I snatched up my hat and gloves and headed for the door. I didn't care how late it was, I needed some fresh air.

Thump! Thump! Thump!

"I won't stand for this, Edwina. Open this door!" A woman in a black velvet evening gown hammered on Mrs. Trevelyan's door with her fists. The chandelier in the hallway and the ostentatious jewels about her ears, wrists, and throat rattled with each knock. Small tendrils of her jet-black hair fell down the back of her long neck.

"Margaret said you were in there," she said. "You're going to have to face me sometime." She pounded on the door again. "I'm not going to stand by while you ruin everything, do you hear? Unlock this door this instant!" The woman yanked on the doorknob, then slammed her hand against the door. "If it's the last thing I do, I'll see that you account for your actions. I'm right, and you know it. I'll take charge and run this meeting. Do you hear me, Edwina? I'll call for new elections."

The woman put her ear to the door. She stepped back and

hesitated for a brief moment. "Very well, I hope you *never* come out."

She pivoted on her heels and stormed down the hallway. Within moments we stood face-to-face in my open doorway. She loomed over me. The creases around her grimacing mouth and squinting eyes suggested that she was in her late forties. But her face was so red and blotchy I couldn't guess what her natural complexion should be.

"And what are you staring at?" she said.

I apologized, retreating back into my room. However, as she glanced inside in the direction of the desk, she grabbed a hold of the door. "You're that new secretary, aren't you?" She craned her head around to see more of my room. "Trevelyan said she was expecting a new secretary this afternoon, 'the best money can buy.' You don't look like much to me.

"Did you see her come back?" she said. Without waiting for a reply, she shouted over my shoulder, "You can't hide forever, Edwina."

I started, glancing over my shoulder, half-expecting to see the temperance leader hiding behind me. "Yes. I'm Mrs. Trevelyan's new secretary. I'm Hattie Davish." I offered my hand. "Pleased to meet you, Mrs. . . . ?"

She straightened her back, put her nose in the air and, putting her hand to her throat, touched a gleaming triple-strand diamond collar. "I'm Mrs. Cordelia Anglewood, vice president and humble servant of the American Women's Temperance Coalition."

"Pleased to meet you, Mrs. Anglewood."

"Well?" She peered down at me. I didn't know how to reply. "Well, girl, have you spoken to her yet or not?"

"Oh, no, Mrs. Anglewood, I've yet to talk to Mrs. Trevelyan. When I saw her, she was . . . preoccupied."

"Ha! Such incompetence." She flicked her hand in the air.

"I always knew Edwina was a fool." And with that, she stomped away.

Why hadn't I taken that hike? Instead I'd lain awake most of the night, ruminating on yesterday's events. Only after typing a list of troubling questions was I able to get some sleep. What I'd read in my typewriter this morning was the rambling of a sleepless mind. Nonetheless, many of my questions were valid.

1. Who is this Mrs. Trevelyan? Does it matter?
2. Why would she send me an urgent telegram? She hasn't even spoken to me yet.
3. She paid for my train ticket, room, board, and a week's wages in advance. What does she expect me to do? See to her correspondences? Throw bricks at saloon windows?
4. Should I resign from her employment? What would Sir Arthur say?
5. Are all of the temperance women here vandals and anarchists?
6. Who would send such vile, threatening letters? Why? Who is J.M.?
7. Who was that dashing gentleman I met tonight? Why was he there?
8. What've I gotten myself into?

Long before the sun rose above the mountains, I dressed in my walking clothes. The long hot bath I'd taken earlier, pumped in from Congress Spring, had relaxed my muscles but had done nothing to soothe my restless mind. But I knew what would— a hike through the town and its hills. With a clear mind and a satisfied curiosity, I'd be prepared to confront Mrs. Trevelyan.

I tucked my white blouse into dark brown ankle-length culottes. Over this, I put on a tan hip-length jacket. I put on my jersey gaiters, not knowing what terrain I might encounter, and slipped my hand lens, secure on a gold-plated chain, over my neck. As the sun filled my room with warm autumn sunshine, I pinned my hat onto my head and slipped on my gloves. Outside, the air was brisk and fresh. My first stop would be one of the springs.

In my room, I'd found a map and description of each spring provided by the hotel. There were over sixty of them, scattered over the hillsides. Several were in the valley that ran through the center of town. One, Crescent Spring, was straight down the hill from the hotel. I scurried down the long wooden staircase that I'd seen the day before. It had hundreds of steps and ended in an elaborate four-sided gazebo, with arches, columns, and carved molding. It loomed above Spring Street, one of the main thoroughfares of the town. A few more stairs and I was standing on a broad platform sidewalk. It still smelled of freshly cut wood. Crescent Spring, less than a block north, was surrounded by a rock wall and another ornate gazebo. Across the street, a small but stately church made of limestone with a single steeple on one side cast its shadow over the spring. I knelt beside it, scooped up cold water with my hand, and drank. It felt good to be outside.

Due to the early hour, there were few people on the street. I practically had the town to myself. The occasional rooster or rattling of the streetcar accompanied me as I followed the winding street as it descended southward down the mountain, passing Congress, Harding, and Sweet Springs. Each spring was a few steps from the street, nestled below a curving wall of rock, with water that had a slight metallic taste.

The entire town was built on various levels of these steep, rocky hills, nothing like the open, rolling plains I was used to. How the invalids that flock to this mountainous town navigated its steep terrain was hard to imagine. Many homes and businesses had ground-level entrances on the first, second, and sometimes third floors. One hotel, eight stories tall, claimed to have six ground floors. Like a crazy quilt, the streets seemed built with no pattern or order, a labyrinth of winding roads intersecting steep paths, without a single street crossing another at a right angle and all at various inclines. To maintain this terraced architecture, the town had erected miles of rock retaining walls. I passed brick, wood, and limestone shops, homes, and hotels lining Spring Street in both directions, most sharing a wall with a neighbor. A few showed the signs of fire damage while many more were under construction.

Every block or so, there was a break between the buildings. Here the town had built steep, narrow alleyways of wooden or stone stairs, allowing the townspeople to walk from one level of the town to the next. Hanging signs, variously positioned down the length of the stairs, indicated businesses' side entrances. One painted mural, of a hand pointing downward, indicated that Steinbach & Sons, cabinet and coffin makers, could be found on the flight of stairs between the fifth and sixth blocks of Spring and Center Streets.

A man in a blacksmith's apron stepped up from one of these stairwell alleys right in front of me. We nearly collided.

"Watch it, lady," he grunted, his breath visible in the cool morning air.

Without looking back, he stomped up the hill. Eager to see what was around the bend, I was grateful for his rude behavior; it saved time exchanging apologies. I continued down the hill.

From time to time I dallied in front of a shop window. The wares in Mrs. Cunningham's Millinery and Dress Shop distracted me for over a quarter of an hour. I pulled myself away from the latest styles of hats when an array of sumptuous cakes displayed in the window of a bakery two doors down caught my eye. Waiting for the shop to open, I read two posters pasted inside the window of Heisendorf's Grocery next door. I had noticed various other posters on my walk. One advertised a health clinic at a bathhouse; another announced an upcoming public ball at the Crescent Hotel. Though several had been torn in half, both "Vote No for Proposition 203" and "Vote Yes for Proposition 203" posters had been plastered on trees and poles throughout town. And like the one in the window, I'd seen many presidential campaign posters; tomorrow was Election Day. Although most had been for Grover Cleveland, I had also seen one or two for James Weaver of Iowa. The one before me was for President Benjamin Harrison.

The second poster in the grocer's window, however, wasn't a campaign poster, nor was it one I had seen before. It advertised the annual meeting of the American Women's Temperance Coalition. It read SPRING INTO HEALTH AND WELL-BEING across the top in capital red letters. PROPOSITION VOTE MARCH, TUESDAY, RALLY AT BASIN CIRCLE PARK, SATURDAY was in large black letters beneath the title. A detailed schedule of the week-long event was listed. In addition to lectures, Bible study, marches, and other organized events, a testimonial gathering was scheduled each day at a different spring. Saloon smashing was not mentioned.

The picture in the middle of the poster grabbed my attention. I pressed my hands to the glass and leaned closer. My breath steamed up the window. I wiped the condensation away with my glove to reveal the face. Her piercing eyes, her stooping shoulders, the mark across her cheek were unmistakable. The picture was labeled, *Our heroic and righteous leader, Mrs. Edwina Trevelyan.*

Yet in the picture her gaze was arresting. Determination stared at me, unlike last night when she appeared dazed, angry, and unfocused. I looked straight back at her image, meeting the challenge.

What kind of woman are you? I wondered.

My culottes fluttered in a gust of wind. Was it merely the cold air that sent a shiver down my spine? Not knowing for certain, I pushed myself away from the window and continued my walk downhill toward Basin Circle Park, forgetting all about the cakes in the bakery.

CHAPTER 5

Basin Circle Park was located at the base of the western mountain, encompassing an entire block of Spring Street. Framed in by two grand hotels at each end, the park's terraced gardens and crisscrossing of stairs led to a towering semicircle cliff of limestone. Circular in design, it centered on an ornate wrought-iron fountain that tapped the most famous spring in town, Basin Spring. It was both a natural and man-made marvel, but I couldn't enjoy it. Unlike the other springs I had visited, there were dozens of people in the park, drinking from the fountain, lounging on the benches, and socializing. The poster of Mrs. Trevelyan had disturbed me, though I couldn't say why, and the unexpected crowd made it worse. In lieu of lingering in the park, I decided to confront Mrs. Trevelyan earlier than I had planned. I needed to get to work.

I headed back to the Arcadia Hotel, taking a different route this time. I climbed several steep blocks of Mountain Street to the top of the hill with the rising sun warm on my back. The buildings were fewer and farther apart here than in the valley. With patches of open woodland and unused pasture, I was able to find several plants that I'd never seen before. I collected a specimen of each before moving on. My walk had taken me back to the hotel grounds in time for breakfast. As I crossed the manicured lawn, my path intersected with that of a woman dressed in a fitted black English riding habit and top hat.

"Good morning, Mrs. Anglewood," I said, recognizing her from the night before.

Cordelia Anglewood, a diamond-studded gold collar pin at her throat, took one glimpse at me, with dirt on my knees and wilting plants in my hands, and then, without a word, continued walking in the direction of the riding stables.

"Oh, don't mind her, dear; she's a sourpuss these days. Too much on her mind."

I glanced up to see an elderly lady in an old-fashioned matron's bonnet leaning over the railing of the hotel's front portico, squinting down at me. Her white frizzy hair was piled up and pulled away from a round face. The lace of her high-collared mauve morning dress couldn't hide a double chin. She had a cherry-red stain on her shoulder. Her thin smile and gleaming eyes radiated either serenity or senility; I couldn't tell which.

"Oh, that's all right," I replied.

From behind the railing, I heard another woman's voice.

"Who can you possibly be talking to in the shrubbery, Lizzie? It's like seeing Moses in a lace bonnet, talking to the burning bush. I thought you wanted me to read this?"

"Yes, in a moment, Lucy, dear."

As I climbed the stairs, I caught a glimpse of Lucy. Although dressed in pale gray, she was an identical, albeit thinner, version of the other woman. She was rocking back and forth, her hands twitching, with a book in her lap. She looked up as Lizzie approached me.

"Good morning," I said.

"Good morning, dear," Lizzie replied.

"Yes, yes, fine morning and all that," Lucy said. She picked up her book again and peered over the spectacles set low on her nose. "Let the gardener get back to work, Lizzie, so we can get back to the passage I was reading."

"I'm Miss Hattie Davish, ma'am. I'm not the gardener. I'm Mrs. Trevelyan's new secretary. I just arrived yesterday afternoon."

"Secretary? So you're Davish." Lucy removed her spectacles and waved them about. "Why on earth are you covered in dirt and dead plants, then?"

"We're pleased to meet you, Miss Davish. I'm Miss Elizabeth Shaw, dear, and this," Lizzie said, indicating the seated woman, "is my sister, Mrs. Lucinda Fry. We're members of the AWTC, you see. We heard that Edwina sent for a new secretary."

"Yes, I'm on my way up to see her now," I said. "I caught a glimpse of her last night but I haven't actually spoken to her yet."

"Oh, dear," Miss Elizabeth Shaw said. "I heard about last night's, ah, incident. You weren't there, were you, dear?"

It was Mrs. Fry who answered for me. "Where else do you think she saw her, Lizzie? Edwina wasn't there to meet the girl's train." She turned to me. "So is it true?"

"I'm sorry, but is what true?" I said.

The old lady licked her lips. "That Edwina went down there, like David facing Goliath, swinging an ax in one hand, a cane in the other, toppling every drunkard that got in her way? That she burned the place down to the ground? I heard there was blood everywhere."

"Oh, it was shocking. I've never witnessed anything like it. Mrs. Trevelyan shattered a window with a hatchet and intentionally started a fire inside the saloon. And yes, several people were injured."

Mrs. Lucinda Fry clucked her tongue. "I knew it. What

was she thinking? She never listens to me. There go any hopes we had for—"

She stopped in mid-sentence when Josephine Piers appeared in the doorway. Mrs. Piers hesitated when she saw the little crowd of women on the porch. She stepped back in retreat.

"Josephine, dear," Miss Elizabeth Shaw said, "please join us. We were talking about Edwina's indiscretion last night."

At the mention of Mrs. Trevelyan's name, tears welled in the woman's eyes. "That indiscretion, as you call it, is God's work, Sister Elizabeth. Mother Trevelyan was destroying that evil place. I'm proud to say I was with her last night." She jutted her chin up in defiance, but her hands were shaking. One hand was wrapped in a bandage. So she *was* one of the women in blue I saw last night. Maybe even the one who left blood on my sleeve.

"We all know you've wielded your share of hatchets and canes, Josephine," Mrs. Fry said. "You also know our feeling about it. This is a temperance organization, not a militia. I don't know how many times I have to say it. We're supposed to advocate moderation in all things, not just in drink. We're supposed to all be on the same side in this fight."

"But we are, Sister Lucinda, each to her own. You serve by writing letters, drinking tea, and raising funds. I serve by smashing bottles with bricks and sitting in prison cells."

"We do appreciate your passion, dear," Miss Lizzie said, "and we could all use more of your youthful energy. It's just that . . ."

Mrs. Lucinda Fry frowned and snapped her book closed. "No harm comes by our letters and tea, unless you count paper cuts. Maybe you'd be happier if we drew blood on the occasional chipped china cup, Josephine?"

"Now, ladies, let's not argue," Miss Shaw said. "This is Miss Davish, Josephine, Edwina's new secretary. Miss Davish, dear, this is Mrs. Josephine Piers, one of Edwina's closest friends and associates."

"Yes, we've already met," Josephine Piers said. "You haven't reconsidered, have you, Miss Davish?"

"Reconsidered what?" Mrs. Fry said.

"Mrs. Piers was kind enough to offer to continue as Mrs. Trevelyan's secretary," I said.

"Josephine, dear, why would you want to burden yourself further?" Miss Shaw said. "You already do so much." She pointed to the woman's injured hand. "And whatever did you do to your hand?"

"I cut it on a broken liquor bottle. But it's merely a surface scratch. I can still serve as secretary."

"No, no, it was nice of you to step in temporarily, but let the girl do her job," Mrs. Fry said. "Knowing Edwina, Davish here has already been well paid."

"Yes, you're probably right. My energy could be better spent. She's only a typewriter. I can serve the cause in many important ways."

"Yes, dear," Miss Shaw said, "just try to be more temperate in your actions from now on."

I was grateful that the conversation came back to the sub-ject of the saloon smashing (*I am not only a typewriter,* I thought).

"Has this happened before, last night, I mean? Aren't you worried about the police?"

"Saloons are the devil's work, home wreckers, the bane of a happy existence, Miss Davish," Josephine Piers declared, her voice rising with each consecutive phrase. "We were doing a righteous and heroic act. God's hand guides us. We shall pre-vail. You'll see. Proposition 203 will be passed and victory will be ours."

"Josephine, dear, we all pray the men pass the proposition, but I can see this is upsetting you. Why don't we go in to breakfast?" Miss Shaw patted Josephine Piers's arm. "Lucy, why don't you go with her? I'll join you in a few minutes."

"Oh, all right," Mrs. Fry said. "Come to think of it, I am starving. Davish, help me out of this chair."

"Poor Josephine, she rarely quarrels with anyone. She must be worried about the convention," Elizabeth Shaw said, watching her sister and Mrs. Piers leave. She picked up a jar of cherry preserves that had been sitting on the railing and unexpectedly scooped several spoonfuls into her mouth. She continued talking as if eating jam straight from a jar was the most natural thing to do. I was astounded.

"And of course, there's the vote. Josephine's quite dedicated and has worked tirelessly for the cause. Like many of our members, she came to us fleeing an abusive drunk of a husband." I recalled the scars on Mrs. Piers's face and shuddered. "Thinking about Cordelia's gruffness this morning, it seems we're all a bit on edge. Nothing good comes from saloon smashing."

"It's true then, Miss Shaw, that Mrs. Trevelyan does this on a regular basis?" I said.

"Oh, do call me Lizzie, dear. And my sister, Lucy. Everyone does, except Josephine, of course. And I'll call you Hattie. My favorite great-aunt, Harriet Shaw, had us call her Auntie Hattie, you know." She patted my knee. "Yes, Hattie, this was not the first time Edwina, Mrs. Trevelyan to you, has caused a great scene." Miss Lizzie Shaw's head swayed back and forth.

"Why does she do it?" I asked. "What does she hope to accomplish?"

"You heard Josephine. Many in the coalition call for such brash action. I fear it may cause a rift in the membership. Lucy and I are very much set against it. Sermonizing, protesting, yes, we can all agree saloons breed evil and destroy families, but we must not condone such violence. Violence is the antithesis of temperance, Hattie. We must all remember that. And Edwina crossed the line again."

"But I still don't understand. Isn't that hypocritical?"

"Yes, there are those, myself included, who would say advocating temperance while participating in anarchy is hypocritical. Yet, as I said, members disagree."

"If so many members disagree with her, why is she still the president of your club?"

Miss Lizzie patted my cheek, then rose. "Welcome to the temperance movement, dear."

"How's Mother Trevelyan, Josie?"

After her insistence, I had joined Miss Lizzie and her sister in the dining room. They had assured me Mrs. Trevelyan wouldn't mind. Miss Lucy, who had claimed to be famished, picked at her food while her sister, after eating everything on her own plate, astonishingly began eating off her sister's plate as well. It was two hours before I was able to get away from the breakfast table. When I did, I headed straight for Mrs. Trevelyan's room. Josephine Piers was leaving as another woman, with thick spectacles and a bulbous nose, arrived. Mrs. Piers closed the door behind her.

"I'm not sure, Eleanor," Mrs. Piers said. "She's not in her room."

"Really? I thought we were supposed to meet her here."

"So did I."

I didn't bother asking the women if I could see for myself. Instead, I set to the task of finding Mrs. Trevelyan, wherever she was. Starting in the basement and working my way up, I made a systematic search of the entire hotel—the storerooms, the laundry, the parlors, the library, the dining room, the ballroom, the hairdresser's salon, the baths, as well as the servants' quarters, the offices, the service rooms and pantry—with no luck. No one had seen her, including the doorman. I took a quick stroll through the gardens, checking every porch and bench, just in case. When I returned to the lobby, I encountered the American Women's Temperance Coalition in full force for the first time. From the number of women I'd seen wearing the sky blue AWTC buttons, I would've guessed no fewer than a third of the hotel's guests were coalition members, here for their annual meeting. But no Mrs. Trevelyan. It was frustrating. Instead of helping the lady with her duties, as I had expected, I spent the remainder of the morning mingling with the crowd inquiring after her whereabouts. Though no one was able to answer with certainty, many members were quick to speculate.

"Did you check the dining room? She likes to linger over coffee."

"She might've had an appointment at the American Bathhouse this morning."

"There's a lot of meetings scheduled for this week. Maybe she's meeting with the other organizers. I'd ask Cordelia Anglewood or Diana Halbert."

"I saw the police earlier; maybe she's with them."

Once, after I introduced myself to a Mrs. Miller, the lady exclaimed, "Her secretary? Too bad. After last night, Edwina probably skipped town."

Now, after talking with coalition members, asking questions, and listening to their gossip, I was no closer to having a face-to-face meeting with my new employer than when I'd started. And I had completed all my work the night before. *Now what do I do?*

CHAPTER 6

I went hiking again. This time I brought my plant press and made it a collecting trip. I was thrilled to find Ozark chinkapin, Arkansas beardtongue, and two species of goldenrod, amazingly still flowering, to add to my collection. Happy and exhausted, I was making my way back to the hotel when I came upon Harding Spring again. A group had gathered below the outcrop of limestone that jutted out over the spring's pool. Cordelia Anglewood stood on top of a limestone rock with Josephine Piers stationed next to her on the ground. It was one of the coalition's testimonial meetings. Miss Lucy and Miss Lizzie shared a bench with a woman with a white toy poodle in her arms, and waved to get my attention. Others I'd met were scattered throughout. I was flattered to be asked to join them and found a bare spot on the grass at Miss Lizzie's feet. Several disapproving faces regarded my plant press.

"What is it with you and dead plants?" Miss Lucy whispered.

Cordelia Anglewood lifted her arms in the air. "Let us pray." Everyone bowed their heads.

"Lord, we thank you for this water to refresh our bodies and for your love to refresh our souls. May we rid this world of the poisons of man and bring the fallen to your sobering embrace. Amen." She raised her head and gazed out at the gathering. "On behalf of the American Women's Temperance Coalition, I would like to welcome one and all. We, a gathering of the faithful, stand here today, as every day, as a force against the destructive power of alcohol and its hurtful effects on society and families. Blessed be they who fight for the sanctity of the home."

Unlike the night before, Mrs. Anglewood was eloquent and welcoming. Her countenance was somber and her gaze radiated the conviction of her words. I listened intently.

"We gather here at the healing waters of Harding Spring to hear the testimonials of those who have suffered from the evils of demon drink. If you have a story to share, please come forward."

Several women stepped forth, including a reluctant one who was urged forward by unseen hands. The woman with the poodle stood up; Miss Lucy grasped the woman's hand.

"Cordelia wants testimony of temperance, Edna, not another story about Charlie."

"Oh." Edna sat down, hugging her dog Charlie close.

"I was a drunk," one woman admitted. "But with the help of Sister Cordelia, I was able to go to the sanatorium and get sober." She smiled at Cordelia, who nodded back. "I haven't taken a drop in four years. Now I have a husband, two beautiful children, and I'm the one to speak at the meetings. I owe it all to the AWTC."

When not at their annual convention, members, it seemed, held weekly meetings in towns across the country, serving as support to families of homes broken by alcohol. They produced educational leaflets, such as how to rid alcohol from the home, and provided refuge for women and children in cases of abuse. Moral, emotional, spiritual, and in some cases, financial support was freely given to all those who sought help in the fight for temperance, for themselves and their families.

"That was me once," Miss Lucy said, suddenly standing and pointing to the previous speaker. "I wasn't always an old lady and I wasn't always sober. One day I was so drunk from laudanum that I drove a horse and buggy two miles down the middle of the sidewalk and straight into my in-laws' house. But I too found salvation in the AWTC. So let that be a lesson to all of you. Temperance works!" A cheer arose as Miss Lucy took her seat. I tried in vain to picture this straight-backed bespectacled old woman wildly riding a horse into someone's front parlor.

"Old Mr. Fry never forgave her," Miss Lizzie whispered to me, "but Oliver did, rest his soul."

Before I could ask more, another woman stood and announced, to applause, that her husband had signed the temperance pledge. She pulled a man into the open space in the middle of the crowd. He held a wide-brimmed Stetson hat in his hands and kept his eyes on the ground.

"This is my man. He used to curse at me and kick our horse. Now he's going to vote Yes for Proposition 203." A loud cheer erupted.

"What is Proposition 203?" I asked Miss Lizzie, whispering. "You mentioned it before."

"It bans the sale of alcohol in Carroll County, dear. We've tried to get it passed every two years for the past fourteen, as allowed by law. But we haven't been successful. That's one reason we're in Eureka Springs. It's on the ballot in tomorrow's election. We are all very hopeful."

"It's one of the most important things we can do, Davish," Miss Lucy said.

"Do you try to influence the ballot in other places as well?" I asked.

"Everywhere we can, dear," Miss Lizzie said. "Everywhere we can."

With a brave countenance and fresh green and black bruises around her left eye, another woman stepped forward and described her harrowing flight from Omaha to Eureka Springs with her three children in tow and a drunkard in pursuit.

"I'd read one of your leaflets. I didn't know where else to go."

When Josephine Piers put her arms around the woman and said, "You're safe now," I think even the battered woman believed it.

Cordelia again took the stage.

"Thank you, brave ladies, for sharing your stories of courage and redemption, and you, good man, for your valiant vote." There was more applause. "Before we adjourn, I'd like to remind everyone of tonight's vigil in the Summer Auditorium at the Assembly Grounds. For our newcomers, it's on the north edge of town, down the hill from Grotto Spring. We will pray for President Harrison's continued guidance and leadership. We will pray that we don't lose our great supporter in the White House, Mrs. Harrison. We will pray for redemption of this land. May God see fit to pass Proposition 203 tomorrow and rid this valley, this entire county of drink." Several women cheered. "God bless you all."

She gave the floor to Josephine Piers, who led the final prayer. Miss Lucy and Miss Lizzie stood, leading everyone in song. Their voices were soft but clear. To my surprise, the meeting ended without an appearance by or single mention of

Mrs. Trevelyan. Yet the moment the women began mingling, dipping their cups in the spring well and socializing in general, Edwina Trevelyan's name was on everyone's lips.

"Cordelia is terrific, but I thought Mother Trevelyan was going to lead the testimonials this year?"

"Where's Edwina? What's keeping her? Surely, nothing's more important than being here?"

"Is it true that Mrs. Trevelyan was arrested?"

I passed through unnoticed as I approached the spring. Josephine Piers spotted me at the edge of the limestone wall encircling the pool. We were both leaning over, filling tin cups.

"Wonderful meeting, wasn't it, Miss Davish? Sister Cordelia's confidence has a way of inspiring the most remarkable testimonies."

"Yes, I've never been to anything like it." And I meant it. The last twenty-four hours had acquainted me with both the best and the worst aspects of the temperance movement. Until yesterday afternoon, I had known very little of what my dear, departed father had called "those teetotalers."

"I rejoice that you decided to join us and partake of the waters."

"These," I said, holding up the cups, "are for Miss Lucy and Miss Lizzie. But thank you for your concern." I hastened back to the sisters without spilling a drop.

"Well, Davish, did you find her?" I handed Miss Lucy a tin cup.

"Find who? Mrs. Trevelyan?"

"No, the vanished crew of the *Mary Celeste*. Of course I mean Edwina."

"Lucy, dear," her sister said, "be nice."

"Well, you saw her this morning. A pack of bloodhounds couldn't have sniffed out Edwina as thoroughly as this girl. Well, Davish?"

"No, Miss Lucy, I haven't seen her yet today. Have you?"

"Come to think of it, no, I haven't."

"Nor has anyone else that I've spoken to. I'm at a loss as to where she could be."

Miss Diana Halbert, a schoolteacher from Memphis, leaned over Miss Lucy's shoulder. "She's hiding with her tail between her legs somewhere."

"Others think so too," I said, "but I'm not so certain."

"Charlie runs with his tail between his legs sometimes," Edna offered.

Several others around me cocked their heads, listening. Conscious of the eavesdroppers, I lowered my voice. "Is it possible she was arrested?"

"No, dear, Cordelia or Josephine would know if she had," Miss Lizzie said.

"What if they aren't telling anyone? The news could be disruptive."

"Come now, Davish. You make it sound so sinister," Miss Lucy said, too loud for my comfort. "I'm sure you type a thousand words a minute and your middle name is Pitman Shorthand, but you have no idea what you're talking about. Cordelia would never do a thing like that."

"Lucy's right, dear. Cordelia wouldn't keep it a secret. She'd be the first one to crow over the news."

Miss Lizzie glanced behind her. Several women, staring in our direction, conspired behind fans. One of them pointed at me. Miss Lizzie lowered her voice to a whisper. "Maybe we should talk about this later, dear. It might prove unpleasant if the others think you're meddling."

"But someone's got to—"

"*You*, secretary." The booming voice, so near, caused me, and everyone around me, to jump. Charlie the dog barked.

"Your meddling has no place here." Cordelia Anglewood gestured to the gathering. "All are welcome who seek healing and inspiration. But you seem intent on spreading rumors and agitation. This is not the AWTC way. I must ask that you please leave." She loomed above me from the top of the limestone wall, casting a long shadow over the ground. She raised her arm and pointed at me.

"Now!"

Josephine Piers took me by the elbow and led me away.

"It's all right, Sister Cordelia," she said over her shoulder. "Miss Davish didn't mean any harm." To me she said, "Edwina's absence is disturbing everyone. Sister Cordelia lashes out sometimes, but she always has the coalition's best interests in mind. Don't blame her for that."

"Of course. I didn't mean to upset anyone. We were merely talking about Mrs. Trevelyan. Do you know where she is?"

"God will show Mother Trevelyan the way home, I assure you, Miss Davish. In the meantime, take pity on us and let Sister Cordelia lead the way."

"Mrs. Trevelyan?"

I rushed down the hallway in anticipation. The door to Mrs. Trevelyan's room was ajar.

"Hello, Mrs. Trevelyan, are you there?" No answer.

This was getting ridiculous. I pushed the door open and saw a vacant room. Except for a pile of papers on the desk, the room was immaculate. The bed was made and a fresh arrangement of azaleas adorned the table. Suitcases were stacked on top of the wardrobe. The trunk I'd seen yesterday was gone. It wasn't my usual way, rummaging through other people's belongings, but that's exactly what I commenced doing. Whether Mrs. Trevelyan was avoiding confrontation by hiding somewhere in town or whether she'd been arrested by the police or had absconded in the night, I needed to know. I could no longer afford to have misgivings about being in someone else's room, uninvited.

I can look and still be discreet, I assured myself.

I scanned her desk. It took great restraint not to organize and tidy up the mass of paper before me. A large pile of telegram receipts pierced on a bill-spike sat on the shelf above the desk. Several correspondences lay open haphazardly on top of one another. An unfinished letter, presumably in Mrs. Trevelyan's hand, was set to one side. Beneath the letters was a copy of the poster I'd seen that morning announcing the American Women's Temperance Coalition schedule. Beneath the poster was a daily calendar. It was opened to Sunday, November 6. The daily schedule of the AWTC had been written in a crisp, printed script. I leafed through the book. There were brief notes in the same handwriting as the unfinished letter on almost every day. For Friday, the entry *Send telegrams, arrange for tickets, GET HD* was written. Yesterday's entry included a brief note about "sermonizing" at a saloon and the words *Mascavarti's response?* underlined. However, today's entry and every other through Saturday, November 12, consisted of the coalition schedule alone. I put the calendar back where I'd found it.

I searched through the desk drawers and found nothing unusual. The large wardrobe, its doors unlatched, contained two capes, a set of slippers, and three pairs of boots. After hanging a jacket that had fallen from its peg, I lingered on her collection of hats: stylish turbans, everyday straw, and one with a Paris label that had a brim larger than I'd ever seen before. It looked brand new. For the number of hats the lady owned, I was surprised by her lack of dresses. Mrs. Trevelyan had fewer than I had.

I checked her nightstand. On top were her Bible, a pair of spectacles, and several remedy bottles: Watkins Liniment, Bromo Vichy headache salts, Radam's Microbe Killer. Not unusual for a woman of her age. By the number of ring stains, more bottles had once sat on this table top. At first, the drawer appeared empty. Sticking my hand to the back, I felt a piece of cloth. It was a handkerchief monogrammed *ERT* in tight navy blue stitches. Edwina R. Trevelyan. Evoking my botanical collection, it smelled of lilac toilet water coupled with another scent, too faint to place. I put it back and, as I closed the drawer, I noticed half of a calling card sticking out of her Bible. I picked it up. Mr. John Martin, Esq.

"Hey, what are you doing in here?" I dropped the calling card. "This is Miss Edwina's room."

A girl, no older than nineteen, her freckled face taut from the pull of her bun, stood in the doorway holding freshly laundered dresses over her outstretched arms. A starched white apron covered her print house dress. A small book was tucked in the pocket.

"Yes, I know, I'm sorry, the door was open." I picked up the card and added it to the papers on the desk. The girl scowled. Walking past me, she set the dresses on the bed. "I'm Hattie Davish, Mrs. Trevelyan's new secretary."

"You could be Sarah Bernhardt herself for all I care. You shouldn't be snooping around in here. Does Miss Edwina know you're in here?"

"No, actually I'm looking for Mrs. Trevelyan. I saw her last night but didn't get a chance to speak to her. I haven't been able to find her all day. In fact, no one seems to know where she is. Do you happen to know, Miss . . . ? I'm sorry; I didn't get your name."

"Mary Flannagan. And no, I don't know where the lady is." She shrugged. "I'm just the maid."

"Did you happen to see her today, Miss Flannagan? Happen to hear where she was going or when she'll be back?"

"I saw her this morning." She yanked on the counterpane, straightening the already straight bedspread.

"You did? When? Did she say where she was going today?"

"I'm sorry, miss. I can't help you." The maid swatted a pillow.

"Can you tell me anything? You're the first person I've talked to today who has seen her."

"Sorry, no. And you still haven't explained what you're doing in here."

"Miss Flannagan, I know you can appreciate my predicament. I'm trying to determine what my situation is. I don't know why Mrs. Trevelyan troubled to arrange for my travel and engage my services. She has yet to avail herself of those services, and has a willing volunteer in one of her coalition members. If I came here under false pretenses, I need to make other arrangements. To tell you the truth, I don't have anything to do. And it's driving me crazy."

"Sorry, miss." The maid shrugged and swatted another pillow. She had to know more than she was telling me. I knew from experience that there was no such thing as "just a maid." Before getting frustrated, I decided to try a different tactic.

"Did you hear about what happened last night at the Cavern Saloon?" The maid stiffened but said nothing. "I was there. It was awful. I'd never heard of such a thing as 'saloon smashing' before. Have you, Miss Flannagan?"

"Oh, call me Mary, will ya? Yeah, I heard. I heard all about it. The righteous lady goes preachifying and instead bashes up the place and tries to burn it down." The maid snatched a dress from the bed and hung it in the wardrobe. "And where were the bloody coppers when you need them?"

"You don't like Mrs. Trevelyan, Mary?" With her back to me, she hung the last two dresses in silence.

"Don't get me wrong, miss," she said, turning around. "Miss Edwina's not all bad. In her way, the lady is good to me. She doesn't ask too many questions, never once raised her voice or hand to me, and she's been very generous. That trunk there is for a charity and it's packed with most of her own clothes." She jerked her head around. "Oh, looks like they took it already."

She hesitated, as if wondering if she should say more. Her lips tightened. "But the lady's difficult, unpredictable too, enforcing her own rules on the staff." She crossed her arms over her chest, punctuating the words with a shake of her head. "And it's not right what she did to that saloon. Not right at all. She deserves to be arrested."

"My impression is that not everyone agrees with her tactics," I said. "And I'm surprised the police haven't been here."

"Oh, they've been here, all right. I saw them in here with the manager earlier this morning."

"Really, when was that?" I procured two glasses of water from the many bottles labeled *Magnetic Spring* next to the nightstand. I handed one to the maid, gesturing for her to sit, and took the next armchair. She swirled the glass for a moment, then gulped down the water. She poured herself another one.

"I don't remember. I've been so busy with these temperance ladies arriving. And this morning has been nothing if not hectic."

"Could you hazard a guess?"

"It would've been well after breakfast. I came by early with the lady's coffee. 'After all the commotion last night,' her words, not mine, she was anxious for her coffee."

"But isn't room service the dining staff's concern?"

"You'd think so. I'm supposed to clean the rooms, not cater to the whims of every highfalutin guest. It seems she doesn't like the waiters from downstairs, so one of the maids has to fetch it. It was my turn this morning."

"After you served the coffee, then what?"

"I laid out her clothes. I was making up the bed when that Miss Cordelia showed up." The maid shuddered. Remembering my encounters with Cordelia Anglewood, I didn't have to wonder why.

Like many people of wealth, Cordelia Anglewood didn't seem to have a high regard for women in service. But then again, Sir Arthur had been like that once too. The first time we met, I'd been called into the study in his rented house in Kansas City. He had always had male secretaries, never entertaining the idea that a woman was competent enough to work for him. But I had come highly recommended from an acquaintance, and he was in a pinch. He was midway through writing an article comparing the Civil War battles that took place in Westport, Missouri, in 1864 when his secretary quit. I had arrived on an hour's notice on a Sunday afternoon, but as a man who expects everyone to be at his beck and call, he was unimpressed. And he told me in no uncertain terms how unimpressed. Then he began dictating, before I had barely time to take off my gloves, before I'd had a chance to sit down, before I had prepared my notebook. But I was quick and competent and had every word he had dictated that afternoon typed up before I was dismissed that evening. He had me back the next day, and my life hasn't been the same since.

"After I fetched a second pot of coffee for them," the maid said, "Miss Edwina gave me the dresses to take to the laundry and then dismissed me, thank goodness." She yanked on a loose thread on her apron. "I didn't have time this morning to run any of her errands."

"Errands?"

"You know, sending telegrams, fetching books, delivering messages, buying train tickets." She said the last pointing at me.

"But why would you be doing what is typically a secretary's job?"

"That's what I wanted to know. Her old secretary, Miss Rippetoe, the one that eloped two weeks ago, and then Miss Josephine usually took care of all that. Miss Josephine must be busy with all the meetings. So it's 'do this, Mary, do that, Mary.' And all on top of my normal work too. I was happy to over-hear Miss Edwina, complaining about 'bungling secretaries,' tell one of the old ladies that she was sending for a profes-sional." She attempted a grin, crinkling her face, showing a chipped tooth. "That would be you, miss."

I smiled back. "Do you remember anything else?"

"No, not really. The last time I saw her, I'd finished clean-ing 230. She was in the hallway, going back to her room. Prob-ably had been to the bathroom again; she's an old lady, you know."

CHAPTER 7

"Vote Yes on 203, Vote Yes on 203, Vote Yes on 203."
Brandishing pro–Proposition 203 banners and pro-Harrison campaign posters, a group of temperance women chanted. They marched, among a gathering crowd, back and forth in front of a one-story whitewashed frame building decorated in red, white, and blue bunting. It was the polling place for today's election.

"Down with Proposition 203!" a man from the crowd shouted.

"Down with you lousy meddlers," another voice shouted at the marching women.

"Vote Yes on 203, Vote Yes on 203, Vote Yes on 203," the women shouted louder.

After leaving Mary Flannagan to her duties last night, I had returned to my typewriter. In lieu of real work, I had kept myself busy by documenting all that I'd learned about the American Women's Temperance Coalition, Mrs. Trevelyan, and possible reasons for her growing absence. I had prepared a list of facts, annotated as to when I had learned each one, how, and from whom. I had kept a separate list of unanswered questions, and another listing tasks I might perform to earn my wages during her absence. It wasn't much.

This morning, after another failed attempt to find Mrs. Trevelyan in her room, I had spent some time attending to the daily stream of telegrams and correspondences sent by both her admirers and detractors alike. But I had been distracted. Was the entirety of this engagement going to be spent making piles of paper and chasing after hints of this woman? Where was she? Why hadn't Mrs. Trevelyan been seen since yesterday morning? Has she been arrested after all? There was only one way to find out.

I had to circumvent the demonstration to get to the police precinct. It was all too reminiscent of the saloon smashing mishap. The chanting escalated into shrill cries and exclamations. Several fistfights broke out. Projectiles flew through the air. A rotten egg soared by, missing my head by inches as I crossed the street. And in the middle of it all was one man.

"Only George Shulman would dare take on the entire Temperance Movement single-handedly," a fellow spectator said when I reached the wooden sidewalk on the other side. In the middle of the street, encircled by a dozen temperance women, a man stood his ground. His thick arms were waving as he shouted eye to eye with a woman several inches taller than him. Instead of a hat, a large bandage covered most of his short, cropped fair hair. "If he can defeat 203, he's got my vote for city council." Men around the spectator concurred.

"Mere placards?" George Shulman was shouting. "Where are your hatchets now? Y'all think you're so high and mighty. You couldn't burn down my bar, so you push for Proposition 203, to put me out of business?"

"Yes, and you would thank me for it," the woman replied, her arms locked across her chest.

"Then it's a damn good thing women can't vote," someone from the crowd exclaimed.

George Shulman raised his arm, as if to toast. "I'll drink to that."

I could still hear the roaring laughter of the crowd as I entered the police station several blocks away. I'd always imagined police stations as dark, cheerless places, but to my delight, and surprise, several species of exotic plants decorated the waiting room: A lemon tree stood in one corner, a flowering fuchsia draped over a plant stand next to the south window, and a shiny green cast-iron plant was in a clay pot on the desk.

"I'd like to speak to the sheriff, please," I said to the clerk. He grabbed a sheet of paper from a towering stack next to him.

"Out of town," he said, without putting down his pen.

"Do you know when he'll be back?"

"Won't be. He took a prisoner back to Berryville."

"May I speak with someone else, then? It concerns Mrs. Edwina Trevelyan, of the American Women's Temperance Coalition."

"It's Election Day, lady; the officers are busy."

"I'm willing to wait."

"Oh, all right, wait here." The clerk lifted himself from his chair and shuffled through a closed door at the back of the room. He returned alone and slumped back down without acknowledging me.

"Excuse me," I said.

"Over there," he said, pointing to a long wooden bench against the wall. A gaunt old man with calico patches sewn on his cap and a bottle clasped between his knees sat with his head back, snoring, at one end. "Someone will be right with you."

A few minutes passed, then an hour. The old man, coughing himself awake, took swigs from his bottle each time before falling asleep again. Several other men passed by me on their way out the door. For a time, I was absorbed with watching a cricket scurry from one shadow to the next until it disappeared altogether beneath the clerk's desk. The hard bench made my back ache. I was forced to stand and stretch my legs several times before a lanky man with a sharply pointed nose, carrying the round, high-crowned hat of a policeman, strode toward me. He stopped briefly, sticking his finger into the fuchsia pot to test its soil moisture, before approaching me.

"You the one asking about the temperance lady?" he said, squinting down at me.

"Yes, my name is Hattie Davish. I'm Mrs. Trevelyan's secretary. I'm concerned about her unexplained absence. I was hoping you might have some information, Officer?"

"It's Jackson, Chief of Police, Miss Davish, and there's nothing to tell." He stroked his thin black mustache.

"So you haven't arrested her?"

"Arrested her? No, we haven't arrested her."

"But I thought you might have, after the other night."

"Oh, yeah, there's a warrant out for the lady, all right. She attacked the Cavern Saloon, its patrons, and its owner." He shifted his helmet from one arm to the other as he viewed the wall above my head.

"I know. I was there." His eyes darted down to my face. I had taken him by surprise.

"Then you know she almost set fire to the place."

"But then why not arrest her?"

"Miss, I went to the Arcadia Hotel. The woman had already left."

"She had? Were you able to track her or determine when and how she left?"

"Miss, I don't know why you're asking me all these questions." He turned away from me to watch another policeman enter supporting a man incapable of walking on his own. They were both splattered with tomatoes and smelled of sulfur.

"Chief Jackson," I said, hoping to recapture his attention. "Could something have happened to Mrs. Trevelyan? The facts don't add up."

"Miss, the facts are simple. The lady broke the law and then skipped town. End of story. I've got better things to do with my time than chase some bottle-breaking fanatic across the Ozarks." He placed his hat on his head. "Now if you don't mind, I have work to do."

But that couldn't be. Before leaving the hotel, I had checked again with the desk clerk. Mrs. Trevelyan was still registered. Could she have left without checking out? From what I had learned about her from her letters, this was not a woman to shy away from controversy. Besides, with the majority of the coalition's members assembled in one place, she had more support for her cause and predicament than at any other time. But then where was she? And what was I going to do now?

I took a detour down two short flights of stone stairs to North Main Street and, after passing the bottom of Tibbs Alley, a narrow staircase of at least a hundred steep steps that connected to Center Street high above, started looking for the Cavern Saloon. North Main Street, unusually flat and wide for this mountainous town, was lined with clusters of buildings, mainly of unpainted wood, that were marked by mud from a recent flood. And it was bustling with activity. Farm wagons, water wagons, and carriages of all sorts fought for room in the street. At the one-story, sprawling wooden livery on the corner, three stable hands frantically tried to groom and house eight horses at once. The two restaurants I passed, one with a second-story terrace, were both crowded with patrons, and the Grand Central Hotel, a long, three-story brick building, with its doors almost continually opening and closing with arriving and departing guests, had a group of young men playing marbles inconveniently in the middle of the sidewalk. I noticed no fewer than four other saloons, all with men loitering about outside, before I found the place I was looking for, between a blacksmith shop, with its telltale rhythmic clank of metal on metal, and Crandell's Tobacco and Fine Cigars.

The first time I had gone to the Cavern Saloon, I had gone out of sheer curiosity, to see the chaos and destruction caused by the temperance crusaders. And now, out of some necessity, I was going there again. But I hadn't known where to find it; Sunday night, I had followed a crowd from the Arcadia Hotel by the glow of fire and street lamps. Today I had to ask for directions, and after several uncomfortable exchanges, I had found a woman with a bright red checkered cloth wrapped around her head, and a bareheaded young boy in a well-used white apron pulling fresh cabbage off a cart on the street a few doors down from the police station. I'd asked if they knew where I could find the Cavern. With a questioning glance and a backward wave of her hand, the woman had sent the youth into the store.

"I shouldn't have to tell you, ma'am, but that's no place for a lady."

"I need to talk to the saloonkeeper about a mutual acquaintance," I said.

When she had finished giving me directions, repeating, "Past Tibbs Alley, now, no use looking for it before," she placed her hands on her hips.

"I hope you're not fixin' to go there right now, ma'am. Old George is in a foul mood. I think he would wrestle his own mama to the ground if she looked sideways at him today. Besides, it's getting late. A lady like you shouldn't be wandering around alone."

I had thanked her for her directions and her advice and

then walked until I found the saloon. Luckily, no one loitered about outside.

I'd never been inside a saloon before. I didn't intend to enter one now. Built into the side of the rocky hillside, I could see how the saloon lived up to its name. I didn't recognize any of the shops or buildings surrounding it and realized that the events of Sunday night must have taken place on the third-story entrance, two street levels above. I waited outside for several minutes until a man emerged. The strong smell of tobacco and alcohol (Now where had I smelled that recently?) accosted me as the doors swung open.

"Excuse me, sir? Would you be kind enough to ask the owner if he would grant me a few minutes?"

The man offered me one long, uncomfortable stare and continued down the street. I attempted this three more times, twice with men going into the saloon and once with another man leaving. However, I waited in vain. I glanced at my watch; I'd been waiting for over an hour and it was starting to get dark. I was going to have to enter myself or abandon my mission. I stood there a few more minutes gathering my courage.

"May I help you, miss?"

I recognized his voice. Until that moment, the men that had frequented the Cavern had dirt under their nails and few words on their lips and were looking forward to a well-earned drink. But I knew when I turned to see him that his dress would be impeccable. I wasn't disappointed.

"Ah, the lovely lady from Sunday night's bar raid." The gentleman I had met two days ago removed his top hat. "May I be of service?"

"Yes, thank you. I was hoping for an audience with the saloonkeeper. Would you ask him if he would step outside and give me a moment of his time? It's about a mutual acquaintance, Mrs. Edwina Trevelyan."

"Mrs. Trevelyan?" The gentleman laughed as he removed

his gloves, one finger at a time. "I'm not sure George wants to talk to anyone about the good and righteous Mrs. Trevelyan. But for an introduction, lovely lady, I'll do whatever is in my power to help you."

"Miss Hattie Davish."

"I'm pleased to meet you, Miss Davish." He took my hand, lifting it against his soft lips. "Walter Grice, at your service." Slightly flustered, I could feel the blood rise in my cheeks.

Walter Grice released my hand. "I must warn you, Miss Davish, George isn't in the best of moods. As you can imagine, Mrs. Trevelyan is not his favorite topic, and with what happened this afternoon . . . But if you would still like to speak to him, I'll get him for you."

"Thank you, Mr. Grice. Yes, I would like to speak to, is it George?"

"Yes, George Shulman."

True to his word, Mr. Grice disappeared into the saloon and emerged within minutes with the man I'd seen standing up to the temperance demonstrators earlier that afternoon. George Shulman, after wiping it on his apron, held out his hand as we introduced ourselves. It was as callused as Walter Grice's hand had been soft.

"Walt says you want to talk to me?"

"Yes, Mr. Shulman. I'm Mrs. Edwina Trevelyan's secretary and—" I didn't get any farther. With a menacing glare at Mr. Grice, George Shulman stormed back toward the saloon. He collided with one of his arriving customers and, without an apology, yanked open the door, shoving the man inside.

"She's missing," I cried. George Shulman stopped, the open door still in his hand, and looked back at me. The dramatic tactic worked, but I felt embarrassed in front of the attentive eyes of Walter Grice. "I know she disrupted your business, but—"

He pointed to his bandaged head. "Is this a disruption? Those women cracked open my skull and almost burned down in one night what I've spent my whole life building." As he let go of the door, someone from inside pushed a chair against it, propping it open. The room beyond was dim, but I could see outlines of men gathering near the open doorway.

He advanced toward me. "You say she's missing? Do you think I care if she's missing? You have no idea what that woman has cost me."

"Good riddance, huh, George," a voice from inside shouted.

"Have you seen her since Sunday, Mr. Shulman?" I said, ignoring the taunt.

"I don't know what you're implying, miss. But I was here all day; I'm here every day."

"Unless you're out campaigning," another voice from inside shouted. "Shulman for city council!"

Someone else chanted, "Vote No on 203, Vote No on 203," his feet stomping on the wooden floor, mimicking the marchers. Several men laughed.

George Shulman, ignoring the ruckus behind him, stopped within inches of my face. "I hope I never lay eyes on that woman again. I could kill her for what she's done to me."

He stomped back into the saloon, shoving the chair away and slamming the door behind him.

"Kill her?" *Did I hear him right?*

"Miss Davish?" My ears were ringing and someone was calling my name. "Miss Davish? Are you all right?" Walter Grice, grasping me by the wrist, glanced at his pocket watch. Taking a few deep breaths, I extricated my wrist from the gentleman's grip.

"You'll have to forgive George, Miss Davish. His behavior is inexcusable."

I straightened my hat. "It's a relief to know he's not always like this."

"No, the Cavern is known as much for its hospitality as it is for its brawls; its proprietor is very popular. George Shulman may even be our new city councilman. No, he's not all bad, Miss Davish. He didn't mean what he said, I assure you."

We stood in silence for a moment or two. A beautiful tenor voice began singing somewhere inside the saloon. The song, met with rowdy applause, was jovial, but I couldn't understand the words.

"You see," Walter Grice said, tilting his head toward the source of the music, "that's typical George; he's already forgotten about your row."

I knew I wouldn't soon forget. "It was nice to make your acquaintance, again, Mr. Grice, but I must be going." I turned to leave.

"Let me walk you to your hotel, Miss Davish, if that's where you're going. It will be dark soon. Let me escort you back."

"That's very kind of you, but . . ."

"It's the least I can do."

Mr. Grice did seem charming, and an escort would be prudent given that night was fast approaching. But the exchange with George Shulman had left my ears ringing and my hands shaking. I needed the solitary walk back to the Arcadia to calm my nerves.

"Thank you, but I'll be fine."

The song in the saloon stopped short, and then we heard shouting and the sound of shattering glass. Before Walter Grice could comment, I hurried away.

It *was* getting late. And I was full of self-reproach before I even reached the Tibbs Alley stairwell. The once-crowded street was quiet of wagon traffic. The horses were all stabled and the marble players were gone. Only the men loitering outside saloons remained. The farmers and the shopkeepers were safely sitting by their firesides, not wandering past saloons, which were blazing with light and full to capacity with questionable characters. The warm glow of the gas street lamps on the faces of the people I passed only reminded me of my foolishness. What was I thinking? The saloonkeeper had threatened to kill Mrs. Trevelyan. Was he in earnest or merely making a boisterous, but harmless claim? Either way, I should never have gone to the saloon. Wanting the quickest route back to the hotel, I began climbing the alley stairs.

With buildings towering up on either side three and four stories high, the only patch of light came from a single lamp, about a third of the way up, illuminating a fragment of an advertisement painted on the wall, *& Sons, Furnishers, Guaranteed.* Music and laughter coming from nearby establishments were swallowed up in the stillness around me as I reached the dim glow of the lantern. I paused in the circle of its light and peered down at the street below. A young couple, arm in arm, strolled by, the streetlight reflecting off the white heron feathers on the girl's hat. Their lighthearted banter persisted as they passed out of sight. I adjusted my bonnet, imagining the wares in Mrs. Cunningham's window and, hesitating only slightly when I turned to face the darkness above, continued climbing with renewed vigor. *When did I become so skittish?*

Two flights of stairs from the top, the alley was pitch dark and I had to use the rail to guide me. I barely missed kicking an empty bottle sitting on the landing. A waft of liquor drifted from an unlit doorway. As I bent to move it, a figure lurched out directly in front of me. In the darkness, I could only make out the outlines of a cloak and hat. I stood up and stepped back, losing my balance. Two hands reached out and seized my shoulders. But instead of attempting to steady me, they shook me frantically.

"You." The voice seethed with rage.

"Let me go," I said.

"Why couldn't you leave it alone?"

"Let me go."

"Why couldn't you keep your stupid mouth shut?"

"Let me go!"

I kicked out and struck a blow with the heel of my boot. The figure yelped, releasing me from his grip. Futilely grasping for a hold, I screamed, powerless to stop my backwards fall. For a few heartbeats, I was airborne. I tried to brace my fall with my hands but my knee hit first, tossing me hard onto my back farther down the stairs. I gasped for breath. Something wet dripped down my face and I could taste blood in my mouth. Cold air pierced the exposed skin on my shoulders and legs; my stockings were in shreds. My right foot was tangled in the torn hem of my dress. My knee throbbed and the palms of my hands stung. I could feel what was left of my bonnet crumpled beneath me, the ribbon band still attached to the hatpin in my hair. But thank goodness, I'd stopped falling.

A man shouted from the street below. Glass shattered as the single lantern crashed against the wall, plunging the alley into complete darkness. I attempted to get up. The sound of advancing footsteps echoed in my ears as the sliver of sky between the buildings momentarily cleared to reveal a brilliant field of stars. Then everything went black.

CHAPTER 8

"Wake up, Miss Davish." A soft, warm hand lightly tapped my cheek. "Come on, now, wake up."

Go away, I thought, groaning at the disruption of my sleep.

"That a girl. Now open your eyes." Sunlight flooded the room as Walter Grice's concerned face hovered above me. I bolted upright, holding the sheet to my chin. He took a step back.

"Mr. Grice, what are you doing here?"

My bandaged hands stung and blood rushed to my head. I was in my bed at the Arcadia Hotel. The memory of the night before flooded back as I sank into the pillows. I gingerly touched my ribs. I felt a bandage on my forehead and knew I'd find similar ones on my shoulder and knee. My head pounded. My whole body ached.

"Everything's all right, dear." Miss Lizzie patted my hand from the other side of the bed. I hadn't noticed her before. Miss Lucy and Mary Flannagan stood behind her. "You're in good hands with Dr. Grice."

"Dr. Grice?" I said. "You didn't tell me you were a physician."

"Have you two already met?" Miss Lucy asked.

"Yes, twice," the doctor said, grinning.

"But you could say we weren't properly introduced," I said.

"I'm sorry, Miss Davish," the doctor said. "Under Sunday's circumstances, I thought it was obvious and didn't need mentioning. You don't have anything against the medical profession, do you?" He laughed as he held my wrist and glanced at his watch.

I said nothing, but tried to pull my hand away.

Dr. Grice raised his head, his smile gone. "Not crazy about physicians, eh, Miss Davish?" I bit back my reply.

"You've suffered several lesions and abrasions, not to mention a possible concussion or broken rib. I recommend a complete examination, but . . ."

"But if I'm merely suffering from cuts and bruises, then there's no need," I said, inching to the other side of the bed. My skin felt clammy and cold.

"Hattie, dear," Miss Lizzie said, "Dr. Grice is an excellent physician. There's no need to worry. You're in good hands."

I sat up, slower this time, and faced Miss Lizzie, my back to the doctor and his expression of concern.

"Oh, I'm sure he is. But I don't need a physician." I removed the bandage from my head. "See? I'm quite all right now." To avoid witnessing Mary Flannagan dispose of the bloody bandage, I focused on the fresh pile of correspondences on the desk. "And I have work to do."

"Oh, your work can wait, Davish," Miss Lucy said.

"Don't be afraid, dear. Lucy and I have known Dr. Grice for years. He's our physician whenever we're in town." I began to shake. "He attends most of our friends as well."

"Did you know that if it wasn't for Dr. Grice, Davish, you might still be lying in Tibbs Alley?" Miss Lucy said.

"It's a blessing, dear, that he was so close at hand."

"Dr. Grice heard you scream," Mary Flannagan said. "You were bleeding all over." She held up the bloody bandage as proof. The room began to spin as waves of dizziness washed over me. "You've been unconscious all night."

"Davish, the way you're acting, you'd think the man pushed you down the stairs," Miss Lucy grumbled. "Now sit up and let him examine you."

I glanced at Walter Grice's face, but couldn't read his expression.

"Must you?" I closed my eyes and clutched the sheet to my chin.

"It's all right, Miss Davish. I've seen enough for today." I dropped back into the pillows, relieved. "Promise me, though, that you'll get plenty of rest. I've left an elixir with the maid. It's to be taken for the pain twice a day."

I eyed the bottle on the nightstand, nodded, and was grateful to watch him pack up his medical bag. He left instructions with the maid and said good-bye to the elderly sisters. My heart pounded in my chest when he approached my bed again and leaned in close. Was it from the gleam in his eye or the fact that I might not have averted the examination after all? I wasn't sure.

"I'll be in your debt, Miss Davish, if you don't mention where we met." He glanced over his shoulder at the Shaw sisters and then winked at me. "I'm not sure they would approve." I closed my eyes and inhaled the sweet scent of his shaving cologne.

"Rest now. I'll be back to check on you later." To my surprise, I almost looked forward to it.

"What were you doing in Tibbs Alley, Davish? And at

night?" Miss Lucy said the moment the doctor shut the door behind him. "You may excel at what you do, but you certainly don't know what you're doing. No common sense whatsoever."

"I wanted to speak with George Shulman, the man who owns the bar."

"You went into a saloon?" Miss Lucy said, flabbergasted. "I'm extremely disappointed in you, Davish. I think we've misjudged you. We thought you were respectable and knew your place."

"But Lucy, dear, Sir Arthur knows Hattie and is an excellent judge of character. He wouldn't have recommended her to Edwina if she was 'that kind of girl.' There must be some kind of mistake."

"There has been a mistake," I said. "I never entered the bar. I would never do that. I simply went there to speak to the owner, George Shulman."

"And," Miss Lucy said, her arms folded tightly across her chest.

"I spoke to him for less than five minutes, saw that it was getting dark, and left."

"Well then, everything is all right, dear. Isn't it, Lucy?" Miss Lizzie giggled, her eyes darting back and forth between me and Miss Lucy.

"I suppose. What did the barman say?" Miss Lucy said, her anger submitting to her curiosity.

"That he hadn't seen Mrs. Trevelyan since Sunday night. He was quite upset that I would even ask."

"Yes, I suppose he would. He's a devil, that one," Miss Lucy said. "We haven't heard yet about yesterday's vote, but if it fails, he's the one to blame. Well, was it worth it?"

I touched my tender ribs and considered the question. I'd been attacked, but I had also gleaned a valuable impression of

George Shulman, of which Mrs. Trevelyan must be told. And I'd met Walter Grice again.

"Yes, I think maybe it was."

"Well, I hope so, Davish. If you rode down the middle of the road like Lady Godiva, you couldn't have gotten yourself into a worse predicament. You're lucky the doctor was considerate enough not to leave you there. Despite his respectability, people will still talk, you know."

"You do take chances, dear," Miss Lizzie said. "A woman at night, alone."

"Whatever were you thinking?" Miss Lucy chided. "It was dark. You should've been more careful and watched where you were going. Maybe you wouldn't have tripped."

"You're right. I shouldn't have been out after dark. But I didn't do it on purpose, Miss Lucy. Someone deliberately pushed me down the stairs."

"Oh, dear." Miss Lizzie patted my hand again. "I had no idea. We had no idea, did we, Lucy? We all thought you tripped. Who could've done such a thing?"

"I don't know. It was too dark; I couldn't see who it was. He grabbed me by the shoulders and jerked me around. I tried to break free, then he pushed me and I lost my balance."

"Oh, dear. Oh, dear," Miss Lizzie said, her hand at her throat. "You could've been killed. Why would anyone want to harm you?"

"I think it has something to do with Mrs. Trevelyan," I said.

"Edwina? Why would you think that?" Miss Lucy asked.

"Because someone wants me to stop asking questions."

I told them what my assailant said. I described the confrontation with George Shulman a few minutes before the attack. As he requested, I left out that Dr. Grice had introduced us.

"It could've been George Shulman; it could've been someone else from the bar who overheard us," I said. "I don't know."

"George Shulman is a violent man. You should go to the police, dear."

"The police weren't too cooperative yesterday, Miss Lizzie," I said. "I don't think today will be any different."

"But your fall? An assault on a respectable young woman . . ."

"Won't change a thing, Lizzie," her sister said. "You know as well as I do the police are not sympathetic to the coalition or its cause. Besides, what do you know about George Shulman?"

"But there must be something we can do, Lucy, dear."

"No, Lizzie, now let's go. Davish needs her sleep. I've seen mothers of newborn triplets look more rested."

"And Mrs. Trevelyan?" I asked.

"Still inexplicably absent, I'm afraid," Miss Lizzie said.

The sisters rose simultaneously, and admonishing me again to rest, closed the door behind them. I obliged and drifted into a dreamless sleep until the door burst open, striking the wall. With the door's crash reverberating in my aching head, Mary Flannagan stormed into the room.

"It's the police, miss. If you're up to it, you might want to get over there. Those lousy coppers are at it again."

I fumbled with my sheets, struggled into my robe, and stumbled out of bed, pausing long enough for my nausea to settle down. I followed Mary as fast as my bandaged knee would allow. The police were searching Mrs. Trevelyan's room. Three men rummaged through drawers, the wardrobe, the bed linen and mattress as Miss Lizzie watched from the doorway. Upon seeing me, she shooed away the maid and tried to persuade me to go back to bed. I recognized the tall, black-haired man in charge. He was wiping dust from the sword fern's leaves.

"Chief Jackson, has something happened?" I asked.

The policeman turned and his face flushed.

"Please excuse her attire, Officer," Miss Lizzie said. "Miss Davish has been recovering next door due to a terrible fall last night. As you can see, she's been quite rattled and doesn't quite know what's she's doing." I'd forgotten I was standing there in my dressing gown and robe. "You'll be able to talk with her after she's had more rest."

"Well, ma'am, miss, there isn't much to talk about."

"There most certainly is something to talk about," Miss Lizzie admonished. "Officer, this young woman was viciously assaulted. Someone pushed her down the Tibbs Alley stairwell."

"Ma'am, if you've got a complaint to file, do it at the precinct. We've got important work to do here."

"But, Officer, Miss Davish could've been killed. Isn't that important enough for you?"

"Ma'am, this town was built into the side of mountains and has thousands of stairs. People fall down them every day. Invalids and women should know better than to be walking around this town alone at night. Now, as I said, I've got work to do." He turned his back on us.

"You're officially investigating Mrs. Trevelyan's disappearance, aren't you?" I said.

Chief Jackson glanced back at me.

"Miss Davish, is it?" I nodded. "Miss Davish, Mrs. Trevelyan is wanted for assault and destruction of property. So, yes, we're trying to determine the suspect's whereabouts."

"Sir?" One of the other officers held up a silver-plated hand mirror. It had been shattered. "Found it under the dresser."

"Good job, Norris. Now look for glass." The officer dropped

to his knees and searched the carpet. "Good day, ladies." The chief dismissed us with a wave of his hand.

"But why are you searching her room now?" I watched as the policeman on the floor gathered up tiny pieces of glass. "Yesterday you said . . ."

"Yesterday I didn't have, ah, certain facts. Now," he said, escorting us to the door, "if y'all don't mind."

Behind him one of the other officers flipped a suitcase upside down on the bed. It was empty. Another dumped hatboxes on the floor, with no regard to their contents' delicate embellishments. Broken flowers, feathers, and bits of straw were scattered across the carpet.

"You should be more careful with those," I said.

"Keep at it, Thompson," Chief Jackson said, pushing us through the doorway.

"But Miss Davish was attacked," Miss Lizzie said. "If I had known how uncooperative you'd be—"

"Like I said, ma'am, file a complaint. As you can see, I'm busy right now. I don't have time to indulge the whim of every woman who demands my attention."

"Sir, I found some more. But this didn't come from the mirror." The officer on the floor held up a large piece of clear, thick glass.

"You can be assured, I will most definitely be filing a complaint," Miss Lizzie said.

"Fine. Now good day to you, ladies. Let's have a look at that, Norris," Chief Jackson said, herding us out of the room and closing the door. "Burke, is that all the luggage?"

CHAPTER 9

"That's not all." Miss Lizzie and I turned to see Mary waiting down the hallway.

"What's not all, dear?" Miss Lizzie asked.

"Remember that trunk I told you about, miss? The one I packed Miss Edwina's old dresses in for charity?" I nodded. "Well, I was surprised it had already been shipped. The trunk was only half-full."

"What does that have to do with anything, dear?" Miss Lizzie said.

Mary looked at Miss Lizzie, then at me and then back to Miss Lizzie. "You're right, ma'am. Never mind." I put my hand on the maid's arm as she turned to leave.

"Mary, what about the trunk?"

"Oh, nothing, except I asked Owen about it. He's in charge of this floor, so he would know."

"And?" I said.

"He said the trunk had been returned to the storage room. So what's in her room isn't all of the lady's luggage, that's all. Her old clothes are in a trunk in the storage room." I was familiar with the storage room, packed to the hilt with empty trunks, crates, and boxes. I had started my search for Mrs. Trevelyan Monday morning in the basement.

"Thank you, dear," Miss Lizzie said.

"Maybe you should tell the police," I said. Mary's eyes widened and, without another word, she fled down the hall and out of sight.

"What a strange girl," Miss Lizzie said. "What difference does it make where a trunk is?"

"Miss Lizzie, I saw that trunk the afternoon I arrived. It was gone the following day."

"I fail to see the significance, dear. Edwina must've had it removed."

"Exactly, which means she must have spoken to someone besides the maid that day. We know so little about where she went or why. Anyone she spoke to may be able to tell us more. We just have to figure out who it was."

"Yes, I see what you mean," Miss Lizzie conceded.

"And why would she store a charity trunk half-full? That seems odd to me."

"She probably got tired of it being underfoot," Miss Lizzie said, "or the maid only thought it was half-full. The girl doesn't seem to be the swiftest of creatures."

Miss Lizzie could be right. Something else could be packed in it. I'd seen Mrs. Piers retrieve something from the wardrobe at the same time I'd seen the trunk. She'd been quick to hide them, but I'm certain they were the hatchets used at the saloon smashing. But I'd searched the room and the police were there searching again. The hatchets hadn't been returned to the wardrobe after Sunday night's raid. Could the coalition's arsenal now be hidden in the trunk? I should go and have a look.

"Miss Davish, you're worrying me."

Miss Lizzie stood next to me, her brow knitted in concern.

We were still in the middle of the hallway outside Mrs. Trevelyan's room.

"I'm sorry, Miss Lizzie. Were you saying something?"

"Yes, dear, you need to go back to your room and rest. If you think it's important, I'll tell the police about the trunk the maid mentioned."

"Yes, that's a good idea." I let the kind old lady guide me back to bed. A pang of guilt struck me, as I had no intention to stay in my room to rest. I was going to look in the trunk before the police rummaged through it.

"Lucy and I'll get you for tea if you're up to it."

Miss Lizzie had barely closed the door when I was up and dressing. Despite the bandages on my hands and shoulder, I managed to don a plain brown and white wool dress and a pair of slippers. I opened my door, peeked both ways for old ladies or policemen and, seeing neither, strode to the elevator. I had ridden in one before. It would be faster than my sore legs could navigate the two flights of stairs and no one would see me. I remember the thrill and amazement I'd felt that first time. I'd taken the speeding elevator car to the twelfth floor of the Manhattan Building in Chicago to deliver some papers to the law office of Burlingame, Carpenter, Carpenter & Rouse. Mrs. Adelaide Washburn had been my employer then.

The elevator doors opened. A young man in a uniform and cap stood inside. I'd forgotten about the elevator operator.

"Which floor, miss?" A bit flustered, I couldn't think of a good excuse for going to the basement.

"The ground floor, please."

We rode the short distance in silence. I can't imagine what he thought when I poked my head out of the elevator before disembarking. Few people were about. A gentleman in one of the rocking chairs held a newspaper in front of his face. It was replete with headlines about the election: CLEVELAND ELECTED—A SPLENDID VICTORY, PROPOSITION 203 VOTED

DOWN AGAIN, SHULMAN BEATS FAIRCHILD FOR CITY COUN-
CIL. Edna, the temperance lady with the poodle, and a white-
haired companion occupied a settee near the window. While
Charlie the dog's eyes followed my movements, the women,
involved in their discussion, never noticed me. The voices
down the hall told me everyone else was at lunch.

I limped down the short flight of stairs. I closed the heavy
basement door behind me, shutting out the faint murmur of
the women's voices. I was surrounded by silence. The air was
chilly and I could see my breath. A long, unadorned hallway
stretched in front of me. Several simple Edison lamps hung
from the ceiling far above. A strong scent of soap indicated the
hotel's laundry was near. I wrapped my arms around me and
started down the hall. My slippered feet scraped against the ce-
ment floor.

I passed several closed doors until I came to one marked
Storage. A faint pungent odor I hadn't noticed the last time I
was here wafted under the door and mingled with the scent of
the laundry. I twisted the knob, and as the door swung open, I
scrambled for a handkerchief and pressed it to my nose. Tears
welling up in my eyes, I skimmed the room. Inside the door,
against the wall, was an enormous steamer trunk padlocked
and labeled *MRS. CHARLES TREVELYAN, ST. LOUIS,
MO.* It was the same trunk I'd seen in Mrs. Trevelyan's room.

I started to gag. I retreated out of the room and ran head-
long into a man, his silk waistcoat crumpling beneath the press
of my hand.

"Dr. Grice!"

"Quick, Miss Davish, away from the door." He compelled
me to move aside and slammed the door shut.

"What are you doing here?" *Was he following me?* I wondered.

"I could ask the same of you, Miss Davish. You're supposed
to be resting." He held a newspaper folded under his arm.

"I know, and I did for some time. I came down to retrieve something from Mrs. Trevelyan's trunk."

"Before the police got here, no doubt." He chuckled. His joviality was infectious, and I relaxed.

"Do you recognize that odor, Dr. Grice? I thought it might be rancid butter."

"Rancid butter?" He took a moment to inhale the scent, then blanched. "No, it's more serious than that. Come, Miss Davish, we have to get the police."

I held the handkerchief to my face and reached for the doorknob. "I'd like to look in Mrs. Trevelyan's trunk first."

Walter Grice reached out toward the door, placing his hand on mine. It felt warm and for a slight moment, I forgot the impropriety of the gesture.

"That wouldn't be wise, Miss Davish." He removed his hand from the door and put his arm around me. "Miss Davish, you're shivering. Your face is quite pale."

Too feeble to resist his embrace, I had the sense he was holding me up.

"It is quite cold down here."

"Yes, let's get you to your room. Then I'll alert the police."

The basement door jerked open as if on cue. A policeman observed us from the doorway.

"What's this?" he said. "Hey, what are y'all doing down there?"

"It's me, Lester, Walter Grice. I'm this lady's physician. She's not well and ignored my advice to let someone else fetch a cape from storage. She almost fainted."

"Dr. Grice," Officer Lester Burke said, "I didn't expect to see you. But I'm not surprised about the lady; Chief says she's a troublemaker." *Me? A troublemaker?*

"Lester, we've got a bigger problem. You'd better get the chief."

★ ★ ★

I'm not certain what happened next. The policeman left and Dr. Grice escorted me toward the door. Then I was sitting on the floor, a few steps from the stairwell, with Dr. Grice's face, for the second time today, hovering over me. His lips moved, his breath smelling of peppermint. It was a moment or two before I understood anything that he said.

"Try to focus on my finger." I followed his finger as it moved back and forth in front of my eyes. "I'm going to take your pulse again." He lifted my wrist, placing two fingers at the base of my hand, and stared at his pocket watch. I didn't resist this time.

"You lost blood last night. You look like you haven't had a decent meal or a full night's sleep in weeks. You may still be suffering from shock. This is no place for someone in your condition. Your body needs rest. This isn't all from last night's fall, either, Miss Davish. Miss Davish, can you hear me?"

I had closed my eyes but opened them at the sound of my name.

"You need rest, lots of pure spring water, and a bath treatment or two wouldn't hurt. And you may not like it, but I need to give you a thorough examination."

I groaned at this. It was all the protest I could muster.

"Good to hear from you again, Miss Davish," the doctor said with a laugh. "Let me get you some water and a few things from my bag. I'll be right back."

He stood up as the sound of rapidly descending footsteps echoed through the passage. Chief Jackson, accompanied by Officer Burke, promptly appeared.

"Doc." Chief Jackson shook the physician's hand. "Burke says there's something going on down here?"

"Yes, Ben, it's unmistakable. Down there in the storage room, third door on the right." The doctor knelt beside me. "Stay right here until we get back."

Officer Burke flashed me a look of concern while Chief

Jackson stared down toward the storage room. Dr. Grice stood and led the policemen down the hall.

"Oh, no, where's that smell coming from?" Chief Jackson grumbled. "I'm betting it isn't from a Limburger cheese factory exploding nearby." They had reached the storage room door.

"You'll want to cover your faces, gentlemen."

All three men produced handkerchiefs, covered their faces, and entered the room. I pushed myself up using the wall and stumbled after them. I paused in the doorway as the three men contemplated Mrs. Trevelyan's trunk.

"Get it open, Burke," Chief Jackson barked.

As Officer Burke struck repeatedly at the lock with his nightstick, I studied part of the myriad of colorful labels pasted haphazardly across the trunk's surface: *Niagara Falls; Boston; Washington, D.C.; Milwaukee; Omaha; New Orleans; The Palmer House, Chicago; Grand Hotel, Mackinac Island; The Peabody, Memphis.* And those were only the ones I could see. To think this was only my second time out of the Middle West.

I heard the lock break. I slipped around the edge of the door and supported myself against the wall. I had a better view of the trunk, as long as Chief Jackson didn't move too much to his right. Officer Burke lifted the lid.

Nothing appeared amiss, except the shameful treatment of the clothing inside. Several black dresses were tangled and piled haphazardly. One, with superior lacework on the matching collar and cuffs, had been rumpled into a ball. Did Mary Flannagan normally pack like this?

Officer Burke reached in to pull out the trunk's contents and revealed a mass of white cotton covered with splotches of dark brown. Tiny fragments of gold-trimmed rose pattern china, probably the remnants of a broken teacup, stuck to the splotches. Waves of putrid smell escaped the trunk, so horrible, the policeman retched. Chief Jackson stepped back as Dr.

Grice took over for the indisposed Officer Burke, who inadvertently now blocked my view.

I pressed the handkerchief tightly against my mouth and nose and held my breath, determined not to draw attention to myself. I didn't last long. I exhaled and gagged. Fortunately my stomach was empty. Officer Burke looked over at me sympathetically but said nothing. The other two men, however, engrossed in their task, didn't notice. A pile of soiled clothing accumulated on the floor.

"Oh my God." All three men spoke in muffled unison.

I forced myself upright quickly and my knees nearly buckled. Nausea rose in my throat as I thrust my way through the men and gaped at what I saw. The birthmark across her cheek was unmistakable. Her blue eyes were partially open in a dull, sunken stare. Twisted in a white morning gown splattered with dried blood, her petite body bent unnaturally to fit the trunk, lay my employer, Mrs. Edwina Trevelyan. Her nightcap, having slipped off her head, was still tied around her neck by a two-inch-wide satin bow. My vision blurred, and then I crumpled to the floor.

CHAPTER 10

At least that's what Officer Burke later told Miss Lizzie. I'd
fainted onto the pile of dresses that had been pulled from
the trunk. He'd been the closest but hadn't been fast enough to
catch me. I didn't know that, though, when I woke in my own
bed several hours later, to the sound of muttering. Remembering the misery of sitting up too quickly this morning, I inched
my way to a sitting position. Mary Flannagan, her auburn hair
the only visible part of her, sat in an armchair with her back
to me.

"Miss Flannagan?"

Startled, she leapt out of the chair, nearly knocking it over.
She whirled around, a book in her hand, Wilkie Collins's *The
Woman in White*. She'd been engrossed in her reading.

"Oh, Miss Hattie, you startled me." She held her hand to
her chest, catching her breath. She tucked her book away and
wiped her eyes with the edge of her apron. "How are you feeling? No one expected you to waken so soon." She fussed
about the bed, fluffing my pillows, tucking my sheets. "Even

so, the doctor's been in twice and those old ladies have been fluttering around here nonstop."

"You don't have to do that, Mary. I'm fine." I lifted the sheets and swung my feet off the edge of the bed, my headache all but gone. "How long have I been asleep? The last thing I remember is . . ."

"Finding the old lady dead," the maid finished my sentence stoically.

"Yes, in the trunk." I pushed away the image of Mrs. Trevelyan lying among her dresses, cold and gray.

"I packed that trunk myself." She shuddered. "Those clothes were to go to a charity. The Salvation Army is what she called it. Sounds like her kind of charity, doesn't it?"

"Yes, but then what happened, Mary?"

"After you found her, you collapsed. You've been unconscious for hours."

I'd never fainted before and now had done it twice in less than twenty-four hours. What was wrong with me? I had a reputation of reliability and competence to uphold.

"Well, I'm fine now. But what about the police? What did they say? What are they doing about it?"

The maid snorted. "Sure, the coppers've been busy, demanding answers, rifling through the lady's room, ransacking the storage area. They've taken over the parlors, and are, as we speak, interrogating the help. I've already had my turn. You can bet they'll be talking to every last one of those temperance ladies too. They've made it very clear that no one was to leave town. Even you're to be questioned. I'm to bring you down, when you're up to it."

I slid out of bed and stood up on my shaky legs. My left knee throbbed. "I'm up to it now." I readjusted my corset, smoothed my dress, and twisted my hair up into a bun. A tinge of pain shot through my ribs. "But do they know what happened? Or why?"

"They didn't say. The coppers aren't telling anyone anything."

And they didn't tell me anything either when I appeared in the ladies' parlor a few minutes later. The airy feel of the room, with its tall ceilings, large windows letting in the afternoon sun, and ivory and sage color scheme, was a stark contrast to the mood of its occupants. The room was full of members of the temperance coalition, most of whom were quietly sniffling behind handkerchiefs or using them to dab at their eyes, red and puffy from hours of crying. Josephine Piers wept openly, clutching her friend Eleanor's hand. Cordelia Anglewood sat on the edge of her chair, tapping her foot, and appeared ready to spring out of the room. Miss Lizzie, her handkerchief clenched tightly in her lap with one hand, mindlessly nibbled on a yeast roll in the other. Miss Lucy, dry-eyed and whose countenance fully expressed her displeasure at me for leaving my bed, indicated with her hand for me to join her on the settee.

"Chief Jackson, have you—" I said.

"Ah, Miss Davish, glad to see you on your feet again," Chief Jackson said, interrupting me. "Now please take a seat. I was asking these ladies to account for their whereabouts the morning of the murder." He consulted a small notebook. "Now, let me get this straight. Miss Halbert, Miss Shaw, Mrs. Fry, Mrs. Stewart, Mrs. White, and Miss Robbins, you were all in the company of others all morning Monday?"

"Yes," Miss Lucy said, speaking for the group.

"Thank you, Mrs. Fry. And Miss McLean and Mrs. Piers, we already know, were being detained at the jail for destruction of property," Jackson said. The two women, with Eleanor still comforting the distraught Josephine, nodded in agreement. "What happened to your friend, Mrs. Sarah Yates? She was the fourth member of your saloon smashing brigade, correct?"

Sarah Yates? I'd never heard the name before. And I'd seen Eleanor McLean several times but hadn't recognized her as one of the saloon smashers. And when had the women been detained by the police? I had no idea. What else didn't I know?

"Sarah left on the 10:14 train Sunday night," Eleanor said. "As far as we know, she hasn't returned." Jackson scribbled something in his notebook and frowned. He swiveled around to face me. "You're a secretary, right?"

"Yes," I said, confused.

"Here." He handed me the notebook. The binding was brown with several coffee ring stains on its cover. "Take notes, will you? I can't read my own handwriting."

I was torn. Part of me was aghast at his presumption, wondering whether this was why he had sent for me, while the other half was grateful to have something safe and familiar to do. I flipped the notebook open to the page the policeman indicated.

"Who's next?" Jackson asked.

I read off the names, one by one, and recorded their responses. Miss Halbert, Miss Lawler, Mrs. Watley, and Mrs. Nason were in the library together planning the day's events. Mrs. Miller had been at the American Bathhouse, Mrs. Anglewood had been out riding, Miss Kiltcher had been meeting with a sign printer in town, and Miss Smith, having packed altogether wrong for the Southern climate, had been dress shopping.

"And now, Miss Davish, where were you Monday morning?" Chief Jackson said when he had gone down the entire list of names.

"I went hiking early, had breakfast with Miss Shaw and Mrs. Fry, then looked for Mrs. Trevelyan. I actually looked in the storage room that morning."

"You what?"

"I wanted to be thorough, so I started in the basement."

"Of course you did. Did you happen to see her trunk in the storage room?"

"No, it wasn't there then. I assume it was still in Mrs. Trevelyan's room. But I was wondering—"

"Well, that about does it for now, ladies." Chief Jackson smacked his hands together. "Y'all are dismissed, but don't leave Eureka Springs until I say so. I'm having the depot watched, just in case. And that includes you, Miss Davish. I may have more questions for you."

Everyone stood, a collective listless gesture. Small groups formed as the women tried to comfort each other. I couldn't share in their grief, having never actually met Mrs. Trevelyan, but I sympathized with their loss. The looks of shock, disbelief, and hopelessness I saw as I looked around the room were all too familiar. I had lost a baby brother and both of my parents by the age of seventeen. My closest friend, Myra, had died of influenza just last August. But none had been murdered, not officially anyway. I knew there was nothing I could say or do to ease their pain. Unbidden tears came to my eyes as these buried thoughts rose to the surface. Before anyone could notice, I wiped my eyes and hastily left the room.

Mary Flannagan was waiting for me outside the door. She motioned me away from the others. "I heard what they said in there. Stupid coppers probably believe everything those women told them."

"Why shouldn't they?" I said, matching her whisper.

"Because at least four of them lied." Not hesitating to see if we'd been overheard, I drew Mary into the vacant library.

"How do you know that, Mary?" My heart was racing, and not only from the sudden exertion.

"I saw them. I saw Miss Josephine and another woman leaving that lady's room that morning. Well, that other woman was Eleanor McLean, who just left the parlor a minute ago. They obviously weren't in jail then." She was right. I had seen Josephine Piers before breakfast and then again afterward with Eleanor McLean outside Mrs. Trevelyan's door.

"That was before you saw the police, wasn't it?" The maid nodded. "They must've gone with the police for questioning, then."

"Maybe, but I also passed that old lady, Miss Lizzie, coming out of here with a dark stain on her dress. It could've been blood."

"More likely she spilt food on herself during breakfast." Mary didn't seem to know anything new after all. I began to relax.

"And what about Miss Cordelia? She didn't tell the coppers she visited Miss Edwina that morning." The maid sneered. "Maybe she did go riding after that, I don't know. She certainly carried her whip with her."

"Why do you say it like that?"

"She's a nasty piece of work, that Cordelia Anglewood. I told you before that she visited Miss Edwina. But what I didn't tell you was that they had a terrible fight. Miss Cordelia raised her whip to that old lady."

I swayed, suffering a sudden wave of nausea. I reached out to a bookcase and steadied myself. "What did the police say when you told them?"

"I didn't tell them anything."

"What? You didn't tell the police? Why not?"

The maid squared her shoulders and looked defiant. "I'm telling you, aren't I? Nothing good ever came out of helping coppers."

"Do you know what the fighting was about?"

"Money, I think, but I'm not sure. I'd come back with the second pot of coffee and missed most of it."

"But you saw her leave, and Mrs. Trevelyan was still alive?"

"Of course, she was even in a good mood."

"After almost getting hit with a horse whip?"

"I was surprised too. She even thought it was funny, laughing a little. When I asked if she was all right, she said not to worry, that Miss Cordelia was 'all bark and no bite.' The old lady had more spirit than I gave her credit for. Too bad she was so unreasonable sometimes."

I didn't ask what she was referring to. What she had already told me was enough, that Cordelia Anglewood had threatened Mrs. Trevelyan the very morning of the murder and that Cordelia and perhaps the three other women had lied to the police. If this was true, who else had lied? Who else was withholding information?

"Well, I'd better get back to work. I still have rooms to clean. But overhearing those women in there, I had to tell you what I knew."

"Thank you, Mary. I need to get back to work too." The maid turned to go, but pulled something from her apron and turned back.

"Oh, I forgot. Dr. Grice left his card, in case you need anything." I took the card.

"Mary, before you go, I forgot to ask you something. Does the name John Martin mean anything to you?" Seeing Dr. Grice's card reminded me of the one I had found in Mrs. Trevelyan's Bible.

She tilted her head, thinking. "No, I don't think so. Why?"

"He might've visited Mrs. Trevelyan before she died."

"Only temperance women were there Monday morning," she said. "I don't know of anybody else."

"He could've visited a day or two before."

"Oh." She gnawed her lip. "I really couldn't say, though I've seen lots of people coming and going from that lady's room. I never met any of them. I suppose her secretary took care of that. Come to think of it, though, I did serve coffee to two of her visitors last week. One was a man."

"When did he visit? Did you catch his name?"

"I remember the lady's name was Sarah. She was a fat woman who arrived in time for lunch on Saturday. She worked on her stitching and talked nonstop about her son in the navy. The man came on Friday afternoon. I was surprised Miss Edwina wanted coffee that late. She drinks a lot of coffee but always said it kept her up at night if she had any after two."

I asked again. "Did you catch the man's name?"

"Now that I think about it, Miss Edwina did call him by name. She called him Joseph or James or something like that. It could've been John. His last name could've started with an *M*, but it wasn't Martin, though. I would've remembered that; my uncle's name is Martin. I didn't stick around to hear what they talked about. I had all my dusting left to do." A note in Mrs. Trevelyan's calendar had listed a name beginning with *M*, but that was on Sunday, not Friday.

"Why do you want to know all this? Do you think the man has something to do with the lady's murder?"

"I don't know, Mary, but I intend to find out."

CHAPTER 11

"What was that all about, Davish?"

Miss Lucy and her sister, who had been waiting for me in the lobby, watched Mary Flannagan dart down the hallway. I wanted to slip away too. My knee hurt and my head was spinning from all that had happened. I wished nothing more than to be left alone to organize my thoughts at my typewriter.

"And shouldn't you be in bed?" Miss Lucy held her hand up before I could answer or protest. She seemed none the worse for the tragedy. "Since you're already up, let's eat."

"I'm so sorry for your loss," I said.

"Thank you, dear," Miss Lizzie said. "It's all been such a shock."

"Yes, I still can't believe it. We worked like beetles pushing dung up a hill and still lost the vote! You did hear, didn't you, Davish," Miss Lucy said, "that Proposition 203 was voted down for the seventh time! And then Edwina, murdered! I don't know if the coalition can take another blow."

I was stunned that Miss Lucy placed the same emphasis on

the loss yesterday at the polls as on the death of her friend. It was an exemplification of an organization putting their cause before individual people. Had I misjudged these kindly old ladies?

We entered the dining room and ordered tea. It was difficult to act casually but I tried. We chatted about small matters— the mild weather, *Harper's* newest fashions, where to buy the cheapest notions—until the waiter served us. I poured. As usual, Miss Lucy was the first to broach the subject foremost on all of our minds.

"Talk, Davish. Tell us everything you know."

"Oh, Lucy, leave the poor girl alone," Miss Lizzie chided her sister while licking her fingers. Cheese biscuit crumbs littered her plate. I was surprised she even had an appetite. I couldn't eat a bite.

"Hattie, dear, we were concerned about you. I'm glad to see you looking more rested, though I notice you haven't touched your food." She took a bite of a tongue sandwich from Miss Lucy's plate.

"Dr. Grice said she's fine, Lizzie. Now, we're here to talk about Edwina, aren't we?"

"Poor Edwina, murdered!" Miss Lizzie used her napkin to dab her eyes. She took a deep breath that sounded like a stifled sob. "And for you to have seen her like that. How awful."

"It was awful, Miss Lizzie," I said. "I can't stop wondering who would do such a thing."

"Well then, let's get down to business, shall we?" Miss Lucy drained her tea and set her cup down deliberately. "If Davish isn't going to, I'll start."

The elderly sisters, almost relishing the moment, were keen to give me their versions of the afternoon's events, as well as details they had gleaned from Officer Burke.

"Dr. Grice carried you himself, dear. He's such a gentleman," Miss Lizzie said, blushing. Then she bit into an apple tart. "He said you were lucky to land on that pile of dresses. Not wanting to take any chances, he attended to you himself."

"Where is Dr. Grice now?" I said.

"He went with the police, dear. Something about an autotopsy?"

"Not an autotopsy, Lizzie, an autopsy, a postmortem examination," Miss Lucy said.

"Does he know how Mrs. Trevelyan died? Or when?" I asked.

"We don't know, Davish. Dr. Grice didn't tell us a thing," Miss Lucy grumbled. "At least that policeman Burke was thoughtful enough to tell us they were taking Edwina's remains to be examined and that Dr. Grice went with them. As far as we know, they're all still there."

"Did the police say anything else?" I said. "Do they have any ideas who did this?" Miss Lucy bristled at the question.

"No, they did not. They've been rude and unforthcoming. You were there during the questioning, Davish. You know everything we do. We haven't heard anything more."

"Of course, rumors abound, dear," Miss Lizzie said. "The police questioned the hotel staff first, and I've heard several of the members whispering about missing jewels." Her hand sought the mother-of-pearl pin at her throat. "What was the maid saying?"

"Yes, Davish, you never did tell us what that maid was fussing about," Miss Lucy said.

"Mary was telling me how several of the ladies lied about their whereabouts."

Miss Lizzie batted her eyes as if dazed. Miss Lucy choked on her pumpkin cake.

"Don't believe it, Davish," Miss Lucy chided. "Did she also tell you that pink flamingos took up residence in the fountain outside? The girl's trying to bamboozle you."

"Why would she lie?"

"Don't sound so surprised. She's a strange one, that girl. Mopes around dusting at a snail's pace, goes up to that Catholic chapel every day. I've even found her lounging about reading! I know it's hard to find good help these days, but I wouldn't put up with that. And why, I ask you, would she want to trudge all the way to that hut in the woods when a perfectly good Presbyterian church is at the bottom of the hill? Davish, now there's a good Protestant name."

I remained silent as I took a sip of my tea. My father had been Protestant, but my mother, who had emigrated from Ireland, had raised me Catholic. But I didn't think Miss Lucy was in the mood for me to explain. "And her family, from what I hear, are a bunch of brawling drunkards."

"Yes, dear, I heard she has a father or uncle or something in Ireland who's in prison," Miss Lizzie said in a conspiring undertone. "Allegedly killed a man. Edwina took a special interest in the girl."

"I gave up on the girl weeks ago," Miss Lucy said, with a dismissive wave of her hand. "Lint coats my chairs and dust flies out of the wardrobe, even with the door closed. Who knows what else she's neglecting."

"But that's Edwina," Miss Lizzie clucked, "wanting to save even the maid from the devil's vice."

"I wouldn't be surprised if we find out she's involved with this whole sordid business," Miss Lucy said matter-of-factly.

"You think Mary might've killed Mrs. Trevelyan? But why?" I couldn't believe it. The idea had never entered my mind.

"Who knows with servants, money, pure vindictiveness," Miss Lucy said. "I heard Edwina tried to be strict with the girl, no courting, no carousing, and no slovenly behavior."

"Well, I know for certain there's some truth to what Mary told me," I said. "Maybe she lied about a few things, but I can't believe she murdered Mrs. Trevelyan. You must be able to think of someone else who would do this."

"I don't think so, dear," Miss Lizzie said. "Edwina Trevelyan was a generous, spiritual crusader of her cause, a role model for the younger women, a genuine leader."

"But what about the threats?" I said, then told them about the threatening letters I had seen. They seemed to know all about them and were calmly dismissive.

"True, not everyone approved of her use of violence, Lucy and I included, but that's not reason enough for someone to do this to her."

"More motivation than Mary Flannagan has, surely," I said.

"No, no, I agree with Lizzie," her sister said. "The American Women's Temperance Coalition has seen a sad day. Granted we're grateful saloon smashing will now be a thing of the past, thank goodness, but her flock will miss her, even if we didn't always agree with her tactics. No, I think Mary's the best suspect."

At that moment, the waiter returned to refill our teapot. We sat for several moments steeping our tea until Miss Lizzie interrupted the silence.

"Of course, that dreadful saloonkeeper could've done it."

"George Shulman?" I said, remembering the threat he had made to Mrs. Trevelyan.

"Yes, dear, him. He showed his penchant for violence by attacking you on the stairs."

"We don't know for sure it was him," I said.

"You may be on to something, Lizzie. The barkeep ran for city council, you know. I've heard he may have even won." Miss Lucy obviously hadn't read today's headlines yet. "And he was vehemently opposed to Proposition 203. He based his entire platform on its defeat. That's why Edwina chose his saloon, you know. And after Edwina almost destroyed his saloon,

a man like that might turn to murder. What better way to en-
sure its defeat than to dispatch its greatest champion."

"But when was he at the hotel? Mrs. Trevelyan's trunk was
in her room on Monday. How did he get in her room? Who-
ever killed Mrs. Trevelyan had access to her trunk."

"He must've come here," Miss Lucy said. Miss Lizzie
squirmed in her seat and stuffed another roll in her mouth.
"What's wrong with you, Lizzie?"

"But he said that he was working all day Monday," I said,
"and I'm sure he'll have witnesses."

"You believe a man like that?" Miss Lucy said. "First the
maid, now the saloon man. I'm disappointed in you, Davish.
I've known toddlers at a magic show that are less gullible."

"I don't know who is and who isn't lying," I said, shaking
my head.

"Just think about it. The barkeep's full of drink more times
as not. And so are his so-called witnesses. He sells liquor on the
Sabbath. What kind of man does that? He must be lying."

"Lucy's right, dear. He's lying," Miss Lizzie said, with unusual conviction.

Miss Lucy abruptly crinkled up her napkin and threw it on
the table. "Why didn't we think of this sooner? He must be arrested. Lizzie, telephone the police. The murderer must be
caught."

"But, Lucy, dear, I haven't finished my tea." She quickly
popped a melon slice into her mouth.

"Yes, well, finish your tea, and then you can call the police."

"Why don't you call? If I call, I'll miss my nap."

"But what about my nap? Davish, why don't you call?
You've got nothing better to do now." Miss Lucy's beady eyes
awaited my response.

"I don't think the police will speak to me." And I didn't

want to speak to them at the moment either. I quickly changed the subject. "From the look of everyone earlier, the members are taking the news of Mrs. Trevelyan's death quite hard."

"Yes, everyone's in shock, dear. We've lost our beloved leader."

"Everyone but Cordelia Anglewood, you mean," Miss Lucy snapped. She was growing increasingly annoyed. "She's always been the commanding type, but this is ridiculous. She's already acting like we've elected her president."

"Isn't she the vice president?" I said.

"Yes, dear," Miss Lizzie said. "But the vice president has no authority to do anything in this situation but call emergency elections. She's doing far more than that, I'm afraid. She's circulating a resolution she wants printed in the newspaper, and she is, even as we speak, making all the arrangements for Edwina's funeral and memorial service. I don't think she's consulted any other members, let alone Edwina's children. Oh, there's Diana Halbert and Kate Dowd." She waved to the two women sitting at a table on the other side of the dining room.

"Mrs. Anglewood's done all this since this morning?" I said.

"Unbelievable, isn't it, Davish? You saw her earlier; she was like a tightly wound top, ready to spin out the window. Edwina isn't even in the ground, and Cordelia Anglewood has anointed herself president. I've aligned myself with Cordelia on many issues, she being the most outspoken against the use of violence. So it pains me to say it, but I for one plan to vote against her. She's dictating that the schedule proceeds as planned while she makes the funeral arrangements. It's almost as if she had been prepared ahead of time."

Miss Lizzie and I stared aghast at Miss Lucy. The silence was uncomfortable as Miss Lucy looked back and forth between me and her sister.

"What's wrong? Why are you two looking at me . . . ?"
She stopped mid-sentence, realization dawning on her face.
She hesitated to say any more.

"Miss Lucy, are you implying that Mrs. Anglewood knew
beforehand that Mrs. Trevelyan was dead?"

"Oh, that's not what you meant, is it, Lucy, dear?" Miss
Lizzie squeaked, an expression of mortification on her face.

"No, no. Goodness, girl, you have a more vivid imagina-
tion than Jules Verne," Miss Lucy said, shaking her head. "No,
I only meant that Cordelia is ambitious and I wouldn't put it
past her to have anticipated this possible occasion, that's all.
Everyone knows she'd sell one of her grandchildren to be
AWTC's president. You're both reading too much into this.
Rumor had it that after the incident at the saloon, Cordelia
was going to call new elections anyway."

"Ambitious enough to have killed Mrs. Trevelyan?" I said.

"Lower your voice, Davish," Miss Lucy said, quickly glancing about the room. "You certainly did hit your head hard,
didn't you? Enough of this. Here, eat some more cake." Miss
Lucy handed me the plate she snatched from in front of her
sister.

"But you just implied that very possibility," I said.

"I did no such thing."

"Hattie, dear, that is wicked of you to say, no, to even think
such a thing," Miss Lizzie said. "Cordelia did not murder Edwina, George Shulman did. Besides, Cordelia was out riding
on Monday."

Cordelia Anglewood had done more than go riding; she
had quarreled with Mrs. Trevelyan, almost striking her with a
whip. A fact she had yet to reveal to Miss Lucy, Miss Lizzie, or
the police.

"Yes, that's what she told the police. And you, Miss Lizzie,
told the police you were with your sister all morning. But
Mary saw you coming out of the library alone."

"Oh, I forgot about that, dear. You're right. I went to use the telephone and returned a book I'd borrowed on the way."

"I think you've forgotten your place, Davish," her sister said coolly, rising from the table. "You accuse Cordelia when you yourself saw Cordelia walking to the stables. And now you accuse my sister Lizzie of wrongdoing? I expect an apology."

"I am sorry if I offended you, Miss Lucy, but a woman has been murdered. Anyone could've done it. And until the police find the killer, even members of the coalition are suspect."

CHAPTER 12

I bolted upright. Someone was trying to open my door. After tea, the Shaw sisters had insisted that I rest again. Still suffering from last night's fall and this morning's shocking events, I must've fallen asleep. The room was pitch dark. I barely remembered getting back into bed.

"Who is it?" I rose, slipping my feet to the floor. I still wore my brown and black pinstriped wool dress.

"Just the maid, ma'am." She jostled a tray laden with a coffeepot, mug, and several covered dishes and shoved the door open with her hip. I hastened over to help her. I pushed the button on the wall, lighting the room.

"Here, ma'am. I thought you might be hungry. You've missed supper."

As I fixed myself a plate, Mary poured the coffee. Despite my hunger, little on my plate looked appetizing. I struggled to eat the dishes of meat and cheese. However, the slices of vanilla pound cake were delicious. I told Mary to help herself.

"Thank you, but no. I'm actually here to give you these." She picked up a stack of letters from the tray. "More mail for

Miss Edwina. Mr. Oxnard, the desk clerk, told me to bring them to you."

"Thank you, Mary. I suppose I am still responsible for Mrs. Trevelyan's correspondences."

"I don't know what you're gonna do with a dead woman's letters."

I took the letters from Mary's outstretched hand and glanced through them. Most were similar to those I'd already seen. However, one was from the Bank of Eureka Springs. I plucked my letter opener off the desk and slashed the envelope open. It contained a bank receipt. One thousand dollars donated to the American Women's Temperance Coalition and deposited in an account at the Bank of Eureka Springs. The name on the receipt was John Martin. I set the letter pile down, with the bank slip at the bottom.

"I'll go through them later. But that reminds me . . ." I wrote a brief letter of my own. I had intended to write it earlier but fell asleep before I had the chance.

"Would you mind taking this to the registration desk on your way out, Mary? I would do it myself, but . . ."

The maid, taking the letter, glanced at the address. "I can take this to Dr. Grice for you, ma'am, if you want me to."

"Oh, no, it's too late."

"Don't you worry about me." Mary waved her hand in dismissal. "I won't be alone, if that's what you're thinking."

"Oh . . . Oh, I see. In that case, that would be kind of you. Are you sure you don't want some of this food?"

Mary squinched up her face and stared at me. "You're a queer one, if I may say so, ma'am. I rather like you."

"Thank you, Mary." I think that was a compliment.

She tucked the letter into the pocket of her apron, hoisted the tray off the table, and with me holding the door open, disappeared down the hall, whistling. She was long out of sight when I heard her holler, "Don't forget to take your medicine."

★ ★ ★

I glanced at the bank receipt again before filing it away. The receipt was dated Friday, November 4, 1892. *One mystery solved,* I thought. I had spent a somber but satisfying hour sorting, organizing, answering, and filing the newest batch of Mrs. Trevelyan's letters. I had related the news of Mrs. Trevelyan's death to several of her correspondents when I came across the receipt again.

It was obviously from the same man as had left his calling card for Mrs. Trevelyan. John Martin must be one of the AWTC's many supporters here for the annual meeting.

Oh, no, I thought. *Could he also be . . . ?*

I quickly leafed through one of the piles on my desk and found what I was looking for, the threatening letter signed J.M. Could this too be the same man? I hadn't made the connection before. I read the letter again, then put a sheet of paper in my typewriter.

FACTS:

1. John Martin left his calling card.
2. A man with the name starting with an M met with Mrs. Trevelyan on Friday afternoon.
3. Within an hour or two of that meeting, John Martin donated $1,000 to Mrs. Trevelyan's temperance cause.
4. A threatening letter, alluding to blackmail, was delivered by hand on Saturday or Sunday.
5. Mrs. Trevelyan was killed on Monday.

Could all this be a coincidence? I reread my list. I don't believe in these kinds of coincidences. I needed to tell the police.

Someone tapped on my door.

"Back already, Mary?" I said, answering the knock.

To my surprise, Josephine Piers, poised to leave, stood in

the hallway. She was dressed in black and held a blue glass bottle in one hand. Her perfume filled the room as she entered uninvited.

"I'm relieved to see you well, Miss Davish. I was on my way to our election meeting upstairs and thought I should check on you. I heard you met with a nasty accident in Tibbs Alley. Then to have found Mother Trevelyan like you did. It must've been horrible. Whenever I picture her lying in that trunk, dead . . ." She started to gasp for air.

"Please sit down, Mrs. Piers." Her eyes filled with tears.

"I brought this for you." She set the bottle down on the table. It was labeled *Basin Spring Water. Bottled by Eureka Water Bottling Co.* I poured her a glass of water.

"I'm sorry for your loss. From what I've heard, you and Mrs. Trevelyan were close. You must be very upset."

"Yes, Mother Trevelyan was my mentor, my guiding light." She dabbed her eyes with a handkerchief. "To find her like that, and then to lose the proposition vote after we worked so hard. Ah, what a devastating blow." As with the Shaw sisters, I wasn't sure what was more devastating, the murder of Mrs. Trevelyan or the defeat of the liquor law. It was baffling. "Do the police have any leads?"

"I wouldn't know. The police haven't spoken to me, except in the parlor this afternoon. You were there. They didn't give us much information."

"What about the doctor? Have you spoken to him?"

"The doctor? No, I haven't spoken to Dr. Grice since this morning."

"No news I can share at the meeting, then?"

"Not that I know of. Do you have any idea who might've done it, Mrs. Piers?"

"She's a martyr to the cause. You've seen the letters, the threats." She hung her head. "God's will be done."

Mary chose that moment to enter the room with little

more than a quick rap for warning. Mrs. Piers leapt from the chair, clutching her chest.

"Am I interrupting something?" the maid said.

"You should knock properly, child," Mrs. Piers said. "What do you want?"

"I have a message for Miss Hattie from Dr. Grice."

"Well, what is it?" Mrs. Piers said.

Mary glanced at me, a flash of concern on her face, before replying. "Dr. Grice said he can call on Miss Hattie in the morning, for breakfast."

"Ah, if that's all, I must be going. Do let us know what he has to say, Miss Davish." Mrs. Piers started for the door. "By the way, Sister Cordelia has chosen me to serve as coalition secretary. As such, I'll need all of Mother Trevelyan's papers. It seems God wanted me to be the secretary after all." She took my face in her hands. Out of the corner of my eye, I saw my own feelings reflected in Mary's cringe. "He must have other plans for you." She released me and headed for the door.

"Mrs. Piers, I don't think—" I said.

"I'll be in the library after luncheon tomorrow. You can give them to me then," she said, interrupting me, and then added with a wave of her hand, "Drink the water too. It'll do more for your health than anything Dr. Grice can give you. It's God's own medicine." And without a backwards glance, she left the room.

CHAPTER 13

The scent of the shortleaf pine was intoxicating. I took a long, deep breath of the fresh air. Despite my jacket and gloves, I wrapped my arms around me as I stood in front of the small, whitewashed frame chapel. I could see my breath in the stillness. I knew now why Mary came here so often.

After an entire day cooped up in the hotel, I'd been eager to stretch my legs outdoors again. Although I'd attended mass at St. Patrick's Church in Kansas City a few days ago, the Catholic Station of Eureka Springs seemed a decidedly appropriate destination after all that had transpired since. I'd followed directions I'd received from Mr. Oxnard, the desk clerk. As Miss Lucy had mentioned that Mary Flannagan came here regularly, I had initially asked Mary for the address. Yet for some unknown reason, she aggressively discouraged my visit and refused to assist me "on account of your health, miss." I didn't believe her and came anyway.

Achy but rested, I had dressed before sunrise intending to hike. But by the time I reached the bottom of the Spring Street stairs, I was limping and perturbed that my injured knee might cut my outing short. The streetcar came to my rescue. I boarded at its Crescent Spring stop. The driver touched the rim of his cap as he took my coin; I was his sole passenger. We made our way down Spring Street, past Basin Circle Park, and then onto the south section of Main Street. The slow, rhythmic pace of the mule as it drew the streetcar along was soothing. I wondered why I'd never ridden it before.

I disembarked near Tablerock Spring, the streetcar's last stop before looping back, and found the road that led to the little church, its small steeple protruding above the pines. I had to hike straight up the hill. Carriage travel on the road, little more than a muddy ditch, would've been near impossible. I set a slow but steady pace. My knee was throbbing by the end, but the brisk air and hushed pine forest alone had made it worth the trip.

I unlatched the gate of the white picket fence. The path and steps leading to the chapel's front door had been swept free of pine needles. I closed the door behind me and stood still while my eyes adjusted to the darkness. Gradually I perceived the rows of wooden pews and kneeling benches. They were all empty. Against the wall to the right, a lit candle lantern cast its glow over the small table beneath it. I was drawn to the ledger left open under the light. Upon closer inspection, it was a prayer request book, with line after line of petitions for healing, money, or both. Mary Flannagan's name appeared several times. Mixed among them was an appeal for Father Mazaret's safe journey and another for his safe return. I flinched at a prayer request, nonspecific and unsigned, for George Shulman. Did he have anything to do with Mrs. Trevelyan's death?

God help him if he did, I thought.

A prayer for temperance caught my eye. Signed by a Joseph Mascavarti, it was dated Monday, November 7, the day of Mrs.

Trevelyan's death. I'd seen that name before. But where? I walked down the narrow aisle. It was elegant and simple, a sacred retreat in the woods. The sacristy was carpeted; the railing was plastered and painted white. The altar, made of highly polished wood, was adorned with a white linen cloth, a single brass candlestick, and a porcelain vase filled with white chrysanthemums. Above the altar was a large, but simple mahogany cross. Against the right wall was a small, ornately painted statue of the Virgin Mary with her arms outstretched. Two rows of pews had been shortened in order to fit a prayer stand in front of the statue.

I approached the altar and, finding matches, lit the candle. I intended to pray for Mrs. Trevelyan's soul, for her friends and family, and for the American Women's Temperance Coalition, a cause close to her heart. I intended to pray for myself. Instead I sat in the front pew, watched the light flicker on the whitewashed clapboards, and reflected on what I knew about the late Mrs. Trevelyan. Although I had never actually met her, I knew that like the temperance coalition, she wasn't all she appeared to be. Temperance crusader and friend to my patron, Sir Arthur Windom-Greene, she was a woman who was both revered and despised, both generous and demanding, who preached temperance and tolerance but resorted to violence and blackmail. She was unlike any employer I had ever had. Did Sir Arthur know what an awkward situation this would put me in? Did he know about her "saloon smashing" crusades? I couldn't imagine that he'd suggest me for this assignment if he did.

The longer I sat there, mesmerized by the shadow play on the wall, the more disturbing the thoughts that came into my mind. Could I have prevented her death? What if I'd been more persistent in meeting with her face-to-face, would she still be alive? Would Sir Arthur think me derelict in my duties?

I knew the answer to all of these questions was no, but I couldn't shake the feeling that I was missing something. Someone had killed her, but who?

The list of possible suspects was growing. Mrs. Trevelyan had received a myriad of letters threatening her, any one of whose writers could've followed through on their threats. The coalition itself was fractured, with only a small faction agreeing with Mrs. Trevelyan's violent policies. The opposing majority was vocal, and almost as hostile in its dissent, if Mrs. Anglewood's protests and threats were any indication. Even Mary Flannagan, her chambermaid, was bitter about something and was vehement that Mrs. Trevelyan should've been punished for the rampage at the saloon. And of course, there was the saloonkeeper. *Did he also attack me? If not, who did?*

I shuddered. *How did I get mixed up in all this? I'm a shorthand and typewriter girl trying just to make a living. Now my employer's dead.*

Suddenly the door opened and the candles flickered. I leapt to my feet, jolted out of my reverie.

"Hello? Who's there?"

I felt my way back to the altar and faced the door. A small man stood with his back against the wall, light from the candle reflecting off something metal in his breast pocket. He turned his hat in his hands.

"Hello," I said again. The man's silence was unnerving. His lips moved, but he didn't reply. "It's so quiet in here, the door startled me."

He cracked open the door. "I didn't know you were here."

"That's all right. Please come in. I don't mind." As I walked down the aisle toward him, sun shining through a crack shed light on his face. He had black hair and wore a thick, bushy mustache. Red blotches sprawled across his skin.

"Well, I do." He jerked the door open wider and slipped outside.

The candle in my hand blew out, so I set it down on the table and followed him out. I discovered him, after a minute or two of searching, leaning sideways against a pine tree. His shoes and the knees of his pants were caked in mud. In the full light, the blotches on his face appeared to be due less to illness than to intoxication. He took a swig from a flask.

"Sir?" I said.

He jumped, hiding his flask in his coat.

"I'm sorry. I didn't mean to startle you."

"You didn't. I mean, what do you want?" he grumbled as he rested back against the tree.

"You can have the chapel to yourself now, if you'd like. I need to leave anyway." For the first time he looked me in the eye. His were bloodshot. "By the way, I'm Miss Hattie Davish, Mr. . . . ?"

"I know who you are. Now leave me alone." He pushed past me and stumbled over an unearthed tree root. "I mean it. Shut up and go away!" he shouted, staggering toward the chapel yard.

Startled, I scrambled down the hill, away from the chapel, without looking back. As before, I stayed on the dry ridge of the road but noticed a new irregular trail of boot prints in the mud. By the time I caught the streetcar on Main Street, I concluded that the man was probably the intemperate Mr. Mascavarti from the prayer request book, or someone like him. *Maybe the coalition members should hold a meeting up there,* I thought, as I boarded the streetcar. I tried to put the unsettling encounter out of my mind and focus on the more pleasant encounter to come.

But what did he mean, "I know who you are?"

"It's extraordinary to see you up at this hour, Walt. And not on a house call?"

A voice boomed across the lobby of the Arcadia Hotel.

The rotund gentleman to whom it belonged reposed in a wicker-backed chair to the right of the grand fireplace. With his shoes on the floor, he perched his stocking feet on the hearth of the fire. The comment was addressed to the man standing in front of the fireplace, rocking back and forth on his heels, warming his hands.

"In a way, you could call it a house call, Sam. I'm here to visit a lady."

Sam lifted his hand in the air. "Say no more, my friend." He turned his head in time to see my labored approach.

"Excuse me, Dr. Grice?" I said.

Dr. Walter Grice whirled around, his face flushed from the fire. The rotund gentleman chuckled under his breath.

"Miss Davish, good morning. You surprised me." The doctor raised an eyebrow. "I expected you to be resting upstairs, not walking through the front doors." He gestured toward his companion. "Miss Hattie Davish, I would like to introduce you to my good friend, the Honorable Judge Samuel Senrow. Sam, Miss Hattie Davish." I took a few more steps forward. "Miss Davish, you're limping. Here, let me help you."

"I'm fine, thank you, Dr. Grice. My knee aches a little. That's all."

Judge Senrow took my hand without rising. "Pleased to meet you, Miss Davish." He cast a sideways glance at Walter Grice. "Now I see why the good doctor was out of bed so early this morning."

"Miss Davish is a patient, Sam." I cringed at this appellation.

"And such a pretty 'patient' too." The judge winked at me. Walter Grice studied the floor.

"Dr. Grice has been a friend to us all during this difficult time. I was Mrs. Edwina Trevelyan's secretary. You may've heard of her untimely death?"

The Honorable Judge Senrow bobbed his head and puck-
ered his lips. "Sad business, that."

"Judge Senrow is acting coroner for this case," the doctor
said. A police officer approached and motioned for the judge
to join him.

"We'll talk later, Walt. Nice to meet you, young woman."
He slipped back into his shoes and snatched up the haircloth
hat on the seat next to him. "Stay out of trouble, you two." He
excused himself and left.

"Thank you for meeting me," I said.

Dr. Walter Grice sat across from me at the breakfast table.
"I'm glad to see you're feeling better, though from your limp,
I'm not sure an early-morning stroll was a wise decision. Did
you take the medicine?"

"I feel much better, Dr. Grice. You don't need to be concerned about me."

"Regardless, you should take it. I'll have someone fetch it
for you."

"Please, Dr. Grice."

"I insist." He called over a waiter, who then sent someone
to my room.

"Thank you, but I certainly didn't ask you to meet me to
discuss my health."

His eyes twinkled, like the first time we had met. "Ah, you
want to know about Mrs. Trevelyan. By the way, please, call me
Walter."

I hesitated, not knowing how to respond. Hadn't we met
but five days ago? Were Christian names appropriate? Wasn't
he my doctor, and I Mrs. Trevelyan's secretary? Had I let my
professionalism slip, just for the sake of a handsome face?

"You're staring, Dr. Grice."

"Do you mind?" Walter Grice regarded me, his thoughts a
mystery, for several interminable moments. I dropped my eyes

to the linen napkin on my lap. A profusion of honeysuckle flowers had been stitched in one corner. "Are we not friends, Miss Davish?"

"Yes," I said. Unlike any physician of my acquaintance, he had demonstrated competence from the moment we met. He'd been gracious, patient, and kind, and had come to my aid more than once already. I pictured myself, unconscious, being carried in his strong arms from the basement of the hotel to my room. "Yes, I do hope so."

"Then I don't understand your hesitation. I grant that we are newly acquainted, but haven't we already seen some adventures together? Or is it because you're a patient? If so, let me reassure you, I keep my professional life separate from my private life."

"That's just it," I said. "I don't have the luxury of separate professional and private lives. I have a reputation to uphold, in both cases."

"Ah." He fell silent for several moments. "Would it make a difference if you knew that my intentions were honorable?" I stole a quick glance at his face. No smile played about his lips, no mischievous twinkle lit his eyes; he was in earnest.

My heart pounded, my hands felt hot. I pressed my palms on the cool linen tablecloth. "But," was all the protest I could muster.

"I'd like to get to know you better, Miss Davish. I'd like to spend more time in your company." He reached for my hand. "If this is agreeable to you, please call me Walter. All my friends do."

What could I say? That our positions in life were vastly different? That as an orphan girl, with no dowry but what she could earn with her own hands and wit, I was no match for a gentleman doctor? That the transient nature of my work hindered my making attachments of any kind? What could I possibly say but, "And, if you'd like, Walter, my friends call me Hattie."

"What in the world are you two doing?" Miss Lucy said, suddenly standing a few feet away from our table. Neither of us had noticed the sisters' approach.

Walter let go of my hand and rose to his feet. "Just getting more acquainted, Miss Lucy. Join us for breakfast?" He helped the old woman to a chair.

"We're not interrupting anything, are we, dear?" Miss Lizzie said, patting Walter's arm as he held a chair out for her, but directing her question to me.

"Ah, interrupting? Um, no, I mean . . ."

"Stop stammering, Davish," Miss Lucy said. "Were you plying Dr. Grice with the millions of questions we have about the murder, or not?" Walter burst out laughing.

"Why are you blushing, Davish?" Miss Lucy said. "If you don't ask him, I will."

From behind her hand, Miss Lizzie said, "I don't think that's why she's blushing, Lucy, dear."

In answer to Miss Lucy's quizzical expression, Walter said, "All right, ladies, I'll answer any questions I can. Only let me eat my breakfast first. I'm famished."

CHAPTER 14

"Then how did she die?"

I sipped my steaming black coffee and nibbled on a soda biscuit slathered with orange marmalade, anticipating the reply to Miss Lucy's question. I was still trying to get the bitter taste of the medicine out of my mouth. Throughout breakfast, Walter, over a heaping plate of spiced pears, poached eggs on anchovy toast, broiled tomatoes, and waffles with maple syrup, had tried to answer our inquiries in vain. And I had tried in vain not to let the blood rush to my cheeks every time Walter smiled at me.

"I can't tell you that conclusively, either," Walter said. "A postmortem should show exactly what caused her death."

"Why then are you sitting here with a tree's worth of syrup running down your chin, shoveling down waffles, when you could be getting us some answers?" Miss Lucy asked.

"Miss Lucy, that's not fair." Walter dabbed his mouth with a napkin. "We have to wait until the next of kin give permission. Her children have been notified, but there's been some difficulty in locating Charles Trevelyan Senior."

"Ha, that's not surprising," Miss Lucy snorted.

"What's not surprising?" I said.

"As far as we know, dear," Miss Lizzie interjected, "Edwina hadn't seen or spoken to her husband in years." She reached over to take a biscuit from her sister's plate.

"Fifteen, to be exact." Miss Lucy swatted Lizzie's hand away. "Stop that, Lizzie. You don't need to eat like you're starving anymore." Her sister seemed duly abashed.

"Charles Trevelyan didn't care much for the American Women's Temperance Coalition," Miss Lucy said.

"Well, the son should be able to do it," Walter said. "The coroner's tied up in Berryville. Judge Senrow is the acting coroner and has asked me to serve as medical examiner. I'll be the one to examine the body."

"But you said earlier that you've already examined her," I said, conscious not to refer to Mrs. Trevelyan as *the body*. "Can't you make some conclusions from that?"

"It was only a brief, external examination. I have yet to perform a thorough, internal autopsy. Any conclusions now would be premature."

"So all you can tell us, good doctor," Miss Lucy said, "is that Edwina was viciously murdered and squashed into a trunk by a person or persons unknown sometime Monday morning or later?"

Walter forked the last pear on his plate and popped it into his mouth. "I'm afraid so," he said. Miss Lucy rolled her eyes and sighed in exasperation.

"That's too bad, dear," Miss Lizzie said, dunking a biscuit in her tea. "I'm afraid we knew all that ourselves."

"What about a man named John Martin?" I asked. "Do any of you know of him?" Throughout breakfast, his name had been on my mind; I seized the first opportunity to broach the subject.

"John Martin?" Miss Lizzie put down her tea with a clatter, spilling some into the saucer.

"Yes, John Martin, Esq. Do you know of him?"

"Know of him? Why, Davish, do you think he killed Edwina?" Miss Lucy said.

Walter Grice looked up from his plate, his eyebrows arched. Miss Lizzie glanced at her sister. "Do you know something we don't, Hattie?" Walter said.

"No, no. It isn't anything like that. At least I don't think so. You know him, then, Miss Lucy?"

"Of course I don't."

"Neither do I, dear," Miss Lizzie said.

"I've never heard of him, either," Walter said. "Wait, the name does ring a bell. Could he have been a patient of Dr. Cantor's?"

"I wouldn't know about that," I said, brushing bread crumbs off the table. "I thought one of you might've known him because he's a coalition supporter and an acquaintance of Mrs. Trevelyan."

"Well, I've never heard of the man," Miss Lucy said. "Why do you want to know who he is?"

I explained that I had come across several correspondences from John Martin that didn't fit into any obvious category. Judging by how Miss Lucy responded to my question, I refrained from describing the contents of the letters, or my true reason for asking. I didn't want my companions jumping to any more conclusions.

"I didn't know whether to place his letters in the personal file or the coalition business file," I said.

"Oh, Davish, what difference does it make?"

"It does make a difference, Miss Lucy. Mrs. Trevelyan's son, I'm sure, will want his mother's personal letters. Josephine Piers, on behalf of the AWTC, has already requested everything pertaining to coalition business. It's my job to make sure that John Martin's letters go to the right person."

"This is a murder investigation," Walter said. "All of Mrs. Trevelyan's possessions, including her correspondences, will be held by the police. I'd say leave all that to them."

"I wouldn't leave anything to them, Hattie, dear, even those silly letters," Miss Lizzie said. "That police chief is incompetent. Consider how little they've investigated your attempted murder."

"My God." Walter knocked the table as he rose half out of his seat and rattled the china. Those breakfasting nearby turned their heads at the sound of the doctor's distress. "What attempted murder?"

"When someone with the strength of Samson shoved Davish down the stairs, of course," Miss Lucy said, "though Lizzie's being dramatic. Tell Dr. Grice what they said, Davish."

"I don't understand, Hattie." Walter retrieved his napkin from the floor, waved off a concerned waiter who had rushed over, and regained his chair. "Someone pushed you down the stairs? I thought it was an accident; I thought you'd fainted or tripped."

"The police concluded that too, dear," Miss Lizzie said, "despite our efforts to convince them otherwise. That's why we don't think they're very competent."

"I had no idea," Walter said. "What happened?" I repeated the account of my encounter with an unknown assailant in Tibbs Alley.

"The last thing I remember was a cry from below, the lantern crashing, and someone running away," I said. "You know the rest."

"And the police aren't doing anything about it, dear," Miss Lizzie said. "Of course, they'll search Edwina's room, but they won't look for poor Hattie's attacker."

"That was me you heard shouting," Walter said. He paused when he saw the startled looks on our faces. "Why are you all gaping at me like that?"

"August gentlemen of your stature, Dr. Grice, do not slink behind young ladies into dark alleyways like tawdry, bungling pickpockets," Miss Lucy said.

"Yes, I thought you more respectable, dear," Miss Lizzie said.

"Oh, you ladies are much too concerned about reputations and appearances." Walter pealed with laughter.

"It's not a laughing matter, Dr. Grice."

"I apologize, Miss Lucy, but I'm a doctor. Hattie left the saloon pale and shaking, so of course I followed her."

"Did you see anyone?" I said.

"Davish told us she went to speak to that saloon man," Miss Lucy said. "What, may I ask, were you doing there, Dr. Grice?" Walter appeared on the brink of laughing again. "Get that smirk off your face, young man, I'm serious."

"George Shulman happens to be a friend of mine, Miss Lucy," Walter said.

"But he sells alcohol and destroys families, dear," Miss Lizzie said.

"Yes, he's in the saloon business, but can I help how my friends make their living?"

"I'm starting to wonder whose side you're on, Dr. Grice," Miss Lucy said. The conversation was heading onto dangerous ground; I had to get back to the question I wanted to ask before the topic of the saloon came up.

"Walter, you said you followed me to Tibbs Alley," I said. "Did you see anyone? Did you see who pushed me?"

Sobriety returned to the doctor's countenance. "No, I'm sorry, Hattie, I didn't."

"Did you see anyone nearby?" I said. "It might be connected to Mrs. Trevelyan's murder."

"Sorry, no. But why do you think it has something to do with the murder?"

"I am a stranger here," I said. "Who else knows me but Mrs. Trevelyan's associates and acquaintances? Which reminds me, do any of you know a Joseph Mascavarti? I met him this morning. I'd never met him before, but he said he knew who I was." No one had heard of him either.

"Do you suspect this Joseph Mascavarti of pushing you, Hattie?" Walter said.

"No, I have no idea who it was."

"Isn't it obvious, dear," Miss Lizzie said, "it was that horrible saloonkeeper." She winced at Walter's sudden frown. "I'm sorry, Dr. Grice, but even before Hattie mentioned her encounter with him, Lucy and I thought he did it."

"George?" Walter said. "Whatever gave you that idea?"

"I have to admit, Walter," I said, "the same idea occurred to me. You saw how he reacted to my questions the other night."

"You don't know George like I do, shouting one minute, singing the next. You remember, he was singing when you left."

"When I left," I reminded him, "glass was breaking."

"Regardless, I was a few yards behind you. I would've seen him."

"The Cavern has a ground entrance on both Main and Center streets," I said. "He could've arrived at the top of the staircase before me. Moreover, I smelled liquor on my assailant."

"Yes, but you see—" Walter never finished his sentence.

"He's a violent man, dear, violent," Miss Lizzie said, interrupting in a burst of emotion. "Shouting vulgarities, smashing glass, and who knows what else." She threw her fork down, sending it clattering onto her plate. "If he's capable of those things, he's capable of anything." Her hands gripped the edge of the table, turning white.

"How would you know, Lizzie?" Miss Lucy said. "You weren't even there." She rose from her chair and grabbed her sister's arm. "Let's go. I've had enough of this. Besides, it's time for my nap." The elderly ladies abruptly took their leave.

"What was that about?" Walter said as he waved the waiter over. He paid the bill, pushed back his chair, and rose.

"I don't know," I said. "Maybe they're still upset about you visiting the saloon."

"Maybe. I'm sorry she has such a negative opinion of George. Has Miss Lizzie even met him?"

"I don't think so. But Mrs. Trevelyan's death has put everyone on edge. If only we knew more."

"I'd better go up and check on Miss Lizzie," Walter said. "I'll be back in five minutes. Then, if you're up to it, let's go for a walk. The painkiller should be working by then." He leaned down and whispered in my ear. "We were interrupted earlier, and there's something I'd like you to know."

"And you call yourself a gentleman? Walter Grice, this is blackmail."

I swatted his arm lightly with my glove as we left the wooded hollow path and approached Grotto Spring. Created by the incessant dripping of water, Grotto Spring was carved deep out of the base of the hill on which the Arcadia Hotel was built. A rocky shelf overhanging its entrance created a natural portico and allowed a bit of light to enter.

Walter and I had strolled around the parklands of the hotel in companionable silence. I'd been content to amble beside him and listen to the rustling autumn leaves underfoot. I had stooped to gather a few fallen hackberry and tulip-tree leaves for my collection when he suggested a visit to Grotto Spring, a hotbed of lichens and liverworts.

"Please just tell me," I said. He shook his head.

"I know you don't like the idea of spa treatments," Walter

said, "but in all seriousness, after what you've been through, you're bruised, sore, and exhausted. A hot mineral bath would do you good."

"How can I be exhausted when all I've done is sleep and lie in bed? Getting back to work, now, that would do me good."

"Hattie, to be honest, when you first arrived I would've guessed you hadn't had a good night's sleep in weeks, maybe months." I couldn't deny what he was saying. When I thought of it, I hadn't been sleeping well.

"And now?" I said.

"I admit there's a little color to your cheeks." He raised his hand to stifle any interruption. "But only because you have been sleeping and lying in bed. Let me prescribe you a spa treatment."

"No, thank you, Walter, spa treatments are for the sick."

"Not always. I take spa treatments, even when I'm well. The therapies help ward off sickness. I prescribe them for all my patients."

"I appreciate your passion and your concern, but spas are not for me. I belong in a typing pool, not a thermal pool."

"What if I tell you all I know about Mrs. Trevelyan's murder?"

"Really? What more do you know?"

"A great deal more than I told the Shaw sisters at breakfast." He had a gleam in his eye. "Can I make you an appointment at the bathhouse?"

"All right, you win." I entered the Grotto Spring cave chuckling. "I'll take one mineral bath."

"Good." Walter scooped up water from the spring with his hands and drank. He sat on the long stone bench that had been built out of the cavern wall. In a hushed voice, he said, "Take a seat, and I'll tell you what I know."

★   ★   ★

"Asphyxiation? Are you sure?" I followed Walter's example and whispered.

Walter had accompanied the police when they had removed the trunk and Mrs. Trevelyan's remains to the police station. There, in the presence of Chief Jackson and Judge Senrow, he had completed a thorough external examination of the dead woman's body and had learned more than he had led us to believe. Mrs. Trevelyan had been killed at least two days ago, though the precise day and time were too difficult to tell; her body had already begun to decompose. He found a gash in her head and tiny pieces of glass embedded in her scalp. Dried blood had clotted in her hair and dripped on the same side of her face and neck. The blood on her clothes could've come from the gash on her head, but Walter wasn't positive. But the blue tints he found around her lips and fingernails, he explained, were signs of suffocation. Walter reiterated that a postmortem examination might lead to more definite conclusions.

"It could've been massive head trauma, but I don't think so." Walter used the same calm but firm tone he reverted to when discussing professional matters. "The gash on her head, although producing a lot of blood, didn't appear significant enough to have killed her."

"Did someone hit her with a looking glass?" I told him how the police had found a shattered mirror hidden beneath the dresser.

"No, the cuts were too deep. I'd say she was hit over the head with something larger, maybe a water bottle, like the ones you saw in her room." I recalled the large glass fragment the police found on Mrs. Trevelyan's carpet.

"And then they suffocated her?" I said.

"Perhaps, though the clothes in the trunk would've been sufficient to do the job; I didn't see anything under her fingers to suggest a struggle."

"Could she have been knocked senseless first?"

"Now, that's a real possibility," Walter said. "It would've been simple to suffocate her before she regained consciousness."

"It could've been a man or a woman then, couldn't it?" I said.

"I think a man most likely. They would've had to carry or drag her body to the trunk. Mrs. Trevelyan was petite, but unconscious she would've been more difficult to lift."

"But there weren't any bloodstains apparent on the carpet." I watched the water trickle down the stone and drip into the spring pool. "Could it have been an accident? Could someone have hit her, seen the blood, and thought she was already dead?"

"And then inadvertently killed her by stuffing her in her trunk?" Walter said, finishing my thought. He stroked his mustache. "It's possible. Air supply would be limited inside a locked trunk."

"And if Mrs. Trevelyan never regained consciousness, never yelled out for help?" I said.

"Or if she did, being down in the storage room, no one heard?" Walter added.

"Hello there!"

Walter and I jumped as two young boys who had been clambering on the hill above us dropped down over the rocky overhang at the mouth of the cave. They each had two large tin pails, which they filled after some time with the slow-moving spring water and then hoisted onto their shoulders. Walter and I said hello to them but waited to speak to each other until the boys started their ascent up the hill and their boisterous voices could no longer be heard. In those few minutes of silence, the full reality of Mrs. Trevelyan's plight hit me.

"How horrid," I said. Walter slid his hand toward me. I grasped it. "We must find out who did this, Walter."

"We? Hattie, I'm flattered, but we don't know the first

thing about being detectives. With all due respect to the Shaw sisters, the police are the best ones to handle this."

I let his hand go. "How can we trust they'll investigate this? They're not even looking for the man who attacked me."

"And I'm sorry for that. But this is a murder case. Let's leave it to the police to find Mrs. Trevelyan's killer."

"Did Chief Jackson or Officer Burke tell you what brought them to the Arcadia Hotel in the first place? My appeal fell on deaf ears. At the time, Chief Jackson was unwilling to follow up on Mrs. Trevelyan's disappearance."

"They didn't tell me anything about that."

"I'm curious," I said, turning to face him directly. "Why didn't you tell me what you'd learned before, at breakfast?"

"To be honest, I'm not sure the Shaw sisters need to know any of this." He felt about the autopsy as I had about the elusive John Martin. We were both protecting the old ladies from distress and any premature details from the rumor mill. A smile crept across Walter's face.

"And . . . ," I said, squinting my eyes in suspicion.

"And until the police release this information, I'm relying on your discretion, again."

"I'm famous for my discretion, Dr. Grice. You keep your patients' secrets, and I keep my employers'."

"Rightly so."

"And . . ."

"And . . ." He chuckled under his breath. "And I got you to promise to take a mineral bath, didn't I?"

CHAPTER 15

"Dr. Grice must be late again."

The doorman, wearing a gray top hat, chuckled as Walter's carriage careered down the drive. "Or else he's showing off that new imported spider phaeton. Only doctor in town that doesn't drive a Goddard wagon. Only doctor in town that risks breaking his neck too."

What more did the doorman know about Walter? I suppressed my curiosity and instead quizzed him on Mrs. Trevelyan and the temperance women. He didn't know much, commenting that "one old lady looks like the next." Once in my room, I fulfilled my last official duty as Mrs. Trevelyan's secretary, collecting all of her papers for Mrs. Piers. Then, free from obligation, I rushed to my typewriter to record everything Walter had said.

In danger of becoming disorganized, I constructed updated lists of questions and facts. When I'd thoroughly considered all points, I sat back and examined my work. The list of questions was far longer than that of the facts, too long; I didn't know where to begin. I began prioritizing the questions and kept coming back to the trunk. I started a separate list.

1. Who did Mrs. Trevelyan speak to about the trunk? And when?
2. When was the trunk moved to the basement?
3. Were other trunks or cases moved to or from Mrs. Trevelyan's room that day?
4. Had the trunk been moved within Mrs. Trevelyan's room that day?
5. Was there a lock on the trunk when it was moved? Before it was moved?

I continued on in this way, grouping questions from the master list into smaller, more manageable new lists. The questions that didn't belong to any other list, I marked *Miscellaneous*. Satisfied, I gathered my packet for Mrs. Piers, selected a couple of lists to work on, and set out to find the young bellboy.

Owen was coming out of a suite on the fourth floor, pushing an overloaded luggage cart. "Sorry, miss, but I've got to get this luggage downstairs. These folks are fixin' to catch a train."

"I only have a few questions."

"Oh, all right, but you'll have to be quick."

I walked beside him. "Did Mrs. Trevelyan speak to you about moving the steamer trunk?"

"Ah, miss, I've already told the police everything I know."

"Please, Owen. Could you tell me what you told them?"

He stopped and pushed the call button for the elevator. "As I told the police, I never spoke to or saw Mrs. Trevelyan."

"Do you know who she did speak to?"

"No."

"Well, do you know when the trunk was picked up from her room?"

"Yeah, around eleven A.M. on Monday. I saw to it myself."

"If you didn't speak to her about it or know who did, then how did you know Mrs. Trevelyan wanted it sent back to storage? The trunk was meant for a charity."

"I had my instructions. As I told the police, the lady had sent her new instructions to the desk."

"New instructions?"

"Sure, her trunk was supposed to go to the depot on Tuesday. Like you said, for a charity. She must've changed her mind."

The elevator arrived. With the help of the elevator attendant, Owen maneuvered the cart inside. "Sorry, miss," the attendant said, "you'll have to wait for the next one."

"Owen, who gave you those instructions?"

"Mr. Oxnard, he was the clerk on duty." As the doors slid closed, he said, "Sorry, gotta go."

I glanced at my list. There were still a few questions I needed to ask. I bounded down the stairs, my knee no longer paining me after taking Walter's tincture at breakfast. I had to admit that my whole body felt better. Owen was outside, loading the luggage onto a wagon. He laughed when he saw me.

"Don't give up, do you?" he said.

"I've got a few more questions, if that's all right."

"Go ahead," he said, turning back to his work.

"Do you remember a lock on the trunk?"

"Sure. I heard the police had to break it to get the lady out."

"Did you move anything else that day for Mrs. Trevelyan?"

"No, just the trunk."

"Do you happen to remember when you got the new instructions?"

"It must've been just before we moved the trunk. She wanted it done right away."

"Any idea why?" I asked.

"Sorry, that's all I know." He scrambled up next to the driver. "Hope that's it. We gotta go."

"One last question. Where in the room was the trunk when you picked it up?"

Owen scrunched his eyebrows together and frowned. "That's a new one. I hadn't thought about it before."

He bit his lip as both the driver and I waited. The two horses bobbed their heads and snorted.

"That's funny," he said. "It was by the tea table. Some of the chairs had been moved back, out of the way, kinda. Usually guests store the luggage out of the way, next to a wall, at the foot of the bed, that sort of thing. Guess Mary thought it easier to pack it from there. Oh well, if that's all, ma'am. Let's go," the lad said to the driver, who whipped the horses into motion.

I too was spurred into action. I hurried to the ladies' parlor and snatched up a pen. I leaned over an end table and jotted down the answers Owen had given me. I also added several new items to my questions list.

6. Did Mary move the trunk near the tea table?
7. If not, who did? Why?
8. Why did Mrs. Trevelyan change her mind about shipping the trunk?
9. When did she change her mind?
10. Did she change her mind?

I stood up and noticed three women, needlework on their laps, with their mouths gaping open on the other side of the room. I tipped my head, then scurried out to the registration desk.

The same stoic clerk, Mr. Oxnard, who'd registered me on Sunday worked behind the desk. I asked if he would answer a few questions.

"I'm sorry about your boss, but I've already told everything I know to the police."

"Would you mind answering a few of my questions? I won't take much of your time." He dropped his elbows on the desk, propping up his chin in his hands, and sighed. "Did you speak with Mrs. Trevelyan about having her trunk moved?"

"No."

"But Owen said that you instructed him to do so."

"I said that I didn't speak to Mrs. Trevelyan."

"Then you did receive the request to have her trunk moved?"

"When did she make it?"

"I don't know exactly," I said. "That's what I'm hoping to determine, when and why. Owen thinks the new instructions came sometime late Monday morning."

"If something was requested on Monday, I would've gotten it," he said. "As you know, I was working on Monday."

"Then you do remember getting the request?"

"No."

"What about the request to deliver the trunk to the depot?"

"I wouldn't know without seeing the specific instructions."

"Then you keep requests on file?"

"No."

"But Mrs. Trevelyan's was a written request? Could she have brought it down herself?"

"Never. If she needed something, someone else, usually her secretary or one of the maids, would deliver the request to the desk."

"So who delivered this one?"

"I have no idea."

"Mr. Oxnard, do you remember anything about Mrs.

Trevelyan's request to have her trunk moved on Monday, either to the storage room or the train depot?"

"No," the clerk said. At this moment, a man in a black poplin hat arrived and waited to be served. "I'm sorry I couldn't be of more service. You could speak to the manager."

"Would he know about Mrs. Trevelyan's request?"

"No, he wasn't working on Monday. I was."

"Well then, no, thank you, that won't be necessary." I stepped aside, but not quickly enough, as the new guest knocked into me as he approached the desk. I nearly dropped the packet of Mrs. Trevelyan's papers.

"Actually, I do have one more question." The new arrival began tapping his foot. "Among Mrs. Trevelyan's papers, there was a letter marked *Give to secretary*. Do you know anything about that, Mr. Oxnard?" To my surprise, he did.

"I addressed them myself after they were found by a cleaning maid, slipped under Mrs. Trevelyan's door."

"Them?" I said. "There was more than one?"

"Of course, there's been a couple. Last one was found Monday morning. I had it sent up immediately."

"To me?"

"Aren't you the woman's secretary?" He turned to the new guest. "Didn't know she was dead then, did we?"

I tried to occupy myself while I waited for Mrs. Piers in the library. Mahogany wood shelves stretched from the floor to the ceiling on all four walls; the entry door and two French doors facing east were the only breaks in their continuity. Overstuffed leather chairs were scattered about the room, a few with matching ottomans. End tables, each with a lamp, were stacked with variously sized piles of books. I browsed the shelves and found an old edition of *Gray's School and Field Book of Botany*. I flipped through its pages but had difficulty concentrating. I didn't remember the letter the clerk said he sent me.

In all of my years of service, I had never mislaid a letter. But then I'd never had an engagement like this one. Regardless, it was inexcusable. I'd succumbed to distractions and put my livelihood in jeopardy. Yet where could it be?

I put the book back and picked up a copy of today's newspaper lying on the table nearest me. I had read a report analyzing Proposition 203's defeat and was finishing an article on Mrs. Trevelyan's death when I heard Mrs. Piers step into the library.

"Ah, Miss Davish. Any news?"

"No, I'm afraid not," I lied. I was bursting with news, but Walter's request for discretion tied my hands. "That's everything." I handed her the packet. She accepted it and thumbed through the stack.

"Yes, everything seems to be in order. Thank you, Miss Davish. You've been most accommodating." She glided toward the door.

"I was wondering, Mrs. Piers, if I could ask you a few questions?"

"Of course. How can I help you, Miss Davish?" She settled in the nearest chair and motioned for me to join her.

"I wonder, since you knew so much of Mrs. Trevelyan's affairs, if you know anything about the request to move Mrs. Trevelyan's trunk back to storage?"

"Isn't that a matter for the police, Miss Davish?"

"Yes, technically, but they haven't confided in me, and the hotel staff can't recall anything definite. It's a puzzle, don't you think?"

She didn't answer me. She picked up the newspaper, which was still opened to the article I'd been reading.

"We've arranged a lovely service for Mother Trevelyan," Mrs. Piers said. She stared at the paper and then gazed out the window. "Sister Cordelia wanted to have it at the Presbyterian church, but I rented the Opera House instead. The Baptists used to hold services there, before they built their church. It has plenty of room, and everyone knows Edwina wasn't a Presbyterian."

"Why not hold it in her church, then?"

Josephine Piers regarded me with an unreadable expression in her eyes. "She was a woman of God, Miss Davish, not one of any church. Her mission was to reach Christian people of all faiths. We should follow her example. The Opera House can welcome all people under one roof. You're expected to pay your respects, Miss Davish."

"Of course." I reminded her of my question: Mrs. Trevelyan's trunk?

"The one they found her in?" she said.

"Yes, the one in the basement."

She thought a moment. "Mother Trevelyan was preoccupied with writing a sermon for the saloon smashing. She mentioned several times that she wanted the trunk put into storage. I volunteered to write up the directive and did so before we went into town Sunday, the night before she died."

Tears welled up in her eyes. I felt sorry for her. She had lost someone very important, someone I'd never known.

"Do you know who delivered the message?"

"I did," she said. "But it's God's message we must deliver now, to continue the good work Mother Trevelyan started."

"Yes, that may be, but her trunk was originally scheduled to go to the train depot Tuesday. When she spoke to you about it, did she mention why she changed her mind? It was half-packed with old clothes destined for a charity."

"I don't know anything more about that dreadful trunk," she said, wiping her eyes with a handkerchief embroidered with yellow lilies. "As always, I'd simply done as she asked. Now," she said, rising from her chair, "I've indulged in this exercise long enough. I must return to my duties. The work is endless, but the cause is just." She laid her hand on my shoulder. "You still look peaked, I'm afraid. You should take better care of yourself."

I ignored her remark. "You delivered the message Sunday night, then? Or was it Monday morning?"

"Josephine, what are you doing?" a voice snapped.

We turned to see Cordelia Anglewood, in full riding gear, the diamond collar pin less lustrous under the electric lights, standing in the library doorway. She glowered at me.

"Are you still here? Now that your services are no longer required, I thought you would've packed your bags and returned to wherever it is you came from. In fact," she sneered, "since Trevelyan was dead before you arrived, you never were required, were you?"

"I've served Mrs. Trevelyan since the moment I arrived Sunday afternoon, Mrs. Anglewood. If you will remember, Mrs. Trevelyan was still very much alive. And I'm still working for her, albeit in a different capacity."

"You're still being paid, you mean."

"No, that isn't what I mean, though I have been paid through the end of the week."

"And then you intend to leave?"

"I've yet to decide when I will leave."

"Ah, I see you've finally relinquished all of Trevelyan's correspondences." She strode into the room and snatched the papers from Mrs. Piers. "Good. Since you're still being paid to serve the AWTC president, I'll return to you anything of a personal nature to which you may respond, including all condolences. And I have a stack of temperance pledges that need to be typed up."

"Mrs. Anglewood, I don't work for you," I said.

"I can tend to the condolences, Cordelia," Mrs. Piers said.

"No, Josephine, you must help me. This woman has been paid and will finish her job. Won't you, Miss Davish?"

"Sister Cordelia is our acting president now, Miss Davish,"

Josephine Piers said, patting my shoulder. "We all must do as she bids, and serve in the ways she sees fit."

"Very well," I conceded, sensing an opportunity. The condolence letters, at least, might reveal something useful. "For Mrs. Trevelyan's sake."

A smirk crawled across Cordelia's face. "And I'll need to approve all responses before anything is posted." She flicked two fingers in the air. "Come, Josephine, we have work to do."

I followed the two women as they left the library.

"By the way, Mrs. Anglewood, I know you told the police you were out riding all day Monday. But why didn't you mention you visited Mrs. Trevelyan that morning? It seems important."

"It's not," Cordelia said, her back to me. "And it's none of your business."

"When did you see Mother Trevelyan?" Josephine asked.

"Before I went riding that morning," Cordelia said. "But it doesn't matter now, does it?"

"It doesn't matter that the two of you argued?" I said. "That you raised your riding crop to her?"

Both women swung around, the velvet-trimmed hem of Mrs. Piers's black dress swishing back and forth, and advanced toward me.

"How dare you?" Cordelia Anglewood shoved the packet of papers at the wide-eyed Josephine and backed me into the wall. She stood mere inches away, her breath hot and smelling of coffee. I turned my face aside. "How dare you imply I had something to do with Trevelyan's murder?"

"Did you?" I whispered. She swung the riding crop above her head.

"Cordelia!" Josephine Piers lunged forward, forcing Cordelia's arm down. She peered over her shoulder, searching for onlookers, before turning to me. "You cannot leave well enough alone, can you, Miss Davish?"

"Let go of me." Cordelia Anglewood, seething, yanked herself free of Mrs. Piers's grip.

"Think about the coalition, Sister Cordelia, Madame President," Josephine Piers said, emphasizing the last word. "A typewriter girl isn't worth the cost to our cause. If you're so adamant about brandishing that whip, join us at the next saloon smashing."

Cordelia Anglewood shook her crop at me. "You . . . ," she stammered with rage, "stay out of my way." She swiveled on her booted heel and, trailed by Mrs. Piers, stomped down the hall.

I have to get out of here.

I raced through the lobby, arousing a string of astonished looks and indignant exclamations from the people I passed. I didn't care. I swung open the French doors that led to the hotel's eastern portico and ran. I clutched my ribs and dashed across the manicured lawns and down the hillside, tracing the same wooded path I had strolled arm in arm with Walter a short time ago. My lungs ached and I stumbled several times before I reached the safety of the cavernous Grotto Spring. Tears streamed down my face, blinding me, as I entered the dark cave and felt my way along the cold stone walls. I dropped onto the stone bench. Someone had left a white enamel cup at the end of it. I picked up the cup and flung it as hard as I could against the opposite wall. I gave in to my frustration and fear and sobbed until I couldn't breathe.

I'd faced challenges here that I never could've imagined while typing manuscript pages for Sir Arthur or taking dictation for Mrs. Madeleine Kennedy. Nothing I'd learned at Mrs. Chaplin's school had prepared me for this. In less than one week, I'd found my employer murdered, locked and suffocated in her own trunk, had been pushed down a flight of stairs, and a moment ago, had been threatened with a whipping or worse. My own dear father never raised a hand to me. I wanted to leave and have nothing more to do with the American Women's Temperance Coalition. I wanted to erase the horrific sight of Mrs. Trevelyan's face ashen and contorted in death from my memory.

Pull yourself together. Un, deux, trois . . .

It's not like I was the one lying on a cold slab in the coroner's office. I pulled a handkerchief from my sleeve and dabbed my eyes. But why was Mrs. Trevelyan killed? Why was I being threatened? Why was any of this happening? I tried to take a deep breath, but a sharp pain in my ribs stopped me short. Something must be done.

I picked up the enamel cup and inspected it for damage. A small chip on the rim was the only evidence of my shameful behavior. I replaced it on the bench. I knelt at the spring and splashed water on my face. I stood, brushed soil from my skirt, and readjusted my hat. A bald, middle-aged man on crutches entered the cave as I was leaving.

"Not scaring you off, am I, missy?" he said, showing a mouth full of missing teeth.

"No, no. There's just something I have to do. Good day."

I had never shied away from a challenge before. Why start now?

CHAPTER 16

"Do you have a Mr. John Martin registered here?"

All afternoon I had searched hotel after hotel, asking the same question. I had visited the Hancock House, the Wright House, and the Pence House, all popular whitewashed frame boarding houses. I had stopped at the Congress Hotel, which proved to be accommodations for black servants. I had inquired at the Lamont Hotel, the Waverly Hotel, and the grand Southern Hotel at Basin Circle Park. I had questioned clerks at hotels with names like the Josephine, the Clara Bell, and the Catherine or at others named for nearby springs, the Sweet Spring Hotel, the Magnetic Springs Hotel, and the Congress Spring Hotel. And still there were dozens left to visit. Yet every hotel clerk gave me the same answer, "No." Exhausted, I took the streetcar up to the Thach Cottage Hotel, high up on the hill. After another disappointing inquiry, I disembarked at my hotel, the Arcadia. The same clerk who always seemed to be behind the desk was poring over a pile of ledgers.

"Excuse me, Mr. Oxnard, but could you do me one more

favor?" He glanced up from his work, rolled his eyes at the sight of me, and sighed.

"What is it now, Miss Davish?"

"Could you tell me if you have a Mr. John Martin registered here?"

He slid the ledgers to one side and drew the enormous registration book in front of him. "When would he have arrived?"

I gave the same answer I'd given over and over all afternoon. "I'm not certain. I do know that he was in Eureka Springs as of last Friday."

He flipped through the book and scanned several pages. "Sorry, no John Martin."

"Thank you." I would have to start again tomorrow. The clerk peered over my shoulder. I turned to see what had caught his attention.

"Davish," Miss Lucy shouted as she and her sister proceeded across the lobby at an astonishing pace.

"Hattie, dear," Miss Lizzie said, panting and bending at the waist, "we found you."

"What is it?" I said. "What's happened?"

Miss Lucy grasped my arm. "Davish, we've been searching all over for you. Where have you been?"

"Why, what's wrong?"

"Oh, Hattie, dear, we have the most monumental news." Miss Lizzie held her hand to her heaving chest. "You tell her, Lucy, I still can't breathe."

"Lizzie and I were right all along. Weren't we, Lizzie?"

"What do you mean?" I said. "Miss Lucy, what are you talking about?"

"That barkeep, Davish." She raised her chin and folded her arms across her chest. "The police arrested him a little over an hour ago. We were right. George Shulman murdered Edwina Trevelyan."

★ ★ ★

The coach was waiting. I would've rather walked, but the medicine had worn off and my knee was again throbbing. Donned in my black Henrietta cloth dress, which I'd worn to my father's funeral, and a new French saucer hat with black satin bow, black feathers, and spotted veil that I'd picked up at Mrs. Cunningham's shop, I joined the multitude of guests ascending into the hired coaches, broughams, and Rockaways lined up in the Arcadia's circular drive. We descended the hillside in a slow procession. I felt at odds saying farewell to a woman I'd never properly met. It was my duty, yet I felt the gesture premature. There was so much I still didn't know.

"It's a lovely night, isn't it, dear?" Miss Lizzie said, sitting beside me, looking up at the sky. Miss Lucy, in a well-used black Directoire bonnet, dozed across from us.

"Yes, it is," I said.

"So crisp and clear. Just look at those stars. With the killer caught, I imagine Edwina is up there among them now, finally at peace."

"I hope so, Miss Lizzie. I truly hope so."

Despite the cool air, the broad doors of the Opera House had been left open, allowing the glow of the gaslight chandeliers and the chords of the organ to spill out into the road. A parade of women streamed into the Opera House. As I helped Miss Lucy through the doors and down the center aisle, we passed women of all kinds, condoling, greeting, and mingling together. There were servants and dignitaries, Southerners and Yankees, old and young. Women held babes in their arms while others flapped fans of ostrich feathers. Some hid dresses of plain wool or cotton under hand-stitched shawls while others flaunted the puffy shoulders of a dress of crepe, silk, or taffeta. On their heads were every shape, size, and style of hat to be found in Eureka Springs. And they were all whispering about the arrest of George Shulman. I had never felt so alone.

My head was still reeling from the array of emotions that revelation had created. I was shocked and suspicious. Any relief I might've felt was negated by the unresolved mystery surrounding John Martin and the menacing letter. And although I myself had argued that George Shulman might've pushed me down the stairs, thus making him a suspect, the near-violent clash I'd experienced with Mrs. Cordelia Anglewood made me uneasy about my own rationale. Could I've been mistaken about my assailant? Could the police be wrong? The arrest of George Shulman alleviated me from any further duty toward Mrs. Trevelyan; I was free to leave Eureka Springs. So why did I feel regret instead of relief? Why wasn't I packing my things right now?

After settling the Shaw sisters into their seats, I located one for myself several rows behind and scanned the crowd for familiar faces. Mary Flannagan, tears streaking down her cheeks, sat a few rows back with a group of girls I didn't recognize. I was touched. It was the first time I'd seen her upset over Mrs. Trevelyan's death. Scattered about in the rows in front of me, I caught glimpses of several coalition members I knew, including the schoolteacher from Memphis, Diana Halbert, who waved when our eyes met. A woman in a black toque with an entire blackbird upon it sat in front of me, blocking my view of the first several rows where the few men in attendance sat: city dignitaries, members of Mrs. Trevelyan's family, and financial supporters of the American Women's Temperance Coalition. I elevated myself from the arms of my chair to see above the bird on the woman's hat and found who I was looking for; Walter sat in the third row with Judge Senrow and Chief Jackson. I was eager to talk to him, but he was too far away for me to capture his attention.

The box seats, normally reserved for special guests during theatrical productions, were empty and curtained, but the stage, overflowing with flowers and wreaths, was set up for the service. In front and center of the stage was a closed casket covered with flowers and silk AWTC banners of sky blue. A podium draped in black crepe stood off to the left with three chairs set behind it. Occupying one of the chairs was Mrs. Josephine Piers, deep in conversation with the rotund man sitting next to her. By his coat, collar, and shallow-crowned dignitaries' hat, he had to be the officiating minister. The third seat was empty.

As the organ music faded to silence, everyone standing scrambled for a seat, except Cordelia Anglewood, who greeted and consoled those in the front row. When the music stopped altogether, she ascended the stairs and took her place at the podium.

"Gentle ladies and gentle men, we are here to remember our dearly departed friend, Edwina Ruth Trevelyan." Bowing her head slightly, Cordelia Anglewood proclaimed, "May God rest her soul." She lifted her head and surveyed her audience. "As her closest friend and successor, I would like to thank you all for attending this service. Let us begin with a prayer from Reverend Little."

The minister, with a book clutched in his hand, replaced Mrs. Anglewood at the podium. Both of the women onstage bowed their heads. As I followed their lead, I couldn't help feeling that Mrs. Piers was the more sincere of the two.

"Most merciful Father," the minister said, reading from the Book of Common Prayer, "who hast been pleased to take unto thyself the soul of thy servant; Grant to us who are still in our pilgrimage, and who walk as yet by faith, that having served thee with constancy on earth, we may be joined hereafter with thy blessed saints in glory everlasting, through Jesus Christ our Lord, *Amen.*"

"Amen," answered those in attendance.

"Most merciful Father—"

Before Reverend Little could add another word, Cordelia

Anglewood was on her feet. The minister blinked at her and muttered something incoherent as Cordelia closed the prayer book, offered the minister her hand, and thanked him, without ever taking her eyes off the gathering. Josephine Piers rose, clasped his hands in hers, and whispered something as she guided the minister to his seat.

"As the first official act as president of the American Women's Temperance Coalition, I move that a Resolution of Sympathy and Respect be adopted on this solemn occasion." Without turning around, she reached out toward Josephine Piers, who placed a tablet in the new president's hand. I wasn't surprised to learn she'd been elected president but was amazed that Mrs. Anglewood's first official act hadn't been to require me to type the resolution.

"Whereas," Cordelia Anglewood proclaimed, "it has pleased our divine leader to take our beloved friend from us; and Whereas, the family circle has been broken with few among us left untouched; and Whereas, the Coalition members feel the loss of our fellow worker; Therefore, be it Resolved that while the American Women's Temperance Coalition does humbly bow in submission to His will, we do not the less sympathize with our esteemed colleague's family, both by blood and by bond, in their hour of sorrow and commend them to His care; Therefore be it Resolved that this resolution be entered upon the minutes of this special meeting of the American Women's Temperance Coalition, Eureka Springs, Arkansas, November 10, 1892."

"Is the motion seconded?" Mrs. Anglewood said.

"I second the motion," Josephine Piers declared before absorbing herself in the task of recording the motion in the tablet Cordelia Anglewood had passed back to her.

Is this a memorial service or a business meeting? I wondered.

"Anyone who would like to come forward and speak on

the behalf of our departed friend, please step forward." Cordelia Anglewood beckoned for others to approach the stage.

Finally. This was, in large part, why I'd attended the memorial service.

Dozens of men and women took the stage, each taking a few minutes to remember "Mother" Trevelyan. All who spoke praised Mrs. Trevelyan for her temperance work, her generosity, her passion, and her faith. One man, to titters and scattered applause, admitted astoundment that "the little lady could wield an ax like a lumberjack." Mr. Charles Trevelyan Junior spoke on behalf of the family and evoked the name of his deceased sister, Ruth, whose death at the hand of her drunken husband had brought Mrs. Trevelyan to the cause. Cordelia Anglewood, as her successor, spoke more eloquently of Mrs. Trevelyan's role as president of the coalition than I thought her capable. Josephine Piers didn't speak at all except to say, "God's will be done," before bursting into tears. The minister, his hand cupping her elbow as she leaned into him, escorted her back to her chair. The evening dragged on.

I'd hoped to gain more insight into Mrs. Trevelyan's character, her life, or her impact on the coalition and its members. I was disappointed. With the exception of her son's revelation, I'd learned nothing new. I was relieved when the minister began to rise from his chair, indicating the night was almost over. Instead Mrs. Anglewood approached the podium.

"In closing I would like to read part of a prayer written by Dr. Alexander Griswold in support for our great cause."

Nonplused over this breach in protocol, the minister commenced toward the podium. Josephine seized the minister's arm and cajoled him back into his seat.

Raising her hands above her, as I'd seen her do at the Harding Spring meeting, Cordelia Anglewood prayed.

"O merciful God, help us to fulfill the duties of our respective stations in life, and to go forward in our Christian course. Give us grace to be temperate in all things, that we may live soberly and righteously. Give thy blessing, O Lord, to all who labor to suppress intemperance. Give success to their benevolent efforts, that they may be instrumental in promoting sobriety and good morals. Help each and all of us to do our duty in the state of life to which it shall please thee to call us, that we may glorify thy name, and obtain everlasting life, through our Lord and Savior. *Amen.*"

Is this a memorial service or a temperance rally? I wondered.

I wasn't the only one. The room was silent. Reverend Little squirmed in his chair. Mrs. Piers stared, without expression, at the back of Mrs. Anglewood's head. Cordelia Anglewood faced the audience with an expression simultaneously challenging and triumphant. The minister stood, after this pronouncement, in hopes of giving a parting benediction, but President Anglewood again ignored him.

"May God keep the old and bless the new leader of the American Women's Temperance Coalition," she said.

"May the devil curse you, Cordelia!" a voice shouted. A woman in a sky-blue taffeta gown and wide-brimmed hat several rows in front of me leapt to her feet. The crowd around her screamed as the woman brandished a hatchet in the air. "You don't deserve to wipe Mother Trevelyan's boots!"

"I'm president now, Selina," Cordelia declared, "and I represent the cause. You will not wave your hatchet at me! Now sit down."

Selina dropped back into her seat, subdued. The crowd murmured with excitement.

"I will not tolerate dissent," President Anglewood said, "not from anyone. For to fight for sobriety and the sanctity of the family, we must be strong, we must be steadfast, we must be united as one!" A cheer rose from the crowd. "God bless the AWTC."

The altercation was revealing. In that moment, Cordelia Anglewood had taken complete, unquestionable control of the American Women's Temperance Coalition. Regardless of what the Shaw sisters thought, could this be a motive for murder? In light of her duplicity, her demonstrated violence, and now her blatant ambition, I was beginning to wonder if the police had arrested the wrong person.

With a wave of her hand, President Anglewood dismissed us all.

A moment or two of confusion followed before everyone realized the service was over. I leapt from my seat and tried to avoid the crush. I succeeded in making my way to the Shaw sisters but missed any opportunity of speaking with Walter.

"I'm in no mood for gossiping over punch and cookies," Miss Lucy snapped as her sister and I stopped in the lobby to sample the delicious cake. "Lead us straight to the coach, Davish."

CHAPTER 17

Despite Miss Lucy's admonishment, the conversation in the carriage returning from the memorial service was nothing but gossip. The elderly sisters and I were accompanied by two other coalition members, Diana Halbert and another woman introduced to me as Miss Pole. The four temperance women talked nonstop from the moment we entered the carriage until we bid each other good night in the hotel lobby. I expected some discussion of George Shulman's arrest but, to my surprise, and gratification, the sole topic of conversation was Cordelia Anglewood. Her blatant use of power, her disregard for tradition, even her choice of jewelry were called into question.

"And was that a brooch she was wearing," Miss Pole said, "or one of those new bottle caps pinned to her neck? At least the steel would shine up a bit. It's such a pity. Mrs. Anglewood used to have such good taste. Thank goodness she only wore the brooch and earrings."

"Yes, dear," Miss Lizzie agreed. "I've often thought Cordelia wears too much jewelry. Though I don't know why she didn't wear her emerald brooch. It would've complemented her dress better."

"Who cares what brooch she was wearing," Miss Lucy chided. "Who wears a green dress to a memorial service?" It continued in this vein for some time.

"Was Mrs. Trevelyan a good leader?" I said. The conversation had turned to the previous night's elections and Selina's objections.

"Granted, she wasn't perfect, dear, using hatchets and all, but no one could say Edwina Trevelyan wasn't an excellent president."

"I agree with you, Miss Lizzie," Miss Pole said, "though I don't think wrecking a few bars is a bad thing. The coalition thrived under Mrs. Trevelyan."

"Yes, Edwina Trevelyan was a superb fund-raiser, a devoted crusader of the cause, and bought us unprecedented political support," Diana Halbert said. "She had correspondences from Mrs. Harrison herself."

"Of course, not everyone agreed with her new plan of action," Miss Pole said. "But overall, she fostered a general spirituality and mutual respect among the members. Only time will tell if Cordelia can do the same." The other women agreed. "She certainly didn't do her best for Edwina's service." A barrage of criticisms about the service, everything from the use of Griswold's prayer as a benediction to the flower arrangements on stage, followed.

"If you don't think Mrs. Anglewood's capable of leading, then why elect her president?" I asked.

"Oh, she'll be an excellent leader, Miss Davish," Miss Pole said. "In this troubled time, the coalition needs a heavy hand."

"It's such a difficult task," Miss Lizzie said, "keeping all of us ladies happy. I often wonder why anyone would want to be president."

"It's an honor to lead, Miss Lizzie," Diana Halbert said. She had been voted vice president.

"Besides the honor, are there any other advantages to being president of the coalition?" I said.

"Are you asking if the president gets paid, Davish?" Miss Lucy said, as painfully blunt as ever.

"Among other things, yes," I said.

"The stipend's a trifling hundred dollars a month and an all-expenses-paid trip to the annual meeting of the Temperance Union in London. But money has nothing to do with it, Davish. Edwina became president because she felt it was her calling. Cordelia's in it for the power. She certainly doesn't need the money. Commodore Anglewood, Cordelia's husband, could finance the entire temperance movement single-handedly if he had a mind to. From what I hear, J. P. Morgan himself once asked him for a loan."

"Yes, dear," Miss Lizzie said. "Commodore has been the coalition's biggest single contributor for years. He's a great supporter of temperance."

Miss Lucy had the last word on the matter as the carriage approached the hotel.

"Well, if you want my opinion, his donations are more about keeping Cordelia away from Chicago than anything to do with our cause."

"Want me to saddle a horse for you, miss?"

The stable boy couldn't have been more than twelve years old. His dark skin glistened with sweat as his back bent over the weight of the bucket he carried. He had the aspect of one well into his workday despite the early hour.

"No, thank you," I said. "But I am seeking someone I could ask a few questions."

"I'm in charge here. Though if it's about after-hours business, you'll have to ask Theo."

"No, you're the one I need to talk to."

I'd had difficulty sleeping after the memorial service. I'd tried all night to convince myself that the monetary gain of being the AWTC president (though far more than I could earn in a month) was not enough to murder someone over. I'd tried to assure myself that my assumptions about Cordelia Anglewood being a suspect for the murder were wrong. I reminded myself over and over that the police had already arrested the killer and that I needed to start focusing on my own future. After my hike this morning, I'd intended to begin in earnest securing my next position. Nevertheless, I had been recapitulating the events of the past few days in my head when I passed the stables on the way in to breakfast. I still suspected Cordelia Anglewood. The conversation in the carriage hadn't quelled my suspicions. I hoped the little stable boy before me might be able to put my doubts to rest.

"What do you want to know?" he said, setting the bucket down with a splash.

"I'm Hattie Davish, by the way."

"Nate." We shook hands.

"Do you work here every day, Nate?"

"Yup, though I get Sunday mornings off for church."

"So you were working here last Monday, then?"

"Yup."

"Do you know Mrs. Cordelia Anglewood?"

"Big, mean lady with black hair, rides the feisty chestnut every day?"

"That's her." I chuckled at the apt description. "Now this is very important, Nate. I want you to think about it before you answer. Did Mrs. Anglewood go riding Monday, at any time?"

Without hesitation, he answered, "Nope."

"Are you sure?"

"Yup."

"But I myself saw her heading for the stables," I said.

"Could she have come without you seeing her? Could one of the other boys have saddled her horse?"

"Nope." He slapped his hands against his thighs, sending dust billowing through the air. "I was here from sunup to sundown, and I never saw her. She's come every day for weeks, but not Monday. I haven't seen her today yet either."

I gestured to the stalls that lined the walls. "You must saddle dozens of horses a day. How can you be so sure?"

He jerked back his collar and showed me fresh lacerations on his shoulder and neck. "I remember. Like I said, miss, she's a mean lady. Monday was the best day in weeks."

"Why, Miss Davish, what a surprise." Walter appeared, wearing a long, starched white coat and a stethoscope around his neck. "You're early for your bathhouse appointment."

I was standing in the doorway of his office. I'd come early, eager to tell Walter about Cordelia Anglewood's lack of an alibi. However, when it came to entering, I couldn't bring myself to do it. I shuddered, recalling the last time I'd visited a doctor's office.

"Did you come early to have a chat with me?" Walter Grice said, his face beaming.

"Yes. I wanted to tell you something I learned this morning. It's related to the murder."

Walter's smile disappeared. "Let's go inside where we can talk," he said.

Walter held the door open with one hand and guided me inside with the other. As we passed through the unoccupied examination room, with its gleaming metal objects and smell of iodine, the room began to spin a bit. Walter's firm grip on my elbow and hand on my back was all that kept me on my feet. I clamped my eyes shut until he helped me onto a settee in his office. I'd been holding my breath. He wheeled his desk chair across from me, sat down, and leaned forward. He kept his gaze on my face while he took my hands in his. He wasn't being amorous, but was yet again inconspicuously taking my pulse. Although my instinct was to pull away, I felt comforted by his soft, strong hands.

"You've had a bad experience, haven't you," he said, in a low, imperturbable voice, "with other doctors?" I nodded, tears welling up in my eyes. I was grateful he didn't inquire further. "I'm sorry, Hattie." He gave my hands a gentle squeeze and then glanced over his shoulder as the postman entered the examination room to deliver the mail. "I'd close the door but I wouldn't want to show any impropriety."

Embarrassed, I extricated my hands and wiped away the tears. "Thank you. I'm fine now." I smiled at him in answer to his questioning countenance.

"Good morning, Jacob," Walter said to the postman. "You can just leave it there on the table."

"Good morning, Doc, ma'am," the postman said as he left.

"I apologize for the interruption," Walter said. "Feeling better?"

"Yes, thank you," I said.

He relaxed back into his chair, grinning. "Good. Can I get you something to drink? Coffee, tea, spring water?"

"A cup of coffee would be nice, thank you."

He rose from his chair and pushed a buzzer on the wall. A thin man with patches of gray hair about the ears appeared in the doorway. He was impeccably dressed, with razor sharp creases down his trouser legs, a starched bow tie, and bleached white gloves.

"Sir?" He spoke with a British accent.

"Theakston, could you arrange for coffee for Miss Davish and me. Use the Kona." Walter, addressing me, said, "My mother sent some wonderful coffee straight from the Sandwich Islands. Would you like something to eat? Knowing you, you didn't eat enough breakfast."

"You don't need to make a fuss on my account, Dr. Grice. Plain coffee is fine. And I don't need anything to eat."

"And bring some of the cake Mrs. Norton brought yesterday," Walter said, addressing his valet again. "Thank you, Theakston."

"Very good, sir." The butler took two steps backward and then disappeared through the doorway. When he was gone, I broached the subject that was the purpose of my visit.

"I'm sorry to hear that George Shulman was arrested. I know you and he are friends."

All the animation vanished from Walter's face. "Yes, thank you." His head drooped. "I never thought it would come to this, Hattie. He's innocent. I know he's innocent."

"That's why I'm here." Walter appeared expectant but didn't interrupt. "I've seen his violent temper, Walter, and I know he had a very good reason to hate Mrs. Trevelyan. You and I were even witness to his threats. But unless the police have more evidence against him than his motive, I know of at least one, maybe two other possible suspects."

"Hattie!" Relief and hope washed over Walter's face. "That's marvelous. Who are these other suspects?"

Theakston's return, with a tray laden with a silver coffee service and several slices of scrumptious-looking cake, cut off further discussion. The butler set the tray on a nearby table and proceeded without comment to pour the coffee. He offered me a cup, black as I like it, and then served the doctor a cup brimming with cream and sugar.

"Will that be all, sir?" he said, setting a cloth napkin on Walter's lap.

"Yes, thank you, Theakston," Walter said. The butler retreated as I took my first sip of coffee. "How do you like it?"

"It's fine, thank you," I said.

Walter wrinkled up his face. "Isn't it the best cup of coffee you've ever had?"

"Oh, I don't know. The coffee is very good."

"Very good? I'll have you know this is some of the finest coffee in the world. Never mind. How about this?" He reached for the cake plate. "Could I tempt you? One of my patients brought this yesterday. She's a very good cook."

Without hesitation, I helped myself to a slice and took a bite, and then another and another until it was gone. Walter watched me over his coffee cup as I reached for a second slice and burst out laughing, almost spilling his drink.

"Now I know the secret to getting Miss Hattie Davish to eat—let her eat cake!"

Despite myself I had to laugh. He was right. I hadn't tasted a cake yet that I didn't like. I finished my third piece as Walter poured himself a second cup of coffee.

"Now, Hattie, tell me all you know about these other possible suspects. Who are they?"

"One is Mrs. Cordelia Anglewood," I said.

"Do I know her?"

"Yes, she's the new president of the American Women's Temperance Coalition, the one who conducted the memorial service last night."

"Ah. What would be her reason, to become the coalition's new president? Doesn't seem like much of a motive to me. She's ambitious, but do you think her capable of murder?"

"I don't know. It's possible. She might've had other reasons as well."

I recounted everything I knew about Cordelia Anglewood, about the threats she hurled at Mrs. Trevelyan's closed door the first time I'd met her, how she was witnessed almost striking Mrs. Trevelyan, how she almost struck me. She was a woman with a temper. I repeated what Miss Lizzie had told me of the disagreements between Mrs. Trevelyan and Cordelia. I told him about her ambitions and how she had lied about her whereabouts.

"She could've lashed out at Mrs. Trevelyan in a rage," I said.

"Maybe." He sounded skeptical. "But you said the chambermaid saw Cordelia Anglewood leave early Monday morning when Mrs. Trevelyan was still alive and well."

"She could've returned after Mary left."

"You don't like this woman, do you?" Walter teased.

"Dr. Grice, I'm being perfectly objective about this," I said, offended, in part because I was afraid that he was right. "It's what I was trained to do. It's all about organization, summation, and an eye to detail." He grimaced as he finished his coffee. "You didn't see the whip lashing she gave that little stable boy."

"You're right, Hattie. She's a legitimate subject." He offered me another slice of cake. "And the other possible suspect?"

"His name is John Martin."

I hadn't told anyone of my suspicions of John Martin: that the money, deposited in the AWTC's bank account in his name, might have been extortion money, that he might have been in Mrs. Trevelyan's room, that he might have been the author of the threatening note, that he might have killed Mrs. Trevelyan. It was too much supposition. I also hadn't told anyone of my search for him and my failure to find him. I'd asked around and no one had recognized the name. He was a mystery, and until now, I alone knew it. So why was I telling Walter?

"Or at least I think it is," I said.

"He's the man you asked about at breakfast yesterday morning, something about an ambiguous letter?"

"I'm sorry, Walter. I lied about that, in a way. I needed to know if anyone recognized the name."

"Why, who is he?"

"That's just it; I don't know." I told him everything, about the note, the calling card, the bank receipt, my futile search, everything. "I'm not sure he has anything to do with Mrs. Trevelyan's murder, but you have to admit how suspicious it looks."

"I agree. I think we ought to go to the police." Walter looked at his pocket watch and then rose from his chair. "We have time before your appointment." He reached out his hand, urging me to rise, but with the mention of the police, my enthusiasm waned. I began to have doubts again.

"The police don't hold me in high regard," I said. "And to tell you the truth, Walter, I'm beginning to wonder why I'm still involved in this." Walter knitted his brow and sat down again. "Instead of thinking about Mrs. Trevelyan's murder, I should be spending my time procuring a new situation. I'm a working typist, a secretary after all, and my current wages will only take me so far. My official obligations to Mrs. Trevelyan end tomorrow."

I stood and studied a painting on the wall. "And except for a few new acquaintances I would miss, I've often longed to be away from here."

I glanced back to regard the impact my speech had had on the doctor. Walter reached up and took my hands, drawing me back to my chair. "If you left, you would be dearly missed."

Abashed by his revelation, I studied the titles of books stacked up on the desk next to me: *Anatomy: descriptive and surgical, Uses of Water in Modern Medicine, Materia Medica and Therapeutics: for physicians and students, Practitioner's Ready Reference Book: a handy guide in office and bedside practice.* Walter touched my chin and gently compelled me to face him.

"George needs my help. The temperance group is against him, the evidence is against him, and even those who voted him into office are turning against him. And I need help if I'm going to prove he's innocent," he whispered as he brushed a stray curl from my forehead. "Please stay and help me." How could I refuse?

CHAPTER 18

"May I help you, sir?" The clerk at the police station addressed Walter as we approached the desk.

"Yes, Miss Davish and I would like a word with the chief. Please tell him Dr. Walter Grice is inquiring. We're acquainted."

"What's this about?" the clerk asked.

"It's regarding the arrest of George Shulman for the murder of Edwina Trevelyan."

At the mention of Mrs. Trevelyan's name, the clerk scrutinized me but continued to address Walter. "I'll see if he's around. Please take a seat, Doctor."

Walter and I had hardly sat down when Chief Jackson emerged from the back room with a watering can in his hand.

"Too bad about George Shulman, eh, Doc? Guess he won't be on the council now. I voted for the man too." The two men shook hands.

"That's what we've come to talk to you about, Ben."

"Let's talk in there then, Doc," Jackson said, pointing to a door on the right.

"Miss Davish needs to be there as well," Walter said. "She has information that might help your investigation."

The policeman rolled his eyes and let out a sigh of exasperation. "Very well," he said, "follow me."

The room was bare except for a long wooden table and four chairs. Wrought-iron bars crisscrossed the window. I had expected to see some greenery, considering the profusion of plants in the lobby; the light was perfect for ferns. With an indication for us to sit down, the policeman closed the door, sat down across from us, and put up his hand.

"Before you say anything, Doc, Miss Davish, I want you to know that we have our man. George Shulman killed that temperance woman. We've got him dead to rights."

"What's your evidence against him?" Walter said.

Chief Jackson counted out with his fingers. "He had means, motive, and opportunity. With your help, Doc, we determined the victim was killed by asphyxiation sometime last Monday. As you are also aware, we have evidence that she was hit over the head first with a glass bottle. We found shards of glass in the trunk and embedded in the carpet in her room. We asked the hotel staff and all of the water bottles in the victim's room are accounted for. Then Burke found the remnants of part of a gin bottle wrapped up among the bloody clothes. Shulman probably hid it there."

"But anyone could've hit her with a gin bottle," Walter said.

"Doc, we're talking about a lady temperance leader. Who else would bring a gin bottle around this woman but the man who held a grudge against her for burning his saloon? It's almost poetic."

"But he says he was at the Cavern all day," Walter said. "Surely someone can corroborate his claim."

"Yes, but not for the whole day," Chief Jackson said. "There are unexplained gaps, a half hour here, twenty minutes there, in which no one knew where he was. But we do."

"How? Where was he?" Walter asked.

"George Shulman was at the Arcadia Hotel, despite his claims to the contrary. He was overheard threatening Mrs. Trevelyan in her room at the hotel Monday morning. And the witness heard the sound of breaking glass." The chief folded his hands behind his head and leaned back in his chair. "There's no doubt. He killed her."

Walter and I stared at him, stunned. Mary had told me about the altercation with Cordelia Anglewood, but this was the first time I'd heard anything about George Shulman clashing with Mrs. Trevelyan that morning.

"That's what prompted you to start investigating her disappearance," I blurted out. "Who overheard the threats? What time did they say they heard him?"

Chief Jackson looked at me out of the corner of his eye before his head followed his gaze. "We received an anonymous telephone call," he said. "Handy device, the telephone. We installed it a few months ago. And yes, we received this information the morning we discovered her in the basement."

"So it was George Shulman who pushed me down the stairs?" I said.

"The two are quite unrelated." He turned to Walter. "It's unfortunate, Doc, but as you see, the evidence is convincing against him."

"But who else could it've been?" I said.

"Even if George Shulman did push you down some stairs, what difference does it make now?" Jackson asked.

"None now, but if you had heeded my concerns, you might've prevented me a lot of aches and pains." I clenched my hands into fists in my lap. "I approached you the day before the telephone tip."

"We don't know for sure that it was even George that

pushed you," Walter said, enveloping my fists with his hands under the table. "Isn't that right, Chief?"

"Something like that," the policeman conceded. "Now, if there's nothing more."

"Do you know for certain that George confronted Mrs. Trevelyan?" Walter said. "I'm not certain that you should believe an anonymous telephone caller."

"Actually, yes," the policeman said. "Although we never discovered where the anonymous tip came from, the information is true enough. The registration desk clerk on duty at the time saw the saloonkeeper bound up the stairs toward Mrs. Trevelyan's room that morning. He couldn't remember the time, but was certain he'd overheard George Shulman all the way from the second floor, shouting something about justice and hypocrisy. We've confirmed this with several others who overheard part of the exchange."

"Sounds like George, all right," Walter said. "It seems idiotic, though, threatening her where all can hear and then killing her. He would be immediately suspected."

"It's a tactic that's been used before. She could've been already dead, for all we knew at the time, and he was covering it up by creating a scene." He rose from his chair.

"Ben," Walter said, "Miss Davish has some information about a few other possible suspects you might want to hear."

"Unless it has to do with George Shulman, it's no use to me."

"But I would think Cordelia Anglewood is as much of a suspect as Mr. Shulman," I said. "She lied about her whereabouts. She said she was out riding all day, but the stable boy I spoke to said—"

"Wait, stop, right there," Jackson said. "What are you doing questioning anyone about alibis? This is a police investigation, Miss Davish, and I won't have you interfering. Now," he said, his face flushed with anger, "this interview is over."

★   ★   ★

The bathing room gleamed in the early-afternoon sun. White tiles reflected the light flooding in through the high windows encircling the room. The room was silent except for the occasional sound of water lapping as someone readjusted in their tub.

I was relishing the warmth of my final soak when I heard Nellie hiss, "The miss was almost done, Fred. What did you go and do that for?"

When I'd first arrived at Basin Spring Bathhouse, I'd been shown into a changing room where I'd exchanged my navy and white striped tailor-made dress and a sailor hat for a black knee-length woolen bathing costume, black stockings, bathing slippers, and cap. When I'd emerged thus attired, Nellie, the bath attendant, intimidating in a starched white cap, dress, and apron, had been waiting for me. It was her responsibility to attend to me throughout the series of baths that Dr. Grice had prescribed. Although she jested and tried in vain to assuage my apprehensions, she took her responsibility seriously. The doctor had put me in capable yet unyielding hands.

The first place she led me was a large, white-tiled room with silver showerheads spaced every five feet. A large copper drain stood in the middle of the room. She switched on the water, adjusted the temperature, and then steered me beneath one of the showerheads. Once I was sufficiently rinsed, she conducted me to a room full of long, rectangular enamel bathtubs. Three women bathers and an attendant were already in the room. It was bright; the sun reflected off the sterile white tiles and, despite towering ceilings, the air was warm. Nellie indicated a bathtub and helped me climb into it. Despite the attendant's encouragement, I had difficulty relaxing in the lukewarm water. I lay there, counting the minutes in my head and fixating on the bottom of my tub, a mosaic of color tiles, goldfish swimming in a sea of brilliant blue. I was shivering by the time Nellie indicated that it was time to move on.

The next room was crammed with strange contraptions including a jungle of metal pipes and a series of metal cabinets, holes cut out of their tops. A woman occupied one of the cabinets. Only her head and the steam surrounding her could be seen. I was beginning to regret ever having met Dr. Walter Grice when Nellie, lifting a latch, opened a front hatch in the cabinet and had me sit on the wooden bench. I cowered as she closed the hatch over my head, securing me inside. She yanked on a handle on the pipe next to the cabinet and steam hissed as it filled the spaces around my body. Being locked in a box filled with steam was a strange sensation. Within a minute, I couldn't see beyond my nose as the mist escaped about my head. Perspiration dripped down my face. Nellie dabbed my forehead with a thick white cotton towel. Within another minute or two, the sense of being trapped lessened and a tranquility I hadn't felt in years fell over me.

Maybe Walter is on to something after all, I thought.

The experience was over almost as fast as it began. Nellie explained, as she freed me from the steam cabinet, that steam relaxed and cleansed the body, but too much could be detrimental. I entered another, smaller bathing room, where there were six claw-foot bathtubs lined up, three on each side. A woman lounged in the second tub on the left. Nellie, indicating the first tub on the right, helped me into a fresh, warm mixture of Sweet Spring and Basin Spring water. It felt cool and refreshing after the hot steam treatment. After fifteen minutes, Nellie indicated I should enter the adjacent tub. This, too, was a mineral spring bath, and was warmer still. After another fifteen minutes, I eagerly climbed into the third bathtub. As I lowered myself in, a faint scent of mint and eucalyptus filled the air around me. I'd never felt so refreshed in my life. I'd lounged in this scented, hot bath for a long time with my eyes closed, letting my mind wander, when the disgust in Nellie's voice as she scolded Fred jolted me upright. The serenity I'd felt a moment ago was gone.

"I'm so sorry, miss." Nellie rushed to my side, blocking my view of the room. She glanced over her shoulder. "Fred didn't know you were still in here. I'd stepped out for a moment. I don't know how this could've happened."

"What's wrong, Nellie?" I said, craning my neck, trying to see around her.

"This has never happened before, miss. Ever, I swear."

"What's happened?"

"A gentleman's in the bath, miss," she whispered. "And of course, there's Fred too." I could see then as Nellie turned that a man in a white uniform was standing in the line of sight of the first tub on the left. His back was turned to us.

"You don't allow men to bathe here?" I asked.

"Yes, miss, of course they do," Nellie said. "Just not in the presence of a lady."

"Oh, of course."

"I'm so sorry, miss," she said, wringing her hands, over and over. "You'll be a prune soon if I don't get you out of that tub."

"Do you think the gentlemen could be persuaded to close their eyes as I exit the bath?" I said.

Nellie's face lit up as if this suggestion had never occurred to her. She dashed over to the male attendant, whispering something I couldn't hear, and then waited while he spoke to the gentleman in the tub. One flick of Fred's head and Nellie rushed back, wrapping me in a towel long enough to cover me from my chin to my feet. I felt ridiculous, shuffling along slowly so as not to trip. I'd plenty of time to regard the men as we passed. Fred, the attendant, was a stocky man with grease glistening in his straight brown hair. When I saw the gentle-man in the tub, I almost lost my footing. It was the man from the Catholic chapel. Enhanced by the heat of the steam, the blotches bloomed crimson across his face, yet the fierceness I'd seen there yesterday had been replaced by an expression of equanimity. The baths were doing him some good. Nonetheless, I was relieved when I reached the changing room.

Nellie helped me out of my wet bathing costume as my mind raced back to my encounter with the man I'd just seen. I still didn't know how he knew me. It wasn't long before my thoughts were full of Mrs. Trevelyan's murder, Cordelia Anglewood's deception, and George Shulman's dire predicament. The serenity of the baths was behind me, yet my body retained the memory. I felt refreshed and warm and hungry.

"Nellie," I said as I fastened my corset, "do you know that gentleman in the bath? I met him before, but didn't catch his name."

I'd asked more questions in the few days since arriving in Eureka Springs than I had since autumn began. But what was I doing asking about this man? He had nothing to do with Mrs. Trevelyan. It seemed indulging my curiosity was becoming habit forming.

"I can check for you, miss."

I joined her, when I finished dressing, in the waiting area, a narrow hall consisting of a wooden desk, a coatrack, and a yellow-flowered settee. Nellie stood behind the desk, poring over a registration book.

"No wonder you overlapped," Nellie said. "The men's baths are full, and obviously overflowing." The male attendant slipped into the waiting room from a side door. "Fred, you shouldn't have scheduled any treatment until two."

"What are you doing?" Fred blustered. He grabbed the book and slammed it shut. "Treatments are confidential." He stalked away with the registration book tucked under one arm.

"Did you happen to catch the man's name?" I asked my attendant.

Nellie glowered toward Fred's retreating figure. "Sorry, miss, but no."

"I'll give you ten minutes with the prisoner, Miss Davish, but no more." Officer Burke, more sympathetic toward me since the discovery of Mrs. Trevelyan's body, led me toward the cell block. "And don't tell the chief I let you in." I promised.

After my baths, I'd been in the mood for some window shopping and a roundabout stroll back to the hotel. As I'd been leaving Mrs. Cunningham's millinery shop, I'd seen Mary Flannagan. I had waved to her. She didn't acknowledge me but instead had ducked around a corner. Something in her behavior propelled me to follow. I kept her in my sights as I descended a flight of stairs until a gig driving past on the street below prevented me from catching up. She disappeared down another stairway. By the time I'd descended the second flight of stairs, she was nowhere to be seen. I plopped down on the bottom stair.

Was Mary purposely avoiding me? Why? Could Miss Lucy be right that Mary wasn't to be trusted? Was Walter the only one in this town who was who he appeared to be? How much more of this could I take?

I had stood up, brushed my dress off, and straightened my hat. No longer content with the distractions of window shopping, I wanted answers. Being in the vicinity of the jailhouse, I had decided to start here; I'd confront George Shulman once and for all.

"Mr. Shulman, someone's here to see you," Burke announced before he left.

George Shulman leapt to his feet. "My darling, again? You shouldn't . . ." He stopped mid-sentence when he saw me. "Who are you? What do you want?"

My darling? I wondered. So someone else had been to visit

him. I'd have to ask Walter about George Shulman's known family or attachments.

"We met Tuesday evening outside your saloon, Mr. Shulman. I'm Miss Davish, Mrs. Trevelyan's secretary."

"Oh, yeah, I remember you. You're the prim and prissy lady who was asking a lot of questions and made some nasty insinuations." He plunked down hard onto wooden plank bench. "What are you doing here?"

"I'd like to talk to you about Edwina Trevelyan."

"There's nothing to talk about. I didn't kill that woman. I'm not sorry she's dead, but I didn't do it."

"Dr. Grice believes you," I said. "I think Chief Jackson wants to believe you. But there's a great deal of evidence against you."

"I didn't do it."

"You claimed to be at the saloon all day, but a witness saw you threatening Mrs. Trevelyan the morning she died. They heard glass breaking. Glass was found in her scalp, Mr. Shulman," I said.

George Shulman blanched. "Someone saw me?"

"And telephoned the police."

"Well, I did threaten the old cow. She'd almost ruined my business. Sure I gave her a piece of my mind, but I didn't kill her."

"What about the glass?" I said.

"A mirror. I smashed a mirror. Those crazy women broke every mirror and window in my place. It was a little payback."

"So you hit Mrs. Trevelyan with a mirror?"

"No! I broke it against the dresser."

"Did you hit her with a gin bottle then?"

"No! I never laid a finger on the old hag. She deserved a good beating, especially after threatening to finish what she started with my bar. But that's when I got out of there, before I really got mad."

"When was this?" I said.

"I don't know. The police asked me the same thing. I don't know. Sometime in the morning, I don't remember. The lady was very much alive. I swear."

"Mr. Shulman, you are hot-tempered and impulsive, and you threatened to kill Mrs. Trevelyan if you ever saw her again. Why should anyone believe you?"

"Because I didn't do it!" He rattled the iron bars with his fists in frustration.

Officer Burke appeared. "What's all the racket?"

I ignored the policeman and approached the bars. "Mr. Shulman, did you push me down the stairs?"

"What? What are you talking about?" the saloonkeeper said.

"The night we met and argued, someone pushed me down a darkened alley stairwell not far from your bar. I believe it was to stop me from asking questions about Mrs. Trevelyan. I want to know, was it you?"

"I didn't push you down any stairs, lady."

"You said yourself you didn't like me asking questions and making insinuations."

"Listen here, lady, if I'd wanted to harm any woman, it would've been that Mrs. Trevelyan. Would've been but wasn't. She insulted me, threatened me, tried to burn down my business, forbid me to—" He stopped short, shaking his head. "I'd every right to, but I didn't. As for you, if you were a man I would've knocked you down, with one punch, right then and there in the street. But I don't go sneaking around and I don't harm women. Get her out of here, Burke."

He threw himself onto the bench, his head in his hands, staring at the floor. I wanted to ask him more, but the stubborn, gruff man was finished talking.

"Shouldn't have let you in," Officer Burke muttered as he escorted me out of the cell block. "Chief said you'd be trouble."

CHAPTER 19

THE WESTERN UNION TELEGRAPH COMPANY
NUMBER *69* SENT BY *TW* REC'D BY *HF* CHECK *24 paid*
RECEIVED at *No. 2 Arcadia Hotel Eureka Springs Nov 11* **1892**
Dated: *Galena, Illinois*　　　　*7:37am*
To: *Hattie Davish*　　　*Arcadia Hotel*

Heard about Edwina Trevelyan, not satisfied with information. Daily update required, relying on your usual discretion, efficiency. If already engaged, cancel, all arranged

A Windom-Greene

"Telegram for you, Miss Davish," the desk clerk shouted as I crossed the hotel's rotunda. Normally very restrained, his boisterousness alarmed me. "It's marked urgent."

I hastened over to the registration desk to take the pink slip from the clerk's waving hand, a profusion of possibilities racing through my mind. The last telegram I'd received marked urgent had brought me to my present predicament.

"It arrived this morning; we've been trying to reach you all day," the clerk said.

I scanned the telegram's contents quickly, almost giggling in relief. Sir Arthur was at it again. I reassured the anxious clerk with a smile before reading the contents more carefully a second time.

As always, my reaction to his telegram was mixed; this hadn't been the first time Sir Arthur Windom-Greene had dictated "If already engaged, cancel" to a telegraph operator. On one hand, Sir Arthur was personable and generous with his vast fortune; on the other, he was a man used to getting what he wanted, when he wanted it. I'd worked on several projects for him and had found him to be a stimulating and rewarding employer. However, his recommendations often compelled me to work in more trying or tedious situations, such as the one I found myself in now. I owed my present position in society to his patronage and didn't begrudge him his demand for absolute loyalty and acquiescence. However, it'd been his influence that had brought me to Eureka Springs and now, at his insistence, I was obliged to stay.

"It says here that arrangements have been made. Can I assume they relate to my accommodations? I was to check out tomorrow," I said.

Annoyance marked the clerk's countenance. "I've been anxious all day on account of your telegram, Miss Davish. Are you telling me that it merely concerned an extension of your stay?"

"It would seem so." The clerk stared blankly at me. "I'm sure, Mr. Oxnard, you've encountered many influential people such as Sir Arthur here in the hotel."

"Yeah," he said.

"So you must know how they tend to approach everything

with a sense of urgency. If I'd known Sir Arthur was going to contact me, I would've been more diligent in checking for messages. I apologize if you had any anxiety on my account."

"Some people," he said, shaking his head.

"Am I correct about my bill?"

With a deep sigh, he checked his registration log. "Yes, funds were wired under the name of Windom-Greene and have been credited to your room, Miss Davish."

"Thank you, Mr. Oxnard. Would you point me in the direction of the telegraph office, please?"

The telegraph office was a tiny room off the hotel's main lobby. The operator, a young man with shaggy brown hair, wearing a bow tie and tan jacket with "H. Floyd" stitched over the left breast pocket, was bent over a telegraph machine on a desk littered with telegrams, ledgers, and teacups. His uniform cap lay on top of a pile.

"Be just a moment," he said, continuing to tap on the key.

As I waited for the operator to finish his task, I glanced at the telegram in my hand. At once I was struck by its similarity to the one I'd received from Mrs. Trevelyan and by the irony of Mrs. Trevelyan's own sense of urgency. Despite her well-laid plans, mine might have been the last telegram she'd sent. Did I arrive too late? I still wondered if I could've prevented her death. What if I had arrived earlier? Pushing the thought out of my head, I wrote a quick response to Sir Arthur, my "new" employer.

"Not urgent, is it?" the operator said congenially. I had the uncomfortable feeling he'd been standing at the window, watching me, for several moments. I was about to say no, then changed my mind.

"Actually, he is expecting a prompt response. It isn't urgent, but if you could send it in a timely manner, I'd appreciate it."

"Of course, that's what they all say." The telegraph operator took my note and payment and glanced over the message quickly. "Nice handwriting, lady." He walked back to his desk. "You should see some of the scrawl I get. Most of the time I can barely make it out."

I understood exactly what he meant. I have spent countless hours deciphering the illegible handwriting of my employers, with Sir Arthur being one of the worst offenders. It confounded me how a man like Sir Arthur, so meticulous in his research, could be so slovenly in his handwriting. But then again, I was grateful for it; that's one of the reasons why he had hired me.

"Do you often get requests for urgent telegrams?" I said.

"Sure, you'd be surprised what some folks call urgent news." He began tapping rapidly on the telegraph machine.

"How about the ladies of the temperance coalition?" I asked.

"I've definitely wired more 'urgent' messages since they've been in town," Mr. Floyd said.

"Did Mrs. Trevelyan, the club's president, send a lot of 'urgent' messages? Or a lot of telegrams in general?"

His fingers slipped on the telegraph key. "Oh no, I misspelled Davish. I keyed a second *v* instead of an *h*."

"Don't worry," I said. "He'll know who it's from."

"As long as you don't mind. . . ." He continued typing in silence. When he finished, he stamped a receipt with the date and time and handed it to me. He leaned forward through the service window and peeked around.

"You're talking about the dead woman, right?" He pulled out his log book. "She always had an urgent message to send. And lots of them."

"Did she send one Saturday or Sunday to something called the Salvation Army?" I said.

"Doesn't ring a bell. What's a Salvation Army?"

"It's a charity Mrs. Trevelyan supported. Could you tell me if she sent or received any telegrams last weekend?"

He flipped through his log book. A lopsided grin spread

across his face. "I see an urgent telegram from Mrs. Trevelyan to a Miss Hattie Davish on Friday, the fourth." I grimaced at his attempt at a jest. "Sorry." He blushed and quickly examined the ledger again. "She sent several Saturday morning and two Sunday afternoon. Nothing to the Salvation Army."

"Could you give me a list?" I said.

"Ah, I don't know. I could get fired."

"Could you at least tell me if anything was wired to or from Mr. John Martin?"

He paused, regarded me for a moment, then returned his glance to the ledger.

"I don't see any John Martin. She sent a telegram to someone with the same initials as John Martin though, a Joseph Mascavarti."

"Joseph Mascavarti? Are you sure?"

"Yeah." He pivoted the log around and pointed. "See for yourself."

Joseph Mascavarti, Elmwood House, 9:18, 7 Nov 1892 Mrs. E. Trevelyan. He turned the log to face him again.

"This was wired Monday morning," I exclaimed.

"Oh, sorry, you only wanted to know about the weekend days, didn't you."

"Oh my goodness, Mr. Floyd, don't apologize. This is extremely helpful. Now think, can you remember who requested this telegram? I've been told that Mrs. Trevelyan usually sent her secretary or a chambermaid down with the request."

Again he consulted his log and hesitated, elucidation dawning on his face. "Oh boy, I remember now. Mrs. Trevelyan brought it herself." He looked up with horror in his eyes. "I was one of the last people to see her alive, wasn't I?"

"Yes. Now tell me everything you remember, Mr. Floyd."

He remembered it distinctly. Mrs. Trevelyan had wanted to wire someone in town. It was highly unusual to wire anything locally and he had told her so. He'd tried to convince her to use the mail, or if she was in a hurry, to have the message hand-delivered; the Arcadia Hotel provided such a service. Or why not use the telephone? But she had insisted, saying nothing but a telegram would command the immediate attention she desired.

I leaned closer to the operator through the window and lowered my voice. "Do you remember what the telegram said?"

His hands quivering, Mr. Floyd shook his head, then proceed to rifle through a filing cabinet. After an unfathomable amount of time, he pulled a slip of paper from the files.

"I don't know why I'm showing you this. I'm gonna get fired." He set the slip down reverently between us on the window shelf.

This time, I was the one to glance over my shoulder to assure we were unobserved.

THE WESTERN UNION TELEGRAPH COMPANY
NUMBER *5* SENT BY *HF* REC'D BY CHECK *14 paid*
RECEIVED at   *Nov* 7 **1892**
Dated: *Arcadia Hotel Eureka Springs 9:18am*
To: *J. Mascavarti*   *Elmwood House*

Contribution received with insufficient funds expect additional response
Mrs. E. Trevelyan

The operator and I regarded each other in silence. "What does it mean?" he said.

It meant that Mrs. Trevelyan had died somewhere between 9:18 A.M. and 11:00 A.M., and that Joseph Mascavarti, whose initials were the second to match the menacing note I'd found among Mrs. Trevelyan's papers, had received the last telegram Mrs. Edwina Trevelyan would ever send.

"I'm not certain," I said. "But it may have something to do with Mrs. Trevelyan's murder."

The wording of the telegram and the fact that Mrs. Trevelyan had personally requested it could leave little doubt that Joseph Mascavarti was a victim of Mrs. Trevelyan's blackmail. And isn't blackmail a motive for murder? But if this was true, then Joseph Mascavarti, and not John Martin, was the one with the motive to kill. *Could it be merely a coincidence that both men share the same initials?* I wondered as the operator whisked the telegram away.

Bolstered now that I knew where to find at least one of the mysterious J.M.'s, I said, "Are you sure you can't give me the list from this weekend too?"

Without hesitating, he pulled the log book closer and scribbled onto a scrap sheet of paper, looking up several times to see he wasn't being watched. He scrutinized the lobby one more time before he slipped it to me. I glanced down at the paper in my hand. In his haste, he had written down everything that had been wired over the weekend, not only those from Mrs. Trevelyan. A few familiar names caught my eye. I folded the paper and slipped it into the pocket of my skirt.

"Thank you, Mr. Floyd. You've been most helpful." I stepped away from the telegraph office window and headed slowly back to my room.

It was a surprisingly long list with telegrams sent from three doctors, two local businessmen, and numerous hotel guests. In addition to Mrs. Trevelyan, several temperance club members had wired messages that weekend: Cordelia Anglewood to a jeweler in Fayetteville, Agnes Kiltcher to a Mrs. Boone in Jonesboro, and Mrs. Elmslie, an elderly lady staying in the room across the hall from me, to Mr. Elmslie in Joplin.

"I said wait, Miss Davish!" a harsh voice commanded.

I stopped in my tracks. I'd been contemplating the assort-

ment of telegrams when I nearly bumped into Cordelia Anglewood.

"Get your head out of the clouds, girl. Now, if you recall,"
she said, "you agreed to write responses to all of the condolence cards. I was about to leave these at the desk, but . . . here
are several more." She thrust the cards and some leaflets at me.
"And as your obligations and commitments are at an end tomorrow, it behooves you to have them completed by then.
The signed temperance pledges are there too."

Taken aback by her businesslike manner, I stood speechless
as she, not expecting a reply, turned to leave. I found my voice,
but stammered. "I spoke to the stable boy. . . ."

She halted, then faced me, glowering. Her hand brushed
her bare throat, smoothed her hair, then twirled the gold stud
in her right ear. "Mine wasn't an idle threat, Miss Davish,"
Cordelia Anglewood said in an eerily calm voice. "I am trying
to lead this coalition and serve its cause. For no apparent reason, you seem intent on undermining my endeavors with your
petty insinuations. You've been nothing but an insolent, incompetent pest since you arrived." She leaned forward, causing me to lean back slightly. Her voice was almost a whisper.
"Once and for all, I'd nothing to do with Trevelyan's demise.
But if you don't stay out of my way, and out of my business, I
won't be able to say the same about you."

I was getting distressingly accustomed to threats but decided it was best to remain silent. Mrs. Anglewood stared at me
for a moment more without blinking, then left. More than
happy to get out of Cordelia Anglewood's way, I returned to
my room, typed my first report to Sir Arthur, and then set to
work on the condolence responses and pledge list as Mrs.
Anglewood had requested. Finally, I was able to immerse myself in a task that made sense. I fell asleep late in the night at
my desk, content.

CHAPTER 20

The chipping black paint on the sign read, ELMWOOD HOUSE.

I was walking back to my hotel, refreshed from my morning hike exploring East Mountain and its springs, including Little Eureka Spring, said to be the best-tasting water, and Laundry Spring, where a woman with bare arms up to her elbows was rinsing linen sheets. It'd been at Onyx Spring where I'd collected sedges, now preserved in the plant press I held flung over my shoulder. Elmwood House was the residence of Mr. Joseph Mascavarti. The telegram suggested that Mr. Mascavarti had been a guest here as recently as a week ago. I dashed up the stairs.

"I'm sorry, miss," the desk clerk said, yawning. "There's no Joseph Mascavarti registered." He took a sip from a cup set on a filing cabinet next to the desk.

"He was wired here this past Monday. He could've checked out since." The clerk leafed through the pages of the registration book and yawned again. I peered over the desk, trying to see for myself.

His head was shaking before he replied. "Sorry." He reached for the cup again. "No Joseph Mascavarti."

"But the telegraph office at the Arcadia Hotel confirms that the telegram was received."

He slurped his drink. "Why would anyone send a wire across town?"

"It's a long story," I said. "Could you check again?"

"Well, we do get telegrams for folks staying in some of the nearby boarding houses. I could check if he picked one up."

"Thank you, that would be helpful." He disappeared into a back office, carrying his mug with him. The clerk reappeared moments later with a tablet under his arm. He drank from his mug as he walked. He clanked the mug down and let out a satisfied sigh.

"Nothing like the first cup of coffee in the morning." He opened the tablet to a particular page and smoothed the paper on the desk. "Here it is, Mr. Joseph Mascavarti, Monday, the seventh."

"Is that a record of the telegram?" I asked, barely able to contain my excitement. "Did he sign for it?" The clerk fixed a blank stare on my forehead and took another slurp of his coffee.

"As I was saying, a telegram for Mr. Joseph Mascavarti, dated Monday, the seventh of November, was signed for by . . ." He wrinkled his nose. and hesitated. "I don't understand. Mr. Mascavarti didn't sign this, a Mr. John Martin did."

I staggered forward, my plant press nearly slipping off my shoulder. The implications reeling in my head, I barely had the faculty to ask what I had asked dozens of times before: "Is Mr. Martin a guest here?"

"Are you okay?" the clerk said. "You look like you got dizzy there for a minute."

"Yes, yes, I'm fine. Could you look to see if John Martin is staying here?"

"Yeah, sure." The clerk retrieved the registration book as I gripped the edge of the desk. His finger traced the entries down the page. When he stopped to take one last swig from his coffee mug, I thought I was going to scream. He turned another page.

"Well . . . ?" I said, almost losing my patience.

"Yeah, looks like Mr. John Martin has been staying with us for several weeks now. He's staying in room 24, second floor, second door on your right."

I thanked him and immediately bounded up the stairs. Once I found room 24, I took a few moments to catch my breath. Was I doing it again? I had confronted George Shulman at the Cavern Saloon, knowing it might not be the best course of action, and had gotten myself shoved down an alley stairwell. Now I was contemplating confronting John Martin, at this early hour, alone. I began to doubt the intelligence of even speaking to this man. I should notify the police. He might be Mrs. Trevelyan's killer. I knocked anyway.

"Can I help you?" A man in his mid sixties answered the door. He had bushy eyebrows, a long white mustache, and a few strands of hair plastered across an otherwise bald head. He was wearing a blue silk dressing gown.

"Mr. Martin?"

"No. What do you want?"

"I'm looking for Mr. John Martin," I said, impetuously adding, "or Mr. Joseph Mascavarti."

The man eyed my hiking costume and plant press. "And you are?"

"I'm Miss Hattie Davish, personal secretary to Mrs. Edwina Trevelyan."

His eyebrow raised as he peered down at me. "The temperance woman found dead in her travel trunk?"

"Yes." It was a crude observation, but true.

"What business, may I ask, Miss Davish, do you have with John?"

"Mr. Martin contributed to Mrs. Trevelyan's American Women's Temperance Coalition. I would like to speak to him on related business." I'm ashamed how easily this half truth came to me.

"Yes? Well, I'm very proud of John. The AWTC is a worthy cause. But I'm sorry, Miss Davish, John's not here right now. I'm Colonel William Walker, John's father-in-law. May I be of assistance?"

"Thank you, Colonel Walker, but it's important I speak with Mr. Martin personally."

"I believe he's taking treatments at the baths, though I don't know which bathhouse. However, I do know he received an invitation from President Anglewood to attend the coalition's event at Magnetic Spring today. But then again, being the secretary, you probably already knew that. You may be able to speak to him there."

I thanked him, apologized for disrupting his morning, and walked briskly toward the staircase.

"By the way," the colonel said, stepping across the threshold into the hallway, "who is Joseph Mascavarti?"

When I arrived back at the hotel, brimming with my discoveries, the lobby, dining room, and ladies' parlor were abuzz with coalition members and talk of today's culminating rally. I was anxious to return to my typewriter so I could sort out everything I'd learned. Colonel Walker hadn't known of Joseph Mascavarti. Yet John Martin and Joseph Mascavarti had to be one and the same. Which meant that he who had left his calling card and had contributed to the AWTC was one and the same as he who had written the threatening note and had been blackmailed by Mrs. Trevelyan. It didn't answer the question of why. Or did it? I was weaving my way through the crowded lobby when I heard, "Davish, there you are!" shouted above the din of the women chatting. I turned and headed for the two white-headed ladies inching toward me.

"Isn't it exciting?" Miss Lizzie exclaimed, clapping her hands together. "Today's the big day. You will accompany us to the rally tonight, won't you, dear?"

"Of course she will, Lizzie," her sister declared. "What else has Davish to do?" The two sisters stared at me expectantly.

"Of course I will, Miss Lizzie. I officially relinquished all of my correspondences and duties to Mrs. Anglewood before breakfast."

"Does that mean you're out on your ear, Davish?" Miss Lucy said.

"Oh, I hope not." Miss Lizzie put her hand to her throat. The motion reminded me of something, but I couldn't quite remember what. "You did hear from Arthur, didn't you, dear?"

"Arthur?" I said.

Miss Lizzie squinted and clucked her tongue against her teeth. "Shame on him. He promised me he would take care of you. What are old friends for if not to do favors for one another?"

"Oh, do you mean Sir Arthur Windom-Greene?" I said. Miss Lizzie bobbed her head. "You contacted Sir Arthur on my behalf, Miss Lizzie?"

"Did I do wrong, dear? I just wanted to help. I thought it best if you stayed, at least until Edwina's murder was solved."

"I knew it." Miss Lucy wagged her finger at her sister. "You really must stop meddling, Lizzie. I insist. Look at what happened the last time."

"Well, you'll be happy to know, then . . . ." I'd missed something. "What did you mean, Miss Lucy, by 'look what happened the last time'?"

"Oh, Hattie, dear, it's nothing." Miss Lizzie patted my arm. I watched Miss Lucy.

"Nothing but trouble, you mean, Lizzie, or should I call you Miss Nosey Parker?"

"What are you two ladies talking about?" I asked.

"Lizzie pries into other people's business, Davish, like the Great Blondin crossing Niagara Falls on a tightrope, that's what I'm talking about. It's a way of life that God never intended. She had no business petitioning Sir Arthur, on your behalf, for a job."

"I'm sure it was kindly meant. I don't think—"

Miss Lucy silenced me with a glare. "And was it her magnanimous nature that compelled her to call the police, enticing them to investigate with her 'credible evidence'?"

My mouth dropped open. I couldn't believe it. "Miss Lizzie, is this true? You're the anonymous telephone caller?"

"Yes, dear. How else was I going to get them to probe into Edwina's disappearance and the attack on you? They didn't seem overly eager to do their job. When George Shulman's name came up, I knew that what I had to tell them would spur some action."

"What did you tell them?" I said.

"That she overheard George Shulman shouting and threatening Edwina the morning she disappeared," Miss Lucy said. "That she heard glass breaking in Edwina's room."

"Miss Lizzie, you saw George Shulman here at the hotel threatening Mrs. Trevelyan?" I said. "What did he say?"

"Well, I'm not exactly certain what he said, dear." She fiddled with her collar and blushed. "They were shouting and yelling in Edwina's room, so I hid down the corridor."

"And when was this?" I said. "Do you remember?"

"During breakfast, dear. Don't you remember I excused myself for a minute? I knew that if I didn't retrieve that book from the library that moment, I would surely forget." Hence the food stains that Mary had mistaken for blood. A blackberry compote had been served that morning.

"Did you check on Mrs. Trevelyan after he left?" I said.

"I'd slipped into the bathroom before he could see me. I was frightened, dear, very frightened." Her lip began to tremble. "When I felt safe to come out, Edwina was gone." Miss Lucy, in a rare act of compassion, patted her sister's hand.

"How did you know it was George Shulman?" I said. "Had you seen him before?"

"I didn't know who he was, dear, at least not until I recognized him standing up to Electra Richards at the protest on Election Day."

"Thank you for telling me this, Miss Lizzie. And thank you for contacting Sir Arthur. He has hired me again. I owe my current situation to you."

"I'm so glad I could help, dear." The elderly lady still fiddled with her collar. Her nervous gesture brought something else to my mind.

"Miss Lizzie, where is your mother-of-pearl bar pin?" I'd never seen her without it.

"Oh," Miss Lizzie exclaimed, pulling her hand self-consciously away from her throat. "How nice of you to notice, dear."

"She broke the clasp taking it off last night," Miss Lucy said.

"I do feel strange without it; it was a gift from our brother," Miss Lizzie said. "It's the only thing I had of value until Lucy married Oliver Fry."

"Davish didn't ask for your whole history, Lizzie. Besides, the rags-to-riches story is clichéd."

"Well, anyway, we're taking the train to Fayetteville on Monday, dear, to have it repaired at a jeweler there. I've heard many of the ladies recommend him."

"We were going anyway, to purchase a few things we can't get here," Miss Lucy said. "But with all this talk of my sister's meddling and clumsiness, we forgot to tell you our news,

Davish." I held my breath in anticipation. "Cordelia Angle-wood received a shock this morning."

"Yes, dear, some very bad news," Miss Lizzie said.

"What news?" My heart raced.

"We don't know," Miss Lucy said, crestfallen.

I closed my eyes and sighed, unable to hide my exaspera-tion. *Ah, to be befriended by the coalition's biggest gossips,* I thought. "How do you even know she received bad news, then?"

"Because we saw her, dear, at breakfast when she received the telegram," Miss Lizzie said.

"And what a sight it was too, Davish," Miss Lucy said, ani-mated again. "I never suspected the woman of even having tear glands. But there she was proud as ever, with tears welling in her eyes. Of course, she acted like nothing happened."

Cordelia Anglewood crying? I thought. This was more than mere gossip after all.

"Josephine tried to comfort her, of course, but was coolly rebuked," Miss Lizzie said. "Cordelia left the dining room al-most immediately. I felt horrible for her."

What could possibly bring the proud Cordelia Anglewood to the verge of tears? My experience left me feeling little sym-pathy for the woman and unable to imagine such an event. I could only speculate. The news of a loved one's death or grave illness would upset anyone. The loss of respectability or posi-tion to a woman of her ambition might upset her. But to the verge of tears?

"We'll tell you if we find out more, dear," Miss Lizzie said.

Several women, arms linked and wearing AWTC buttons, marched past us, singing.

> *Now the temp'rance army's marching*
> *With the Christian's armor on;*
> *Love our motto, Christian Captain,*
> *Prohibition is our song!*

"Enough of this prattle," Miss Lucy said, "we're going to miss all the festivities. It's settled, then. Davish will spend the day with us." She frowned, noticing my plant press and appearance for the first time. "But properly attired and without the dead plants, please, Davish."

Magnetic Spring acquired its name by imparting magnetic properties to anything that came into contact with it. As a testament, the Arcadia had on display a pewter dinner plate with a fork, a knife, a hatpin, a pair of spectacles, and a tin of kippered herring, all magnetically attached. I was skeptical but hadn't had time to test the "magnetizing water" for myself. I had brought an extra hatpin for the purpose. However, the Shaw sisters viewed the spring in a different light. As we rumbled down the gravel road toward it, they revealed to me that this spring, said to cure drunkenness and addiction to medicines containing alcohol and laudanum, symbolized their cause. Among themselves they called it "Temperance Spring," and to some it was akin to holy water. It was one of the reasons the AWTC assembled in Eureka Springs. All attending members gathered here on the last day of every annual meeting. I felt honored to be invited.

The morning had turned cloudy and cold after a more promising, bright sunrise. Therefore the large pavilion built over the spring was filled to capacity with coalition members and cure seekers hoping to stay out of the imminent rain. I was surprised to see such a large crowd, but the sisters assured me that by the time the program began, the pavilion would be overflowing and the crowd would be spilling out into the surroundings. The path the hired coach followed was no more than a rough trail, and although several other wagons and buggies had made the trip, I was concerned rain might convert the trail to mud. I leaned forward and asked the driver to stop on a grassy patch several yards from the pavilion.

"Maybe we should watch from here inside the coach?" I said. "The trail's muddy beyond this grassy patch and I don't see any more benches or flat rocks available to sit on."

"You're right, Davish. Lizzie and I will watch from here, but you should go and get closer. This is your first time at Temperance Spring."

"Yes, dear, and make sure to drink the water," Miss Lizzie said.

I was about to insist on staying with them when Mrs. Anglewood, Miss Halbert, Mrs. Piers, and a few other coalition members approached the other end of the pavilion. Accompanying them was the man I'd seen twice before, at the chapel and yesterday at the baths. More than my curiosity was piqued now. I disembarked and the sisters handed me their tin cups to fill.

"Do you see that man with Mrs. Anglewood?" I said. "Do either one of you recognize him?"

"Davish, why are you whispering?" Miss Lucy asked.

"This could be very important," I said, "and I don't want anyone else to hear. Do you know that man?"

Miss Lizzie studied the figure I pointed to. "I've never seen him before, dear."

Miss Lucy, alternating between squinting and holding up her spectacles, watched him trail the coalition women through the crowd. "No," she whispered. "No, Davish, I've never seen him before either. Who is he?"

"I don't know."

"Then why . . . ?"

I didn't wait for Miss Lucy to finish her sentence. I swiftly wove through the crowd toward the group gathering at the far end of the pavilion. I needed to get closer, unnoticed, to the man with whom I kept crossing paths. I stood behind an old, lanky gentleman wearing a crushed top hat and faded morning coat. Although stooped over, he was tall enough to conceal me. I glanced around his thin frame whenever I could.

As before, Cordelia Anglewood officiated. She was in an unusually jovial mood.

What is she up to? I wondered. At breakfast the woman supposedly had tears in her eyes and now she was beaming at the gathering. She welcomed everyone and explained to the uninitiated the significance of meeting at Magnetic Spring on the last day of the American Women's Temperance Coalition's Annual Conference. She held her arms open wide before her while introducing the minister, the same Reverend Little from Mrs. Trevelyan's memorial service, who gave a benediction. As before, she invited anyone to step forward and give testimonials to the power of temperance. There were many, a great deal many more than on the previous occasion, yet Cordelia Anglewood, clasping her hands before her, bobbed her head in response to each account. She then read, from the list I had typed the night before, the names of those who had made the temperance pledge.

"May God forever keep you in his sight," she said.

During the entire proceeding, I kept myself out of her sight but kept the man on her left clearly in view. Although he remained next to Mrs. Anglewood throughout, he rarely looked at her or at anyone else. Instead, he shifted his weight from one foot to the other and studied the roof of the pavilion or contemplated the shine on his shoes or gazed down the trail. He licked his lips incessantly and, despite the chill, periodically pulled a handkerchief from his pocket and dabbed his brow. Once, after a particularly stirring testimonial given by a man and his wife, standing hand in hand, he raised his eyes to the ceiling, closed them, and moved his lips as if in prayer. My interest in him grew as the meeting lengthened. However, when the testimonials concluded, I'd yet to learn his name.

He was silent and still as those around him began to whisper and stir. I noticed, for the first time, Colonel Walker among the crowd; he was talking to the men beside him and gesturing toward Mrs. Anglewood. Mrs. Anglewood's commanding voice settled the gathering down.

"Before we part and ask Reverend Little for a final prayer, I've a few announcements to make," she said, without a hint of her usual disdain. "First, I would like to invite you all, members and well-wishers alike, to the rally tonight at Basin Park Circle. The program will begin at eight P.M. sharp."

Then she motioned to the man next to her, urging him forward. Several inches taller than him, Cordelia put her hand on his shoulder. I'd never seen Cordelia Anglewood touch anyone before.

"And second, I would like to acknowledge our special guest. Everyone, I would like to introduce to you a man who, unknown to us until quite recently, has unexpectedly out of the goodness of his heart and his belief in our cause given the AWTC one of its largest single donations to date." Applause followed her announcement. She projected over the noise, waving her arms for the clapping to stop. "He preferred to remain anonymous, his humility being a lesson for us all. But I wouldn't have it." This explained his reluctant presence at her side as well as Cordelia Anglewood's peculiar buoyant mood. "It's my pleasure to acknowledge this generous friend of temperance, Mr. John Martin."

CHAPTER 21

"Are you all right, miss?"

Upon hearing John Martin's name, I'd stumbled into the bent old man in front of me, knocking the hat from his bald head and clutching his coat to keep from falling. The tin cups that I'd been holding clattered to the ground. Cordelia Anglewood's announcement had rattled me as much as when she had raised her whip at me. The man I'd been seeking all this time, I'd already met, twice. I'd seen him in the Basin Spring Bathhouse, and I'd spoken to him at the chapel. And to see Cordelia laud the man whose "contribution" to the cause was actually blackmail money, in front of the entire membership of the AWTC, was disconcerting. Either she had no idea about the man's true motivation or else she was the most brazen woman I'd ever met. Chills went down my spine.

"Miss, are you all right?" the old man said again.

"I'm so sorry." I handed the old man his hat and brushed his rumpled sleeve. I straightened my bonnet, brushed my skirts, and gave the gentleman a brusque curtsy. "Please excuse me."

I disregarded the old man's wide-eyed expression and set out toward the retreating figure of Mr. John Martin, who, alone on foot, was heading up the narrow trail away from town. The meeting had concluded and the crowd was dispersing.

"Davish," Miss Lucy called from the carriage. "Where are you going? You'll never get back to town going that way." I waved, then picked up my pace.

I caught up to John Martin at Mystic Spring, a hillside spring a little less than a half a mile up the hill from Magnetic Spring; he was alone. Instead of drinking from the water gushing from a rocky outcrop, he sipped slyly from his flask.

"Mr. Martin, may I have a word with you?" I said. He deliberately lifted the flask for another drink and finished its contents before acknowledging me. The initials *J.M.* were engraved on it. I suppressed a shiver.

"You. What do you want?"

"I'm Hattie Davish. We met before, at the Catholic chapel and at the Basin Spring Bathhouse."

"Yeah, Miss Busybody, I know who you are. Like I said, what do you want?" Menace filled his slurred words. "I've had enough of the likes of you for one day." He pushed past me, almost staggering.

"I'd appreciate a few more moments of your time, Mr. Mascavarti." *There, I said it, no going back now,* I thought.

He stopped short. "What did you call me?"

"I know Mrs. Trevelyan was blackmailing you, Mr. Mascavarti."

His shoulders slumped. His head dropped to his chest. He grumbled incoherently. I watched as a crow landed on an overhanging branch and drank cautiously from the spring.

"How much do you want?" He wheeled around to face me. "It doesn't matter. I don't have any more. I told that hag I didn't have any more." He flung his arms loosely in the air, then pointed his finger at me. "And now I'm telling you. I don't have any more."

I backed away from him, stumbling slightly on the mossy rocks; the crow took flight. However, he halted his advance and stood, slightly swaying, staring at the ground. It started sprinkling.

"I've had enough of all of you," John Martin said. "Why couldn't you keep your stupid mouth shut?"

I gasped. "What did you say?"

He lifted his head, his eyes fixated on a point over my shoulder. He fumbled with something on his lapel without looking at it. It was an AWTC pin. He threw it to the ground.

"Why did you have to start asking questions?" he said. "Little Miss Busybody, demanding answers in the street where everyone can hear. You should've done what I told you and left well enough alone." He dropped his head into his hands, his body slightly shaking. "Now you've ruined everything."

"You? You pushed me? Why?"

His head bobbed feverishly. "Must I keep paying and paying?" He ground the pin into the path with his heel. "I thought, with her dead, I was finally free. Then you came along. Why won't you leave me alone?"

"You killed Mrs. Trevelyan?" I said.

He put his hands over his ears. "Shut up! Shut up!"

"Did you kill Mrs. Trevelyan?"

He wobbled where he stood, but his voice was low and steady when he spoke. "I told her I couldn't pay any more. And like you, the witch wouldn't listen."

He suddenly lunged forward, grasping wildly with his arms. He stumbled, slipped, and tumbled face first onto the slick grass. I leapt back, spun around, and ran.

Rain pelted me by the time I reached the streetcar stop. My shoes and the hem of my dress were thick with mud.

Water dripped from the brim of my hat. My neck ached from looking behind me. I had imagined John Martin in pursuit as I ran, but I didn't see him again. Soaked through and shivering, I rode the streetcar back into town. I wanted to go straight to the police, but propriety and practicality insisted I change first. Chief Jackson would never take me seriously if I appeared at the police station in such sodden disarray. The stop at my hotel room would give me a chance to write my report for Sir Arthur as well. The typing would calm my nerves.

I took a hot bath, changed into a warm blue and green plaid wool dress with smart lace ruffles at the cuffs and collar, sent my soiled clothes to be laundered, and then sat down to work. I typed an extra copy of both my reports for the police's perusal. Chief Jackson wouldn't welcome my summary, but I was confident that he wouldn't be able to dismiss the information. It felt good to be working again, every keystroke a victory against fear and chaos. I didn't even mind being interrupted, which I was several times, once by a chambermaid wanting to make up my bed, which I'd already done, and once by another delivering a tray of coffee, soup, biscuits, and cake sent to me by Miss Lucy, who wrote on the card, *Missed you at lunch—EAT.* I inquired after Mary, but neither maid had seen her today.

I typed with one hand, and with the other, ate two biscuits (dipped in the soup) and a piece of cake. I had finished my second cup of coffee when Josephine Piers arrived with a question about one of Mrs. Trevelyan's letters. I clarified the reference and returned to my typing.

"I heard you were helping the police," she said, glancing at the partially finished report in my typewriter. "Have they learned anything more about Mother Trevelyan's death?" She leaned over my shoulder and took the top of the paper in her hand. Before she could read too much I grabbed the paper and ripped it out of the typewriter.

She stepped away from the desk. "Who is Joseph Mascavarti?"

I placed the report face down, away from her prying eyes, and answered her with a question. "I saw Mr. Martin at the testimonial this morning. How long have you known him?"

"We didn't know who Brother Martin was until we became aware of his generous donation. We found the bank receipt among Mother Trevelyan's papers this morning. His desire was to remain anonymous, but Cordelia . . ."

Mrs. Piers glanced at the door, left slightly ajar when she had entered. The door swept inward and Cordelia Anglewood marched into the room. She was attired again for riding, though the diamond collar pin had been replaced with a simple horseshoe-shaped pin of silver.

"Josephine, how long does it take to ask a simple question?" Cordelia said.

"Is there anything else I can help you with, Mrs. Piers?" I said. Cordelia Anglewood glared at her associate.

"No, thank you, Miss Davish. I'd simply hoped you'd heard something more about Mother Trevelyan."

"That's a matter for the police, Josephine, and you know it." Cordelia Anglewood, dismissing the conversation with a slight flip of her hand, headed out the door. "Are you coming? We've wasted enough time here already. I need to dress for dinner."

"Thank you for your help with the letter from Brother Smith, Miss Davish. I never could read his handwriting." She approached the door. "I rejoice to see that your stay in Eureka Springs has done you good, Miss Davish. You're still far too thin, but your cheeks have color and your eyes have a spark that I haven't seen before."

"Yes, let's hope you're able to take your newfound health with you when you leave," Cordelia Anglewood said, reaching in and slamming the door behind the retreating Mrs. Piers.

Un, deux, trois . . .

I finished counting to ten and found myself refreshingly undisturbed by Cordelia Anglewood's veiled threat. I started a new list.

1. Did Cordelia Anglewood previously know of John Martin? Or of Joseph Mascavarti?
2. Did she know about the blackmail or does she believe the money is a donation to the cause?
3. If she believes it's an honest donation, what would she do if she discovered it was otherwise?

I finished my report, adding an entire previously unintended section on Mrs. Cordelia Anglewood. Although John Martin/Joseph Mascavarti had as good as admitted his guilt, the police needed all of the evidence before them to convict Mrs. Trevelyan's murderer, even if that meant exposing the American Women's Temperance Coalition's new president's threats, cruelty, and lies.

"Hattie, I mean, Miss Davish," Walter corrected himself, "you have impeccable timing." I'd come to tell Chief Jackson about John Martin and was surprised to find Walter and Jackson already in conference. "Please join us, have a seat."

Burke, having escorted me, awaited Chief Jackson's word. The chief indicated the chair next to Walter. Burke rolled his eyes and left. "We were talking about George," Walter said, his voice suddenly sullen. "It doesn't look good."

"I was telling Dr. Grice that without an alibi, George Shulman is the best suspect we have," Chief Jackson said. "And with those temperance ladies picketing his saloon and calling for justice, I'm transporting him to the courthouse in Berryville Monday morning." This was the first I'd heard about the picketing, but it didn't surprise me.

"The AWTC's meeting ends tonight. I'm certain that—" I said.

"Most don't emerge until midday or later," Jackson said, interrupting me. "That's why I'm leaving before dawn, less of a crowd. And simply because their meeting is over, Miss Davish, doesn't mean they're gonna stop. Lots of these women spend the winter here."

"What if I have information that might help cast suspicions elsewhere?" I said.

The policeman raised an eyebrow. "Haven't I heard this before?"

"Give her a chance, Ben," Walter said. I handed Chief Jackson the summary of all of my findings about John Martin/Joseph Mascavarti and about Cordelia Anglewood. He flipped mindlessly through the pages.

"John Martin? Cordelia Anglewood? You can't be serious, Miss Davish?"

"Yes, I'm serious, Chief Jackson," I said. "Very serious. I've been threatened by one and practically confessed to by the other." Walter gaped, his expression a mixture of concern and wonderment. The policeman was unfazed.

"All right, I'm a fair-minded man," Jackson said. "Let's take Cordelia Anglewood first. She has an alibi and no real motive."

"Gaining the power and prestige of the coalition's presidency might be enough of a motivation for Mrs. Cordelia Anglewood. She was seen by a chambermaid threatening Mrs. Trevelyan with her riding crop the morning of the murder. She lied about riding that day. I spoke to the stable boy; he never saw her."

"Miss Davish, you trust the word of a stable boy and a maid over a pillar of the community? Come now. Do you know who Commodore Anglewood is? He's one of the richest men in Chicago. He could buy his wife the position. She didn't need to kill to get it."

"What about John Martin, then?" I said. "He essentially confessed to me that he killed Mrs. Trevelyan." I appealed to Walter. "He admitted to pushing me down the stairs and tried to attack me again this morning."

Walter leapt from his chair, sending it screeching across the floor.

"Where's the devil? I'll—"

"I'm okay, Dr. Grice," I said, waving him away. "I ran away before he could catch me."

"Ben, this man must be stopped," Walter said.

"What man?"

Walter ignored the policeman. "Are you sure you're okay? If you were running, you must've taken your medicine this morning." Without taking his eyes from my face, he eased back into his chair. "Did he say why, Hattie, why he attacked you?"

"I was asking too many questions." I described all that I could remember of the conversation.

"He must've heard you talking to George," Walter said. "He must've been at the Cavern that night."

"That's what I thought too," I said. "The door was open. Anyone inside could've heard us talking about Mrs. Trevelyan's disappearance."

"Uh, 'em," Chief Jackson cleared his throat. "Excuse me, but could someone explain to me what you're talking about?"

I turned back toward the policeman. "John Martin wrote a very sinister note to Mrs. Trevelyan. The full text is in the report. I believe Mrs. Trevelyan was blackmailing him, though I haven't discovered why. Maybe it had to do with the heinous crime he referred to. In the letter, Mr. Martin threatened to harm Mrs. Trevelyan if she didn't leave him alone. And he's the one who pushed me down the stairs."

Chief Jackson put his hand up to silence me.

"Enough of this, Miss Davish. I've seen the threatening letters to Mrs. Trevelyan. They're nothing new."

"But—" I said.

"But that's beside the point," Jackson interrupted again. "John Martin couldn't have killed your Mrs. Trevelyan. He's a drunkard, and yeah, maybe his liquor got the best of him this morning when you confronted him, but that's all it was."

"But what about—"

"And that applies to your regrettable encounter with him on the stairs as well," Jackson said. "But he didn't kill anyone. The fact is, we arrested him for public intoxication the night before the murder. He couldn't have done it. He was locked up right here."

"But . . ." I was stunned. That John Martin was an inebriate made sense, and I should've realized it sooner. I'd seen him drinking this morning as well as on the day I met him at the chapel. Intoxication could indeed account for much of his behavior. Yet my instincts told me John Martin/Joseph Mascavarti was also a dangerous man. He'd pushed me down the stairs. But if he was in police custody Monday morning, he couldn't have killed Mrs. Trevelyan. Or could he?

"When did you release Mr. Martin?" I asked. "Was it before eleven A.M.?"

Chief Jackson ignored me. "I'm sorry, Doc, I don't like it any more than you do, but I've got to take George Shulman to Berryville. The sheriff's been notified and Judge Senrow has already signed the papers."

I was unwilling to give up. "Did you know that John Martin is an alias for Joseph Mascavarti?" I blurted out.

"No, I didn't." He hesitated, twisting his mustache between his fingers. "But it doesn't matter."

"What about—"

"Miss Davish." The policeman cut me off again and rose

from his chair. "This discussion is over." He held up my report and waved it at me. "It's obvious from this, and your unauthorized visit to the prisoner, that you've ignored my repeated requests not to interfere in this investigation." The report dropped to the desk with a thud. "I've endured your presence for Dr. Grice's sake, but you've gone too far, lady. You're not to interfere again. Do you understand?" I nodded, my cheeks burning with frustration.

"If I see you here again, I'm tossing you in a cell." He waved his arm and nearly shouted, "Now get out of here."

"Now what do we do?" I said.

Walter had offered to buy me dinner at the Grand Central Hotel, the hub for train travelers, a few blocks from the jailhouse. An eclectic mix of laborers, merchants, and leisure travelers filed in and out of its unpretentious dining room. I felt right at home.

"We wait," Walter said, shoveling poached potatoes onto his fork. Walter relished everything set before him, the soup, the lamb and beef in mushroom sauce, the peas with lettuce, *and the wine*. He'd been elusive about his stance, most likely for professional reasons, but now I knew Walter's views on temperance. His secret was safe with me.

"Despite his posturing and bluster, I know Ben is a decent policeman," Walter said. "He answered your question, didn't he?"

Before we'd left the station, Walter spoke to Chief Jackson in his office, repeating my question about John Martin's release. To my vexation and relief, the chief had offered Walter a straightforward answer; all prisoners were released at 9:30 A.M. Monday morning. Mrs. Trevelyan's murder occurred between 9:18 A.M. and 11:00 A.M. John Martin could've received the blackmail telegram, gone to the Arcadia, confronted her, and then killed her before the bellboy moved the trunk. The timing would've been close, but possible.

"He has your report, and I've no doubt that he'll read it thoroughly. No matter how much he may dislike getting his information from a woman, he'll have to consider it." Walter swirled his wine and regarded me with a mischievous glint in his eye. "In the meantime, I may have to chaperone you more often. You tend to invite danger, Miss Hattie Davish."

"I don't know why," I said. "I'm just a lady typewriter."

Walter laughed and held his glass up in a toast. "A charming and clever one at that."

Over dessert, I broached the subject of George Shulman. "Do you know, Walter, if George Shulman has any romantic attachments?" I selected a thick piece of nut cake, sliced off a piece of cheese, and took heaping servings of the pickled peaches and the orange jelly.

He sipped his coffee. "Not that I know of. Why?"

"It may mean nothing, but when I visited Mr. Shulman in jail, he mistook me for someone else at first, calling me 'my darling.' "

"That's peculiar, Hattie. Now that you mention it, I think George was courting someone. I'd heard him teased about it by the boys at the bar. But that was a while back; I'd assumed it got called off. If that's the case, I'd guess it was probably his sister, Gertie, he mistook you for. She keeps house for him."

"You're probably right," I said. "Of course his sister would visit him."

But then why did George Shulman say "my darling" the same way Walter said "Hattie"?

"Is something wrong? You don't sound convinced."

"Mr. Shulman mentioned that Mrs. Trevelyan forbid him to do something," I said, "but he didn't say what. Do you know what it could be?"

"Besides selling liquor? No. Why?"

"I'm sorry, Walter, but I think there's more to George Shulman's story than what he's telling the police. And I think it's connected to the woman he thought I was."

"And you don't mean his sister Gertie, do you?"

"No, I'm afraid not."

CHAPTER 22

"What's going on here?" Walter said, slightly out of breath. We had climbed straight up several flights of stairs from the restaurant on Main Street.

A crowd gathered in Basin Circle Park, the physical and social center of town. Tonight, the park was fitted with a stage and hundreds of folding chairs. The street lamps blazed, colorful paper lanterns hung from the trees, and dozens of torches, placed periodically along the curving stone wall that encircled the park, lit up banners staked in the ground. Among them were banners that read: TEMPERANCE LEADS TO HEALTH, WEALTH, AND HAPPINESS, or AGITATE—EDUCATE—DO NOT INTOXICATE, or LIPS THAT TOUCH LIQUOR SHALL NOT TOUCH MINE, or TAKE THE PLEDGE, GET ON THE WATER CART. Bunting decorated every lamppost, stone wall, and fountain. It was wonderful.

Hundreds of people mingled, their voices and peals of laughter reverberating off the buildings that surrounded the park. Musicians set up their instruments on a pavilion built on a rocky ledge halfway up the hill. Everywhere people were

drinking, from tin cups, champagne glasses, and beer mugs.
Though every glass was filled with spring water, the whole
atmosphere was festive and exciting, more reminiscent of an
Independence Day or New Year's Eve celebration than a rally
to the cause of temperance. And to think I'd considered skip-
ping it.

"The rally!" I said. "I'd almost forgot. I promised Miss
Lizzie and Miss Lucy to meet them."

"I'll help you find them," Walter suggested. "They've got
to be around here somewhere."

As we traversed the crowd, we were stopped repeatedly by
patients and friends who wanted to chat with Walter and wish
him well. He had a jest, a smile, or a pat on the back for each
one. I felt proud to be on his arm. His gaiety seemed boundless
until a man in a crushed brown duck hat mentioned how
much fun George Shulman would've been, had he been there.

"We should toast his health, don't you think, Walt?" the
man suggested.

"Ah, but George wouldn't restrict himself to a water
toast," Walter said.

The man roared at the jest and slapped Walter on the back.
Officer Burke chanced to walk past, acknowledging us with a
nod. The man bid Walter a jovial good-bye as both he and the
policeman disappeared separately into the crowd. The corners
of Walter's mouth drooped.

"I'd toast to George Shulman's health with Coca-Cola if it
meant getting him out of jail," he grumbled. "That's the irony
of this whole sordid business, Hattie. George doesn't drink
liquor. He prefers cocoa and coffee to beer and brandy. He
runs the saloon because it's the family business."

I was shocked. "Why didn't he just say so? So much of
what has happened could've been avoided had the temperance
ladies known."

"George has principles, Hattie, and didn't want the temperance group dictating how he made a living. But I'm afraid you're right. His principles may land him in the gallows." Walter's countenance clouded over for a moment, but he didn't dwell on the thought as I might have, and as quickly as his gloomy disposition had arrived, it was gone.

Eventually I espied the Shaw sisters and left Walter behind me, conversing lively with yet another acquaintance, and threaded my way through the crowd. I'd gone a few yards when John Martin swaggered in my direction. I was mortified at the thought of facing him again. I twisted around, trying to lose him in the sea of people, and in my haste nearly collided into the old woman I'd met waiting for the public omnibus the afternoon I'd arrived. She wore the same old black bonnet but carried a new walking stick.

"Oh, my, you look rested, miss," she said. "Last time I saw you, you were as taut as a fat man's suspenders. I wouldn't have recognized you."

Can that have been less than a week ago? I wondered. It didn't seem possible.

"The springs are doing you good then, miss?" I stood on my toes and peered through the throng. "Miss?" The old woman shouted over the din of the crowd. I dropped back onto my heels.

"Oh, thank you, and how are you? I'm sorry," I said, "but I don't think I ever caught your name."

"It's Gunning, Sarah Gunning. Thank you for asking, miss. It's kind of you to remember. Ah, my gout isn't much improved. Harding, Sweet, Gadd, Rock House, and Iron, so far none of the springs have helped." She pointed to the fountain in the middle of the park with her stick, almost hitting a passerby. "I'm leaving this here Basin Spring for last. It's done wonders for some others I've met at the Piedmont House. That's where I'm staying." She pointed, with a gnarled finger this time, toward a group of old ladies sitting in folding chairs to the left. "They're here at the rally. Would you care to join us?"

"Thank you, Miss Gunning, but I've friends waiting for me."

"This is grand, isn't it? I wouldn't have missed this rally for the world." She watched as coalition members and their well-wishers flocked by, oblivious to my subtle hint. I watched, loathing the moment John Martin might appear.

"I really must be going," I said. I fidgeted with my collar and then my gloves.

The old woman put a hand on my arm and continued, blind to my distress. "I wanted to see Mrs. Trevelyan with my own eyes, you know, but alas, I'm too late. Poor Mrs. Trevelyan. You did hear what happened?"

A shiver went down my spine. It was almost more than I could bear. Even now Mrs. Trevelyan's murder permeated the gaiety around me, and at any moment her killer would be upon us. Where was Walter? Why hadn't he caught up to me by now? The old woman gripped my arm tight and leaned closer.

"I heard," she said in a conspiring tone, "that her personal secretary found her dead in a wardrobe, hanging from a hook like nothing more than a kitchen bib apron, strangled with her own best lace." The old woman licked her lips and edged closer. "And that the secretary, crazed by the trauma, has been seen scaling the mountains, barefoot and bareheaded, every morning, searching for her mistress's killer. She collects dead and dried-up bits of plants and animal hair and bones, and brings them back to the hotel." The band started up and the woman yelled over the music. "Girl's gone completely mad."

Aghast by the ghoulish rumor, I stared at the woman in horror. Then a group of women passed. One of them bumped against me and dropped her black lace handbag. She and an-other woman were outlandishly attired in identical dresses of puce and black stripes and enormous black Gainsborough hats with puce muslin roses. As I stared at the comical duo stooped over to retrieve the bag, I caught a glimpse of John Martin, a few feet away. He was arguing with Cordelia Anglewood, gesturing with a clenched fist, while she pointed down the hill. I couldn't tell what they said, but I could guess. I stood mesmerized by the confrontation, acutely aware that I wasn't involved this time. *Better Cordelia Anglewood than me,* I thought.

Colonel Walker and Josephine Piers emerged out of the crowd. The former gripped John Martin's shoulder; the latter took her place next to Cordelia, clasping her hands before her in supplication. None seemed too happy. Cordelia Anglewood raised her hand. Torchlight reflected off the wineglass she held in her hand and, for a moment, lit a patch of John Martin's blotchy red cheek. She threw it at him. It shattered at his feet. I flinched, but he didn't move. Cordelia blanched in surprise. Could Cordelia Anglewood have met her match? It was frightening to think so. But she recovered herself quickly, glowering at John Martin and everyone around her. She shouted something about retribution. John Martin jerked out of his father-in-law's hold and stalked away in the opposite direction. Ever the peacemaker, Mrs. Piers tried to follow. The old woman next to me craned her neck, tracking the retreating figures' path through the multitude. I took a deep breath, relieved to see them all go.

"Don't tell anyone," I said, emboldened by John Martin's sudden departure, "but you have that only partly right, Miss Gunning." She cupped her ear with her hand, licked her lips, and tilted her head toward me. "I did find Mrs. Trevelyan, but she was suffocated by her dresses, not strangled by her lace." My plant press and morning hikes aside, the old woman had something right. "And I will find her killer."

The woman's jaw dropped, and her walking stick clattered to the ground. I indulged in a moment of guilty satisfaction in the old woman's reaction, then excused myself and hurried to meet up with Walter.

"Welcome one and all to the American Women's Temperance Coalition's Annual Temperance Rally."

Prodigious applause erupted at President Anglewood's greeting. The park was filled to capacity, every chair was filled, every available space to sit or stand was occupied. I sat between Walter and the elderly Shaw sisters near the stage, on a folding chair the sisters had saved for me. John Martin was nowhere to be found.

Candles were passed down the makeshift aisles and lit, as Mrs. Anglewood explained, "to signify the Holy Spirit that lives in us all." She called for a moment of silence in the memory of the late President Trevelyan. The rowdy crowd hushed as the flames of hundreds of candles flickered in the slight evening breeze. The moment felt sacred; a true memorial for a woman who, despite her faults, had devoted her life to the temperance movement. I bowed my head.

For the first time I could sense the love, the pride, the veneration, and the loss Mrs. Trevelyan's followers felt for her. And in that moment I regretted never knowing her. Several women stifled cries with their handkerchiefs held tight against their mouths. Miss Lizzie dabbed her eyes. Josephine Piers broke the silence by reading the coalition's mission and charter. Her voice quivered with emotion. I raised my head, tears in my eyes, and caught both Walter and Miss Lucy watching me. Abashed, I tried to ignore their stares and followed the proceedings on stage.

Cordelia, appearing to have recovered from her altercation with John Martin, proceeded to introduce all the dignitaries seated on the stage with her, including the mayor of Eureka Springs and several visiting coalition branch officers, many of whom I'd seen at Mrs. Trevelyan's memorial. She invited them all, one by one, to give a speech, and graciously thanked each one. The rally again became festive as dozens of water toasts were offered. Josephine Piers raised her champagne glass first.

"In honor of God, the glorious cause he has called us to, and to the coalition's new president, who will lead us to victory." Cordelia, in turn, raised her glass to victory.

People cheered and proposed new toasts. The town clock struck ten o'clock and someone called for a song. The first, a boisterous but appropriate hymn, was led by Diana Halbert, followed by temperance songs I'd never heard called "Willie Has Signed the Pledge" and "Girls, Wait for a Temperance Man." The tunes were catchy and I tentatively joined in the singing. Everyone was intoxicated with the spirit of the rally, including me. I mentioned my surprise at the raucous crowd to Miss Lizzie.

"We're here to celebrate what brought us all together in the first place, dear. With the killer behind bars, it's time to put the tragedy of the past week behind us," she said.

I refrained from telling her that I didn't share her conviction that the right person had been arrested or that I would probably never be able to forget the past week, ever.

"By the way, you have a lovely voice, dear," Miss Lizzie said. "You should use it more often."

I stayed as late as I could, enjoying the congenial atmosphere. But the events of the day eventually caught up with me, and I was tired. The American Women's Temperance Coalition, Miss Lizzie and Miss Lucy included, were still singing and drinking Basin Spring water when Walter escorted me home.

I couldn't sleep. I had gone through the motions of changing into my nightdress, washing my hands and face, and giving my hair a hundred strokes with a brush, knowing that last night, when I had slept better than I had in years, had been an aberration. Temperance songs reverberated in my mind and I couldn't stop thinking. I lay in bed for an hour or more before slipping onto the balcony. It sounded so peaceful. Carriage wheels rattled on the street below and a few singing voices came from the direction of the Spring Street staircase on the edge of the hotel's parkland. People were still returning from the rally.

I returned to my room and typed up another list.

1. Why was John Martin also known as Joseph Mascavarti?
2. Why was Mrs. Trevelyan blackmailing John Martin? Was there a connection between the blackmail and the alias?
3. Having sent a threat, did John Martin follow up on it? He confessed as much.
4. If so, was there a witness to place John Martin in Mrs. Trevelyan's room that morning, as there were for George Shulman and Cordelia Anglewood?
5. Where was John Martin between 9:30, when he was released from jail, and 11:00? Do the police know?
6. Where did Cordelia Anglewood go after leaving Mrs. Trevelyan's room? Not out riding. Did she come back to see Mrs. Trevelyan again?
7. Why were Cordelia and John Martin arguing at the Rally?

I fell asleep in the early-morning hours, but during a pleasant dream, Walter's amiable countenance metamorphosed into the red, blotchy face of John Martin. I woke with a start, disconcerted. Only one thing would help. I lit the lamp on the night table and carried it to the desk. I tucked my legs under me in the chair and retrieved from a drawer my copy of the report I'd given the police. I slipped the last sheet of the report into my typewriter and added an addendum, comprising John

Martin's arrest for public drunkenness and the time he was released from jail. I added a note of speculation, that Cordelia Anglewood must be unaware of his arrest or she would never have showcased his generosity at a coalition meeting. *Maybe that's what this evening's argument was about.* I plucked the paper out of the typewriter, feeling composed again. I attached it to the report and attempted to review the facts objectively.

Mr. John Martin, also known as Mr. Joseph Mascavarti, had been blackmailed by Mrs. Trevelyan. He'd been arrested for public drunkenness, and upon his release from jail Monday morning had received Mrs. Trevelyan's wire demanding more money. Within an hour and a half she was dead. Did he kill her? Did he get drunk and, wanting to confront her, come to the hotel, bringing his gin bottle with him? It was the most likely scenario. Could it have been an accident? I doubted it. Pushing me down the stairs just to stop me from asking more questions demonstrated his desperation and proclivity toward violence. And he had a reason for wanting Edwina Trevelyan dead. He must've killed her. Otherwise why would he lie about his whereabouts?

But then so had Cordelia Anglewood and George Shulman. They too each had a reason to want Mrs. Trevelyan dead. And who else could be lying? Who else wanted her dead? The more I thought about it, the more I realized that almost every reason to suspect John Martin could also apply to several others. I was dumbfounded. How could one woman have so many followers and at the same time have so many enemies? In Mrs. Trevelyan's case, of course, I thought I knew the answer. What I didn't know was which one of them had killed her.

The moonlight was enough to see by, but at times the path, weaving its way down through the glen behind the Arcadia, was completely dark. But I was determined and, having come this way twice before, was confident that I could find my way back to Grotto Spring. I thought fresh air would help me clear my head. I was wrong. The question of Mrs. Trevelyan's killer still rumbled through my mind as I made my way down the woodland path, armed with a candle and a small specimen jar.

The rain had washed away the dust and pollen, leaving the air crisp. I relished the fresh scent of autumn leaves and fallen pine needles. The soft rustling of damp leaves beneath my boots and an occasional hoot of an owl were all that broke the early-morning silence. When I reached the top of the hillock that led to the spring's rocky cliff ceiling, I lit the candle. Something scurried off through the leaves. I'd been confident about navigating the path in the dark, but wasn't as sure about the ridge.

Crouched low to the ground, with one hand to anchor me, I crept down the hillside. Halfway down, my candle went out. Yet I persevered. At the bottom, I brushed the soil and leaves from my skirt and straightened my hat. I relit the candle and, poised to enter, peered into the cavern. The light only pierced a foot into the gloom. At once, I felt apprehensive. I'd come to collect liverwort specimens I'd noticed in Grotto Spring before; safe in my room, it was an appealing place to spend a few peaceful moments before daybreak. But I hadn't considered that I might wake a sleeping animal or a wandering tramp taking refuge inside. I listened for the gentle rise and fall of someone or something sleeping.

"Hello?" I called, more timidly than I'd like to admit.

The wind rustled in the trees above; a roosting bird took flight. I called again.

"Hello? Is there anybody in there?"

There was no response. No late-night revelers or skittish wildlife emerged.

Reassured, I hoisted my candle above my head and entered

the cave. I took a few steps toward the back of the cave and the noiseless trickling source of the spring, and hesitated again. The previously dry cavern floor was slick, dampened from the previous morning's rain. I steadied myself against the cavern wall and lifted the candle higher.

What is that?

Something white was on the ground in front of me. I was jittery and almost dropped my candle. But it was only the enamel mug I had shamelessly thrown against the wall yesterday; its owner had yet to retrieve it. I felt ridiculous for over-reacting and yet again regretted venturing out alone in the dark. I would get my liverworts and go.

I moved swiftly, steadying myself against the cavern wall, and aimed for the spot near the spring where I had seen a large population of the plant earlier. But I never made it. Instead, I nearly stumbled over something in the dark. I felt foolish, letting my nerves get the best of me, as I lifted my candle.

What is it now, I wondered, *a branch, a forgotten walking stick?*

It was an arm, with pearl buttons on its shirt-sleeve cuff.

I screamed. I couldn't help myself. There, next to the stone bench, sprawled across the cave's floor, was a man, his head lying in a small pool of liquid. He wasn't moving.

"Is anybody there?" I shouted.

I held the candle up and frantically circled around hoping to confirm that there wasn't. My candle reflected off something metal on the floor. Suddenly I began to panic, breathing erratically, perspiring and feeling my heart pound hard in my chest. I felt paralyzed, trapped between the darkness and the body on the floor, the way out impossible to reach. As I listened for the sound of an unseen assailant's footsteps, I became dizzy and knelt down beside the body.

Blood caked his hair and streaked down his temple and cheek. His eyes were partially closed. I put my candle to his lips; the flame didn't waver. A pebble that had been stuck to his face fell back into the dirt, leaving behind a tiny indentation. I became nauseous; I recognized the face! I leapt to my feet. The heel of my boot snagged my skirt, rending my hem and tripping me. I dropped my specimen jar and my candle, plunging the cavern into darkness, and fell to my hands and knees. Blood splashed on me. I cried out as a sharp pain shot through my injured knee.

Why does this keep happening to me?

I slammed my hand into the ground. Tiny pebbles lodged themselves in my palm. A moment of calm came over me as remorse for indulging in self-pity replaced my fear and anger. I knew what I had to do. I scrambled to my feet and, as fast as my knee would allow, raced from the cave, each step distancing me from the body of Mr. John Martin.

CHAPTER 23

"Walter! Walter!"

I gasped for breath and pounded on the door again.

Mr. Theakston, Walter's valet, finally opened the door. He was wearing a blue and green plaid dressing gown. His eyes flew open in surprise.

"Miss Davish, it's six o'clock in the morning," he said.

"Get Dr. Grice," I said. "Please!"

He checked up and down the street, blocking my entrance. I'd no patience for appearances or conventions. I pushed past him into the dimly lit hallway.

"Miss, this is highly irregular," the valet lectured as he hurriedly closed the front door behind me. "Unless you are . . . Oh my!" He seized my arm and set me down in the hall chair. "Stay right here, I'll get the doctor."

As he disappeared down the hallway, I caught a glimpse of myself in the hall mirror. Did I really look that ghastly? My carefully combed hair was now tousled; masses of curls had loosened and fallen haphazardly about my shoulders. *Where is my hat?* The palms of my hands were scraped and streaked with soil. One of my favorite dresses was ruined; splotches of blood stained the skirt, and strips of fabric, caked with blood and dirt, hung partially attached to the hem. Lines of perspiration and soil mixed with tiny specks of blood streaked across my face and bodice. I was mortified that anyone should see me like this. As I began wiping away the grime, Walter, disheveled and still pulling a dressing gown around a pair of striped silk pajamas, raced down the hallway. He immediately began to examine me.

"Walter," I said, "I know I look a fright, but I'm all right. It's not my blood."

"Just stay quiet," he said. He swept me up into his arms and rushed me to his examining room. Countless metal instruments gleamed as Mr. Theakston lit the lamps. The doctor laid me down, loosened my collar, and reached for his stethoscope. I felt my breathing catch in my throat.

"Walter, this isn't necessary."

Despite my declaration, the doctor continued his examination, leaning closer, placing the stethoscope on my chest.

"Please, Walter, let me up. I don't like this room." I struggled to sit up.

"Hattie, calm down. Just stay still and breathe deeply." He held me down with one hand on my shoulder and spoke in his particular professional manner, which alarmed me all the more.

"Please, Walter, it's not my blood. Please let me get up." My breathing quickened and my fingers started to tingle and go numb.

"There's nothing to fear here. I won't hurt you. Now, just try to breathe deeply."

On the brink of panic, I clutched at his arm. "Stop, Walter, stop," I said. "John Martin's dead!" Walter's head snapped up. "This is his blood, not mine. I found him at Grotto Spring, lying in a pool of it."

"What? What are you talking about?"

"He wasn't breathing, Walter. I think he's dead." To my absolute relief, he lifted his stethoscope away from my chest and took a step back.

"Who, Hattie? Who's dead?"

"John Martin, the man I told you about, the one Mrs. Trevelyan was blackmailing, this is his blood." I struggled again to sit up. Walter helped, supporting me until I had my legs dangling off the side of the examining table. "I ran here as fast as I could."

"You're all right, then?"

"I'm exhausted, and my knee hurts, but otherwise I'm fine. Can I get down now?"

The doctor held me at arm's length, studying my face. "Let me see your knee."

I looked dubiously at the shiny metal objects mounted on the wall in front of me. "It just aches. That's all."

"I'll be the judge of that, Miss Davish," Walter chided.

"What about John Martin?" I said.

"You're my priority right now. It'll only take a minute."

My hands trembled as I slid my skirt up, revealing my legs. My petticoat was intact but ruined; the scab from my fall down the stairs must've torn off and blood had seeped through. Walter snatched a pair of scissors from a metal tray. I recoiled from him as he sheared off a square patch of the cotton fabric, exposing my bare knee. He retrieved a bottle from a shelf and dipped a wad of cotton into it.

"This might sting," he said. He swabbed my scrape with the cotton and then clamped a bandage over it.

"Ouch!" I jerked my leg away from him. It didn't sting; it burned. I knew I shouldn't have mentioned my injured knee.

He noticed my hands and reached for another wad of cotton. I quickly resettled my skirt and hid my hands in its voluminous folds.

"Okay, okay," he said, putting the cotton back, "I'm done." My whole body sagged forward in relief. "You're still suffering from your exertions and shock, so I'll have to keep you under observation." Before I could protest, he continued, "Otherwise, with the exception of your knee, you do appear uninjured."

"That's what I've been trying to tell you," I said. "I'm fine."

Walter exhaled deeply, then chuckled. "I've heard that before."

Relief washed over his face as he abruptly wrapped his arms around me. A pang of guilt hit me. Why didn't I trust him more? He was a physician, yes, but he did seem only to want to help and heal me. Hopefully I wouldn't have occasion to worry about it again.

Walter's calm, professional demeanor returned as he helped me down from the table.

"Now, about John Martin," he said, "tell me everything you can."

I matched his mood, composed myself, and relayed my outing to Grotto Spring and the subsequent discovery of John Martin's body. Walter remained silent and attentive throughout, stopping me but once to clarify a point. When I finished, the doctor sprang into action.

"He may still be alive. If you're well enough, we should go immediately." He indicated the basin Mr. Theakston was filling with steaming water. "This is the best I can offer you at the moment. It'll take a minute or two for me to get ready."

He grabbed a large leather satchel and disappeared from the examination room. A few minutes later, after I had time only to wash my face and hands, Walter stood before me dressed, composed, and prepared. I was impressed. As we left, he snatched an overcoat from the hall tree and put it around my shoulders.

He regarded my hair, still in disarray. "I don't suppose you'd like to wear one of my hats?" he said.

I glanced at the hat rack. Walter sported some of men's finest. I weighed the impropriety against the practicality of the idea and then chose a brown derby and stuffed my unruly curls up inside the roomy crown. I stole a glance at myself in the mirror and was pleased at how I looked.

"Maybe they should design derby hats for women," I said. "It's very comfortable and doesn't require a hatpin."

Amusement flashed across Walter's face. I didn't mind; his jests helped divert my thoughts from the morning's ordeal. He grabbed a similar hat in black and escorted me to the phaeton waiting outside. The carriage's folding top was raised. Mr. Theakston, holding the horse's bridle, handed Walter the reins.

"Telephone the police," Walter instructed his valet. "Have them meet us at Grotto Spring."

Walter snapped the reins. We lurched forward and I gripped the arm rail with one hand and held on to the hat with the other. The horse galloped down the street, mud flying as it ran. What I had seen of Walter's wild driving the other morning was not, as I had discovered, the good doctor in a rush. This treacherous speed was normal for him. We reached the spring in minutes. Walter halted the horse abruptly and, without a word, handed me the reins.

"Oh, no, don't give me the reins," I protested. But Walter leapt down, grabbed his satchel and a lantern, and ran into the dark cave.

I gripped the leather straps, my knuckles turning white; I'd never handled a horse before. I waited for the animal to rear up at any minute or to bolt and gallop away with me and the phaeton careening behind. Instead the horse swished its tail, bent its head, and snipped off blades of grass, silently chewing.

"Good horse," I whispered. *This isn't so hard after all*, I thought and relaxed my grip.

The stillness of the environs around Grotto Spring surprised me. The roaring of the wind as we galloped through the deserted town had made me forget how quiet it was at this early hour. Though the sky was growing light, sunrise was still a good half hour or more away. From the time I'd discovered John Martin, little more than half an hour had elapsed. I sat listening—to my racing heart, for Walter's returning footsteps, for the arrival of the police—but I heard nothing but crickets chirping and leaves rustling in the trees towering above me. How I loved this time of day.

The horse snorted, its breath visible in the predawn light. Taking its cue, I inhaled deeply, taking in the clean, fragrant morning air. I felt calm for the first time all morning. For a few moments, I allowed myself to forget why I was there. My race to Walter's and the subsequent panic being in his examination room seemed a distant past by the time he returned. He placed the lantern on the ground as he removed his stethoscope from around his neck. When our eyes met, he shook his head.

"He's dead," he said, returning his satchel to the carriage. "I'll need more time in order to determine the cause. It's a lot to ask, but would you take notes?" He handed me the tools of my trade, a notebook and pencil. "The police will need the information as soon as they get here."

Fortified by a familiar task to perform, I followed closely behind as Walter reentered the cavern. When we reached the prone figure, Walter set the lantern down. Its light revealed more than my candle had. A flask, the same one I'd seen John Martin carry, sat on the bench. Dried leaves and paper litter accumulated in a corner of the cave. And blood was everywhere: on the man's head, spotted on his jacket, shirt and cravat, puddled on the floor beneath him, on the wall next to him where it had splattered when I'd tripped, and smudged on the stone bench that lined the side of the wall. I felt a wave of revulsion churn up from my stomach. I clutched the notebook and took a deep breath, somehow finding the fortitude to take notes. Walter examined the bench and the wall before kneeling down beside the body. He dictated as he worked.

"The body is cold to the touch. The muscles are stiff." He peeled back one of the man's eyelids. "The eyes have filmed over and hypostasis has set in. And there's a faint smell of alcohol about his lips." He methodically probed the man's entire body. "There's a single wound, on his head, roughly two inches above the ear. The scalp is punctured and bruised, hence the excessive blood, but has already started to heal. The skull feels fractured, possibly causing internal bleeding. Blood and hairs, consistent with those of the dead, are on the edge of the bench. He must've hit his head there. I'd say at this point that blunt force trauma to his temple was what killed him. I'll know more with an autopsy."

"Is that your official opinion?" a man said from behind us. We both stood up, startled by the voice. I held up the lantern. Chief Jackson, with a shadow of a man behind him, entered the cave. "Didn't mean to startle you, Doc. I got your message." He indicated the man behind him. "You know Norris." Officer Norris nodded in acknowledgment.

"What do we have, Doc?" Jackson said, after a brief glance at me and my hat. "Your servant mentioned a body and blood."

Walter told what he knew as Chief Jackson leaned over the body and then examined the cave. When Walter finished, Chief Jackson turned to me.

"So, Miss Davish, you found the body." I confirmed that I had.

"And the man was dead when you found him?" I told him how I'd placed a flame next to the man's lips. "And it didn't flicker?"

"No," I said.

"I'm not surprised," Walter said. "This man's been dead for hours."

"Good to know, Doc," the policeman said. "And you didn't touch anything, young lady?" I said I hadn't. Jackson picked up the Crusher-style hat lying on the ground.

"Not even the hat on his head?" He chuckled, obviously pleased with his pun. I repeated I hadn't touched anything.

"Good." He wagged his finger at me. "You have a peculiar knack for finding dead bodies, don't you, Miss Davish?" Before I could respond, he turned to Walter. "And you think it was an accident, Dr. Grice?"

"I didn't say that," Walter said. "But from what I can tell, he hit his head here," he pointed to the man's temple, "on the corner of that bench," he pointed to the corner darkened with blood, "deep enough to cut into the scalp, fracture the skull, and cause severe bleeding. It was probably the blow to the head and not the loss of blood that caused his death. He may've had intracranial bleeding. I don't know. The floor is slippery, but I can't say if that's what caused him to fall."

"As I was saying this afternoon," the policeman said, "this man was a well-known drunk." He picked up the flask, unscrewed the cap, and sniffed its contents. "See here? He'd been drinking." Jackson punctuated his words with a wave of the flask. "He probably was sitting here on the bench, got up to leave, slipped on the wet floor, and hit his head. Any evidence to the contrary?" The policeman held a stern face on me while addressing Walter. "Doc?"

Walter rubbed his chin as he stared down at the body on the floor. "That seems reasonable." He turned to me. "Hattie?"

Chief Jackson glared at Walter. My gaze drifted from Walter to the policeman to the man I'd been convinced was Mrs. Trevelyan's murderer. If he had killed Mrs. Trevelyan, then his death by a drunken-induced fall was ironic justice, and the ordeal was over. I should feel satisfied and relieved. I didn't feel either.

"What do you think, Hattie? An accident?" Walter repeated.

John Martin was a known drunk and could've easily lost his balance and fallen; I'd seen him acting erratically myself. And all the evidence indicated his death was an accident. But what was he doing here? What would the police do now? With John Martin dead, would we ever know for certain that he was Mrs. Trevelyan's killer or why she was blackmailing him? What if it wasn't an accident? And what if he wasn't the killer?

Despite my desire for a more orderly solution, and to the amazement of both Walter and Chief Jackson, I reluctantly agreed. I was too exhausted to argue. Chief Jackson nodded in satisfaction and walked back to the cave's entrance, where sunlight now filtered in. He disappeared from view, but a moment later, two men carrying a stretcher appeared and, with Officer Norris as escort, carried the body away.

"He pushed me down the stairs, Walter." I stared, unseeing, at the cave's entrance. "He may've killed Mrs. Trevelyan." My whole body began to shake. "What was he doing here?"

Since discovering Mrs. Trevelyan dead, images of her contorted in the trunk, with a dull unseeing gaze, had plagued my dreams. Now, even while awake, images of John Martin haunted me. His body was gone, but the blood remained. I closed my eyes and tried to relax, but instead of blackness I saw blood everywhere, on the floor, on the corner of the bench, on my skirt, my knee, my face.

"Let's get you out of here." Walter put his arm around my shoulders and led me into the sunshine. Despite its warmth, I couldn't repress the shivering. A small crowd had gathered and several policemen were keeping them from approaching the spring. Chief Jackson and Officer Norris were off to one side, near Walter's phaeton, questioning people, including the two boys Walter and I had encountered during our first visit to Grotto Spring. I wanted to warn them. I wanted to tell Walter not to let the boys see the blood, but I couldn't voice the words. Walter helped me into his phaeton and wrapped a horsehair blanket around my shoulders. Chief Jackson approached several minutes later.

"Well, didn't learn much," the policeman said in answer to Walter's query. "Those boys there claim to have heard our deceased talking with someone last night, but I don't put too much into that. The man was drunk and was probably talking to himself." Walter agreed. "But, just to be thorough, we'll do a sweep of the cave and let you do a full autopsy, Doc, if you want. Though I'm guessing we'll still come up with the same answer, accidental death." He regarded me. "Sorry, Miss Davish, no murder here."

Walter and I left Grotto Spring, and any investigation, in the hands of the police. The crisp chill of the breeze as we wound swiftly up through the woody hollow toward the Arcadia Hotel cut through me. In less than a week I'd found two dead bodies—first my employer in her steamer trunk, and now one of the suspects in her death, in a wet spring cave. Until last Wednesday, I'd only seen two dead bodies in my whole life, those of my mother and father. I was still shaking.

And I kept coming back to the same questions over and over. What had John Martin been doing there? Would the police be able to prove he'd killed Mrs. Trevelyan? Then other questions cropped up. When had he gone to the spring? I had seen him the night before at the rally. Did he leave the rally and go straight to Grotto Spring, or did he have other encounters, other things to do first? How would Colonel Walker react? He had attended the Magnetic Spring meeting and the rally. Would he be shocked to learn his son-in-law was a drunkard? How was John Martin's death going to affect the reputation of the coalition? What would Cordelia Anglewood do when she found out?

"Mrs. Anglewood isn't going to like this," I said.

Walter jumped at my comment; it was the first thing I'd spoken since exiting the cave. I hadn't realized I'd said it out loud.

"What do you mean, Hattie? What does Mrs. Anglewood have to do with this?"

I explained how John Martin had been honored yesterday and hailed as a patron of the American Women's Temperance Coalition, and how I'd seen them arguing the night before.

"Despite the sum of the contribution, Cordelia Anglewood wouldn't have gone public if she'd known that John Martin was a drunk. She would've accepted the contribution for what it was without announcing it at the Magnetic Spring meeting. If everyone finds out that John Martin, the AWTC's champion of the moment, died of an inebriation-induced accident the night of the rally, she'll be humiliated."

"It won't do her cause any good, either," Walter agreed. "By the way, I've been meaning to ask you something."

"What?"

"Why on earth were you at Grotto Spring at six o'clock in the morning?"

"I couldn't sleep," I said. "I'd noticed liverworts on the walls of the cavern when you and I were there. So I thought I might collect some specimens." I had forgotten about my jar; it must still be lying in the Grotto Spring cave somewhere. "I still haven't gotten a sample."

Walter laughed. "Oh, Hattie, what am I to do with you?"

CHAPTER 24

"Come with me to Pivot Rock this afternoon," Walter said as he helped me from the carriage. "You need a pleasant distraction. I'll have Theakston pack us a picnic lunch." I stared at him, my eyes blurry with fatigue. "Catch up on your sleep while I perform the autopsy. Then I'll cancel all my appointments and spend the afternoon with my favorite patient."

I cringed at the last word but held my tongue. "That sounds wonderful. I have to finish my latest account for Sir Arthur, so I'll meet you on the rotunda at one o'clock."

"Until one, then." Walter flicked the switch and sent the horse and carriage careening down the driveway.

Relieved and grateful to have work to focus on, I went straight to my room. Someone had sent breakfast. I changed out of my bloody clothes into my favorite muslin wrapper and took a few sips of lukewarm coffee. My hands were unsteady, but the typewriter keys felt reassuring under my fingers as I chronicled the events of the morning and evening before.

Once the report was completed, a wave of relief washed over me. I curled up in bed and immediately fell asleep.

When I awoke, the sun had almost climbed to its zenith. I felt refreshed. I shook off the morning's events as one would a bad dream. I carried my bloody clothes to the washroom, leaving them to soak. I was drinking the rest of the coffee, though now thick and cold, when, after a cursory knock, Miss Lucy, followed by her sister and Mary Flannagan, entered the room.

Miss Lucy eyed the partially eaten breakfast tray. "As I suspected. The girl didn't even touch her food. Mary, go fetch Davish some lunch." Mary left and the elderly sisters sat down.

"We heard about what happened, dear," Miss Lizzie said, helping herself to the breakfast tray. "How dreadful."

"Davish, you do have a knack for morbid adventure," Miss Lucy said. "You should be sitting down." I complied.

"I assure you I'm fine, Miss Lucy. I took a nap and feel completely refreshed. It was a nasty business, though, I agree."

"Well, then, Davish, tell us everything."

I relayed the morning's events: my early-morning hike, discovering the body in the Grotto Spring cavern, and running to Walter's house, being careful to gloss over the blood and the ghastly wound to the dead man's head. To be honest, I avoided the gory details as much for my own sake as for the elderly ladies'.

"Walter sent for the police and they deemed it an accident," I said.

"An accident, huh? Oh, well," Miss Lucy said, disappointed. "Anyway, we've got news too, Davish."

Mary Flannagan arrived then with a lunch tray.

"Mary, I've been meaning to ask you something," I said.

"Miss?" Mary frowned.

"My room has a similar layout to Mrs. Trevelyan's," I said.

"Could you show me where the trunk was when you were packing it for the charity?"

Mary raised an eyebrow, but her shoulders relaxed. "About there." She pointed to a spot near the tea table, the same place the bellhop had found it.

"And Mrs. Trevelyan?" I said. "Where was she sitting?"

"The missus sat there," she said, pointing to the chair Miss Lucy now occupied, "while I brought over clothes from the wardrobe."

"Stop pointing at me like that, girl," said Miss Lucy, whose eyes widened at the shift of everyone's focus. She breathed on her spectacles and began rubbing them rapidly with a handkerchief. "Don't you have something useful to do, Mary, like tending to the monsters of dust accumulating under my bed? I do believe I'll wake up one morning to find myself consumed by them." The maid remained, awaiting my reply.

"That's what I wanted to know," I said. "Thank you."

I poured the sisters' tea and invited Mary to join us, much to the chagrin of Miss Lucy.

"Thank you, Miss Hattie, but I've got chores to do."

"Maybe another time, when you have a break," I said.

"I don't know why you insist on treating that girl like you do, Davish," Miss Lucy said after the chambermaid had left. "Even she has enough sense to know better."

"Yes, dear, I have to agree with Lucy. She is just a maid."

"I myself am just a secretary."

Miss Lucy dismissed me with a wave of her hand. "Nonsense, Davish. Now, do you want to hear our news or not?" She didn't wait for a response. "Did you know that our worthy president has checked out of the Arcadia Hotel?"

"Why is that surprising?" I said. "The coalition's meeting ended last night, didn't it? Maybe she changed her mind about staying on for the winter. She probably went home to Chicago."

"No, no, Hattie, dear," Miss Lizzie said, "she couldn't have left."

"You know as well as I, Davish, that the police specifically told several people, including Cordelia, that they weren't to leave Eureka Springs until the investigation was concluded."

"According to the police, the investigation is concluded," I said.

"Besides that, dear," Miss Lizzie said, "Cordelia's husband is joining her here for Thanksgiving."

"Are you saying that another American Women's Temperance Coalition president has gone missing?" I said, hoping this was just Miss Lucy indulging in exaggerated gossip again.

Miss Lizzie patted my hand. "No, no, Cordelia's not missing, dear, she's merely checked out."

"Thank goodness."

"Don't you understand, Davish? Cordelia Anglewood, the proud, the rich, the haughty," Miss Lucy said, to sounds of Miss Lizzie's distress, "has checked out of the Arcadia Hotel and is now staying at the Hotel Byron." She said the last word with a triumphant flourish. In my search for the elusive John Martin, I'd visited the Hotel Byron. It was small but respectable, catering to middle-income families and the aged.

"Why would Mrs. Anglewood leave the Arcadia for the Hotel Byron?" I said.

"Exactly!" Miss Lucy said, slapping her knee for punctuation.

"We don't know, dear," Miss Lizzie said, taking a napkin and dabbing at a blob of marmalade that had dripped onto her shoulder.

"We do know, Davish, that her bill was paid here until yesterday, and that after the rally, the woman packed her things and moved . . ." She hesitated for dramatic effect.

"In the middle of the night!" Miss Lizzie and Miss Lucy

exclaimed simultaneously. The door burst open. We all jumped and stared at the puzzled maid.

"My, you startled us, Mary, dear," Miss Lizzie said. "Do you always enter a room like that?" The maid wrinkled her brow and said nothing.

"And she keeps interrupting me," Miss Lucy said, annoyed.

"Don't mind us, Mary," I said. "We're all a little jittery, that's all."

"I came to tell you, Miss Hattie," the maid said, "that I sent your dress, petticoat, and stockings downstairs to the laundry; the bloodstains were too difficult for me to get out. And before you say anything, don't worry. I know Sally downstairs and it won't cost you a ha'penny."

Both sisters stared at me, Miss Lizzie wild-eyed, her sister squinting with suspicion.

"Bloodstains, dear?" Miss Lizzie said.

"Free laundry?" her sister said. "If that's the case, girl, I've a few things you can take down."

I ignored the former comment. Mary ignored the latter. "Thank you, Mary. I doubt anything's salvageable, but please thank Sally for trying."

"Sure." She began clearing the cups, saucers, and plates.

"One more piece of news you might be interested in, Davish, if you're finished discussing your laundry."

"But, Lucy, dear, the maid mentioned blood," Miss Lizzie said.

"The girl exaggerates, Lizzie. I'm sure if there was something to it, we would've heard about it. Now," Miss Lucy said, facing me again, "about my other news."

"Oh my," I said, "it's been an eventful morning. I'm not certain I can handle any more news."

"Yes, dear, it has been an eventful week," Miss Lizzie said, plucking the last cracker from the tray.

"The news you might be interested to know, Davish," Miss

Lucy said, with a hint of exasperation, "is that the police are transporting the murdering saloonkeeper to Berryville in the morning. Justice will be served. As sure as rum turns to ruin, he'll hang. The police this morning said—"

A crash of falling china interrupted Miss Lucy, as Mary, who had finished her task and was in the process of leaving, tipped the contents of the tray onto the floor. She dropped to her knees. I rushed to her aid.

"I'm sorry, miss," Mary said, groping, through tearing eyes, at pieces of shattered china. Suddenly, she leapt to her feet.

"It's all right, Mary. I'll help you clean it up."

"No, miss, there's nothing you can do. I'm sorry, but . . ." She shook her head frantically. Without saying another word, the maid flew out of the room, leaving me on my knees, dumbfounded, surrounded by little bits of broken white china scattered across the floor.

"That looks much nicer on you than my derby did," Walter said, indicating my bonnet, a recent purchase from Mrs. Cunningham's. He'd been waiting for me in the lobby. "In fact, all of you looks lovely, and rested."

"I don't know. I was starting to take a fancy to that hat." I laughed at my own joke, pleased with the compliment.

"Ready for our picnic?" he said.

"Do you mind waiting a few minutes more?" I said. "I want to check on something."

"I'll be in the gentlemen's parlor."

"Good, I'll be right back."

Mr. Floyd was hunched over the telegraph machine. His face grew somber when he saw me. He rose and met me at the open service window.

"Did you hear?" he said.

"Hear what?"

"About that man, you know," he followed a passerby with

his eyes as he spoke, "the one the dead lady sent the local wire to." He referred to the death of John Martin. "Everyone's talking about it."

"Yes, I heard. It's horrible."

He nodded vigorously in agreement. "What a coincidence."

"Yes, you could say that," I said. "Could you do me another favor, Mr. Floyd?"

He leaned in toward me. "If I can."

"Cordelia Anglewood received a wire yesterday morning. Could you tell me anything about it?"

After the conversation with the Shaw sisters, I had begun to wonder about Cordelia Anglewood's unusual behavior. What would cause the steel-hearted woman to cry at the breakfast table, then act the gracious host the rest of the day? Could she be hiding something? Why else would she move to another hotel in the middle of the night? The police still insisted George Shulman was Mrs. Trevelyan's killer. I still wasn't convinced.

"You know I shouldn't, Miss Hattie," the telegraph operator said. "Telegrams are confidential. I told you about the others because the lady was dead."

"I understand the need for discretion, Mr. Floyd, and I wouldn't ask if this wasn't important. Your previous assistance was invaluable."

"Invaluable?"

"Yes, you helped establish an approximate time of death, which may be key in discovering Mrs. Trevelyan's killer."

"Really? All right, I'll help you again, but you can't tell anyone. Mrs. Anglewood could get me fired." I nodded my assent. "The lady actually received one and sent one. The telegram she received was from her husband."

"Do you remember what the one from her husband said?"

"Sure, all it said was *No*."

"Simple and unrevealing," I said. "Oh well. And the one she sent?"

"I don't remember much about that one, what it said or who it was from. I wasn't paying much attention. It was marked urgent, of course," he said, rolling his eyes, "and I was concentrating on getting it out."

"Do you remember where it was sent?"

"Let me see." He thought for a moment. "I think it was Fayetteville."

"Thank you, Mr. Floyd. I hope not to impose on you again." I was disappointed, and started to walk away.

"That lady also received a money wire about a half hour or so ago," the telegraph operator hissed under his breath. I halted.

"Did the wire come from Chicago, from her husband?" I said.

"I don't know. I wasn't on duty until one, so Amos received it. But I came in a little early, won't do that again," he muttered under his breath, "and had to deliver it the moment I came in. It was addressed to the Arcadia Hotel, but the lady had checked out. I had to go all the way to the Hotel Byron to deliver it. I just got back. She didn't even tip me."

"Is there a record of it?"

Mr. Floyd pulled a tan-colored ledger from a shelf mounted above the window. He scanned the page with his eyes, flipped to the next, and continued scanning. "Here it is. No, it didn't originate in Chicago."

"Fayetteville, then?"

He gaped at me as he closed the book. I'd guessed correctly.

"If that's the case, then I'd like to wire something myself, Mr. Floyd."

"If I'm gonna get fired, the least you can do is call me Hank."

"Hank it is, then," I said, writing out my brief message. "Ask for a response, please, and, Hank," I said with a laugh, "mark it 'urgent.'"

"Miss Davish?" I turned to see Colonel Walker, in a brown regulation army hat, approaching. He carried two large suitcases and a bulky envelope tucked under one arm. "You found my son-in-law?"

Images of John Martin's body and the blood everywhere flashed into my mind. I reached out for something to steady myself but then found I had no need. I faced the colonel with my hands laced together in front of me, composed.

"Yes." Out of the corner of my eye, I saw Hank's jaw drop.

"They tell me it was an accident. Is that true?" He let the suitcases drop with a thud.

"I don't know, sir," I said. "The police think so."

"But you don't?" His blue eyes were piercing, reminding me of Mrs. Trevelyan's photograph.

"Yes, I do think it most likely, Colonel. It's just that . . ."

"That you believe there's a connection between the death of your temperance leader and my son-in-law?" *How would he know that?* I wondered. "I'd known John for years, Miss Davish, as a levelheaded young man, a loving husband to my daughter. He was a teetotaler, for goodness' sake. Then we came here." He held out the envelope he was carrying. "This was at the bottom of John's suitcase; I found it this morning." In large scrawling letters, it read *For Joseph Mascavarti.* To my consternation, I recognized the handwriting.

"Do you recognize this, Miss Davish?" he asked.

"Not the envelope, Colonel, but the handwriting. Mrs. Trevelyan addressed it."

"John was family and he's dead. I don't speak ill of the dead. But I don't want anything more to do with him, or his entanglements." He spat out the last word as if he had a bad taste in his mouth. "Here, take it." The colonel thrust the envelope at me. "Keep my daughter out of it, if you can." He picked up his suitcases.

"Shouldn't you give this to the police?" I said, turning the envelope over in my hand.

"You knew about John's true identity before anyone else, didn't you?"

"I believe so."

"Well, there's your answer," he said. "God knows he had me fooled, and I don't trust the police, Miss Davish. I trust you to do the right thing."

I rushed into the gentlemen's parlor the moment Colonel Walker walked out the Arcadia Hotel's front door.

"Walter, come look at this," I said. Seven astonished faces looked up from their newspapers or billiards game to gawk at me. I froze.

"Hattie," Walter exclaimed, leaping from his chair, grabbing my arm, and escorting me out of the room. "You know women aren't allowed in there."

"I'm sorry, Walter, it's just that . . . Come in here and see this." I motioned for him to follow me to the library. "I haven't had a chance to read every article, but . . ." I dropped the envelope on the table and sat down.

"What's this all about?" Walter pulled a chair up next to me.

"See for yourself." I slid the envelope toward him. He pulled out some newsprint. He dumped the remaining contents of the envelope on the table, picked up the closest article, and began to read. I eagerly reached over and did the same.

"This article's from the *Chicago Tribune* about the murder of Ruth Mascavarti by her husband." Walter paused. "Joseph Mascavarti."

"Known to us as John Martin," I said. "He allegedly killed his wife by pushing her down a flight of stairs."

"Like he did to you. Hattie, I had no idea."

I sat on the edge of my chair. "Keep reading."

" 'Joseph Mascavarti, a clerk at Dunn, Dunn, and Steele, is suspected of killing his wife of three years in an intoxication-induced rage by shoving her down the three flights of stairs at their apartment building on North Green Street,' " Walter read out loud. " 'Neighbors alerted the authorities after hearing the couple's violent argument. Mrs. Mascavarti died later at the Chicago Hospital for Women and Children from injuries incurred in the fall. The suspect fled the scene and is still at large.' " He skimmed the rest of the article. "Oh my God, Hattie, Ruth's maiden name was Trevelyan."

"Exactly," I cried. "Ruth Trevelyan Mascavarti died in May 1877. That's around the time Mrs. Trevelyan joined the coalition and became estranged from her husband. Her son even mentioned it at the memorial service."

"So John Martin, who was also this Joseph Mascavarti who killed his wife, was Mrs. Trevelyan's son-in-law?"

"Yes. It would explain why she was blackmailing him," I said. "She probably hated him and wanted to make him pay, literally, for what he'd done."

"And she knew he would pay it," Walter said. "He couldn't risk having his past revealed; he had too much to lose. If he hadn't had the misfortunate of meeting his first mother-in-law after all this time, he might've gotten away with it. Where did you get all this?" Walter slid the newspaper articles back in the envelope.

"Colonel Walker, John Martin's father-in-law. He said he didn't trust the police, so he gave it to me."

"Where did he get it?"

"In John Martin's suitcase. Mrs. Trevelyan met with someone last Friday; I'm guessing it was her son-in-law. She must've confronted him with these articles, then made her blackmail demands. That's about the time Colonel Walker said John started drinking again."

"Ironic. The man starts drinking again after seeing a temperance movement leader," Walter said, shaking his head. "So he paid her a thousand dollars," Walter said. "The money that the coalition thinks was a donation to their cause."

"Yes, and since it went to the AWTC and not to Mrs. Trevelyan personally, in a way it was," I said. "But then she demanded more."

"Sounds like a good motive for murder."

CHAPTER 25

"You haven't told me about the autopsy," I said.

Walter and I had traveled in companionable silence toward Pivot Rock. Walter had concentrated on driving the carriage through the mountainous terrain, while I, despite the breakneck speed and the brisk wind on my face, had endeavored to classify trees: oak, hickory, shortleaf pine, maple, hackberry, Ohio buckeye. As we journeyed through the countryside toward the celebrated "natural wonder," I attempted to put all thoughts of murder and temperance and secret pasts out of my mind. But the disconnected facts and inexplicable events of the past week continued to creep in my mind and disrupt my moments of tranquility. Frustrated, I finally gave up and asked Walter what was foremost in my mind.

"I was wondering when you were going to ask," he said. "It's as I thought, his blood had high levels of alcohol, and intracranial bleeding was the cause of death. The angle of the incision and contusions on his head as well as the position of his body, when accounting for the effect alcohol had on the muscles, match the trajectory of a backward, sideways fall toward the bench. The police examined the cave and found a partial footprint on a dry patch next to the bench that matches John Martin's boot. So it was much like Chief Jackson supposed."

I pictured John Martin setting his flask down beside him, rising from the bench in a stupor, and after taking a few precarious steps, slipping, falling, and cracking his head on the stone bench. *Ironic justice indeed,* I thought.

"Judge Senrow, as coroner, has officially ruled it an accident."

"Walter, I think we're here." The end of the road approached swiftly and I braced myself against the rail.

Walter jerked back on the reins and the carriage halted abruptly at the end of the gravel road, less than a foot away from an enormous old hickory tree.

"We can discuss this further, if you'd like, when we return," he said, lifting me down from the phaeton. "In the meantime, Miss Davish, let's enjoy this beautiful spot."

We found a mossy piece of ground a few feet from the rock formation itself to spread out the blanket and have our picnic. Striated and pale gray in the afternoon sun, the curiosity we had traveled several miles to see wasn't disappointing. Standing alone in a mossy clearing, Pivot Rock was twice the height of a man. The base of the pedestal rock was less than two feet wide, yet with a top broad enough to accommodate an omnibus. I insisted we not sit too close; the top-heavy rock appeared, to me at least, to be on the verge of tipping over. A well-trod path, through oak–sweet gum forest and along eroded limestone ledges, led to the clearing and beyond.

I sampled everything Walter had packed: cold fried chicken, potatoes in mustard sauce, sharp Cheddar cheese slices, boiled beans in vinegar, taking seconds of the pound cake and stewed apples. Walter had a glass of champagne, and the ginger beer he offered me as we lounged lazily after our meal was delicious. We made an unspoken pact beneath the lengthening shadow of Pivot Rock not to discuss the police, Mrs. Trevelyan, or anything related to the tragic events of the past week. Instead we laughed about the Shaw sisters' endearing contradictions, reflected on the beauty of the late-autumn afternoon, and took turns reading out loud from Whittier's *Poems of Nature,* which Walter had thoughtfully tucked into the basket. It was all that Walter had promised as a "pleasant distraction" and more.

All too soon, Walter said, "We should head back; it'll be dark before long."

I suggested a brief hike of exploration before returning. I'd been eyeing the path that meandered away from the clearing all afternoon, wondering what I might find around the bend. Walter agreed. The hike was short and steep but well worth the effort. I'd been rewarded with two new specimens for my collection, a forest wildflower I'd yet to identify and several leaves from the rare Eureka Springs hawthorn tree, when we came across a small cluster of Eastern red cedar atop an escarpment with a thrilling view of the valley below. The fragrance of the trees, as they brushed against me, brought to mind the last time I'd encountered the scent. I crushed a few needles in my hand, breathed in the fragrance, and then lifted my upturned palm.

"Walter, does this scent remind you of anything?"

He touched the tips of my fingers as he inhaled the fragrant needles. It was a small but intimate gesture that almost took my breath away. I quickly brushed my hands off on my skirt.

"Gin."

"Exactly." I was simultaneously exuberant and appalled. "I last encountered this fragrance on one of Mrs. Trevelyan's handkerchiefs. It was faint but undeniable. I wasn't able to place it until now."

With the implications of my discovery settling in, we turned back.

"Do you realize what this means?" Walter said, offering me his arm. "Either the killer used the handkerchief to clean up and left it behind . . ."

"Or Mrs. Trevelyan had more than one dangerous secret," I said.

The sun was below the horizon when Walter, promising to return for dinner, bolted around the hotel driveway. The moment his carriage disappeared from view, I dashed up the stairs and ran straight to Mrs. Trevelyan's room. It was imperative to determine whether indeed the coalition's late hatchet-wielding, saloon-smashing temperance crusader had had a secret drinking habit. Although the police had searched Mrs. Trevelyan's room, I decided to look again.

I wondered if the police had left Mrs. Trevelyan's possessions or whether the hotel had given the room to another guest. I tried the door. It was unlocked. Neither scenario was right; the room was empty. I scoured it anyway. I opened every table drawer and every wardrobe door and searched under every piece of furniture, even lifting the mattresses. For my efforts, I found several slivers of glass, a blue feather, and a small piece of molding cheese, but nothing of any significance. Next I searched Mrs. Trevelyan's bathroom. I knocked three times before entering. The room was vacant but far from empty. Both washstands were covered with ladies' toiletries, as they had been the day I arrived. I was lucky. The police hadn't removed or disturbed any of Mrs. Trevelyan's belongings; dust had settled on the perfume and Magnetic Spring water bottles.

I examined the top of the washstand and the shelf above it, systematically reading all of the labels, and checked each bottle by scent for any hint of alcohol. I found nothing unusual. As I suspected, the washstand drawer contained piles of the plush hand and bathing towels. I removed the towels in order to check the back of the drawer and uncovered a stack of hand- kerchiefs matching the one I'd found in Mrs. Trevelyan's nightstand drawer. Why had there only been one in her room? Did these too carry the scent of gin? As I lifted the handker- chiefs out, the drawer tipped toward the floor and a four-sided dark olive bottle, lying on its side, slid forward. My heart skipped a beat. Could the beloved, controversial, and infamous president of the American Women's Temperance Coalition have been an intemperate hypocrite, a betrayer of everything that those around her held dear? I stared at the bottle a few moments, unsure I wanted to know the truth. But I had to know. I uncorked it and sent the aroma of juniper wafting through the room. I felt dispirited and enlightened at the same time; I'd found Mrs. Trevelyan's cache of gin.

It all began to make sense: Mrs. Trevelyan's lackadaisical at- titude toward Cordelia Anglewood's threat to whip her, her preference for Magnetic Spring water, the frequent trips to the washroom that Mary mentioned, even her flushed cheeks and unfocused gaze I noticed the night the temperance leader as- sailed the saloon. The bottle weighed heavy in my hand. I had to tell the police. Mrs. Trevelyan herself had supplied the weapon of her demise, not George Shulman. I tucked the bot- tle under my jacket and replaced the remaining contents of the drawer.

As I approached my room, I was startled to hear someone moving about within. I cracked the door open and watched, mortified, as Mary Flannagan searched frantically through my desk, pulling out drawers and sending papers flying to the floor. She grabbed my letter opener, hid it in her apron, and sprinted toward the door. I dodged back into the bathroom, barely avoiding meeting her in the hallway. Her head twisted this way and that. Loose hair strands sprang haphazardly from

her forehead and bun. Her eyes were red and swollen. She disappeared down the hall. I hid the gin bottle in the desk in my
room, checked the condition of my typewriter, and cringed at
the sight of my work flung about the floor. I struggled with
the urge to reorganize the mess, but I'd have to leave it for now
if I wanted my letter opener, a gift from a former employer,
back. I raced to catch up with Mary.

I followed her down staircases, through back alleys, and
across many winding streets. We navigated through a yard of
hanging laundry and kept to the back of the hotels. The sun
no longer reached many of the paths, and I had no idea where
she was going. To keep her in my sights, I often drew too near.
Twice Mary glanced over her shoulder and forced me to duck
behind a parked wagon. Otherwise, she was oblivious to
everything around her. Behind one hotel, I almost stepped on
a stray cat raiding a hotel's garbage. It hissed at me, but Mary
didn't pause or turn around. I thought she hadn't heard and
was inching forward when suddenly she froze in the middle of
an alley. I darted into the shadow of a doorway.

"Is someone there?" She twisted her head in my direction,
brandishing the letter opener. She stood still, listening.

Do I typically breathe this loud? I wondered.

I tried to hold my breath, fearful she would detect my
presence. Then a darker thought crossed my mind. This was
Mary Flannagan, the maid, who had been kind, if not always
truthful, with me. So why was I suddenly afraid of her? Was it
her threatening stance with the letter opener? Was it that I had
witnessed her complete lack of regard for my belongings and
papers? Was I starting to realize that Miss Lucy had been right
about Mary all along? I dismissed this outright but knew of no
other explanation. She turned away again but proceeded more
slowly.

She had left the alley before I continued after her. I crept
forward in the dark along the alley wall and, peering around

the corner, was amazed. The police station loomed in front of me. Despite the numerous times I'd been here before, I'd never arrived by such a circuitous route. There were no signs of the maid. I'd lost her again. Yet the last time I'd followed Mary, I had ended up in the same place. She had to be close by.

"George, George," someone whispered. I moved in that direction.

It was Mary, standing beneath a barred window of the jail-house. "Here, I brought something that might help you."

I crouched behind some brush, flinching at the crunch of dried leaves beneath my feet. She either didn't hear me or didn't care because her glance never faltered. I watched as Mary tossed my letter opener to a pair of waiting hands. George Shulman's face filled the window.

"Ah, love, what am I to do with this?"

Here was George Shulman's "darling." No wonder she felt bitterness over the assault on the saloon and reacted strongly to Miss Lucy's callous remarks about George Shulman hanging. Mary had hinted that she had a beau. And Mary's and George Shulman's names had both appeared in the prayer book at the chapel; they probably even met there. I silently reproved myself for my ignorance. I should've known. Walter had thought George no longer had any attachments, but here was Mary, in her desperation to help him, arming George with a stolen letter opener. I suddenly felt ashamed for eavesdropping on such a private conversation, but had no way to leave unde-tected.

"You can defend yourself," Mary said. "I won't let them hang you. I won't."

"It would be worse for me if they found this." George Shulman tossed the letter opener back on the ground. It landed a few feet away. "There now, let's hear some more of that book you've been reading. You stopped just after the girl Marian's diary entries."

Mary fumbled with the book in her pocket. When she accidentally dropped it on the ground, Mary collapsed in on herself, falling to her knees. She covered her face with her hands and sobbed.

"Mary, dear, don't cry. I'm innocent. They'll find out who really did it."

"They're sending you to Berryville in the morning," she shouted. "Don't you understand, George? My da was innocent too, but he rotted away for years, until he died in his cell. The coppers aren't even looking for someone else."

"Oh, it's all that hypocrite's fault." George rattled the bars and spat. "In life, she was a tyrant, keeping us apart with threats of reporting you to the hotel. She knew they'd throw you out without any references. Now someone's murdered the old hag, and I'm to blame for it."

"Don't talk ill of the dead, George. It's bad luck. Besides, she did some good, all those charities and such. You know she paid me well. So what if she liked a nip now and then?" I gasped, dumbfounded at this revelation. Mary knew about Mrs. Trevelyan's habit. *Who else knew?* I wondered.

"But what type of woman objects to us being together because I sell liquor for a living, while she's drinking gin-loaded coffee?" the barkeeper said. "Even after we took the temperance pledge with her as a witness!" Mrs. Trevelyan knew that George Shulman didn't drink and yet she targeted his saloon anyway. She must've been more fanatical than I'd thought.

"All that matters now is that she's dead," Mary said. "And they're going to hang you for her murder."

"What about that secretary lady? Or Doc Grice? They said they were going to help."

"I don't know," Mary said. "I think they're trying, but the coppers aren't listening." George rested his head on the bars, all the spark gone from his eyes.

"Well, let's hope they start listening," he said.

Mary jumped to her feet, brandishing her fist. "I'm not going to let them hang you. I'll do whatever it takes. I'll say I killed her, if I have to. I'll fight those coppers with my last breath."

"No! I'll let them hang me before I let them get their hands on you, love. I couldn't bear to lose you."

"You'll never lose me, George Shulman. Never."

"Then promise me you won't do anything foolish, Mary. And that you'll marry me the day I get out of here."

"Ah, you're a fool, George Shulman." My heart broke as I watched Mary slump to her knees, her body shaking as she cried.

Walter held the door for an older couple as I mounted the hotel portico steps. He had arrived early for our dinner date.

"What are you doing coming from out there? It's going to rain any minute," he said, peering over my shoulder at the darkening sky. "I thought you had work to do."

"I did," I said, breathing hard from my brisk walk back to the hotel, during which I'd promised myself that I'd help Mary any way I could. "Walter, George Shulman's innocent. We have to do something to prove it."

"I've always thought so. But, Hattie, what convinced you?" I wasn't prepared to tell him everything just yet.

"Is there somewhere in town we can grab a quick bite to eat?" I said.

"Sure, we can get a nice broiled steak at Fletcher's Grill-room in twenty minutes. Why?"

"Let me get something from my room and then I'll tell you all about it on the way."

Still not used to Walter's reckless driving, I clung to my hat with one hand, the railing of the phaeton with the other, and squeezed the bag I had retrieved from my room tightly between my knees as I relayed everything I'd overheard between

Mary Flannagan and George Shulman. Large raindrops splashed onto the top of the phaeton.

"What incredible news," Walter exclaimed, oblivious to the declining weather. "The hotel chambermaid and George Shulman courting? Many eligible ladies have attempted to snag George Shulman. But wouldn't you know it would be Mary Flannagan of all people he takes to." A peculiar expression grew on his face but was quickly replaced by a wide grin. "Cupid works in mysterious ways." Then he noticed the bag clutched between my knees. "What do you have in the bag?"

"Evidence for the police," I said.

Walter raised his eyebrows. "I take it that's where we're going after dinner?"

"Walter, I think we're here."

I pointed to a building, which we were rapidly approaching. He glanced up at the sign, and we suddenly skidded to a halt in front of Fletcher's Grillroom on Armstrong Street. True to Walter's boast, we ordered, were served, had eaten a hearty steak dinner, and were on our way to the police station in less than an hour.

We rode in silence for several blocks, both of us most likely thinking about the importance of our meeting with the police. If we failed to convince Chief Jackson that George Shulman was innocent, the policeman would take him to the sheriff in Berryville in the morning. We couldn't help George Shulman in Berryville. But despite Chief Jackson's earlier dismissals, I was feeling more confident with each block. I glanced at the bag on my lap again.

The rain pelted down now and the streets were thick with mud. We rumbled over a wooden bridge that spanned a ravine and crossed over to the usually busy thoroughfare of Main Street, though its nickname, Mud Street, was more appropriate today. The wheels slid on the mud, but Walter didn't slow his pace until we reached Montgomery Street and nearly tipped over making the turn. The one fully lit building on the dark street, the police station was a beacon in the rain. Nonetheless, when we entered, shaking the rain from the umbrella, it was as still as one would expect late on a Sunday evening. A lonely clerk, holding a broadsheet between his hands, peered over the newspaper at us.

"Can I help you?" he asked.

"Yes, we'd like to speak to Chief Jackson," Walter said.

"Can't this wait until morning?"

"What now?" Chief Jackson had seen our approach.

"We've found out a few things you need to know," Walter said.

"Doc, it's been a long day. It's late. It's Sunday and the missus has already telephoned twice. I should've been home with my slippers on hours ago." Walter sat down on the bench, folded his legs, and set his hat in his lap. "Oh, all right. If you're going to be that way, let's go into my office."

He led us to a cluttered room, filled with a desk, three chairs, a sofa, and numerous bookcases. One barred window revealed a view of the livery down the street. Every bookcase, the floor, the sofa, and two of the three chairs were stacked with piles of tablets and typewritten paper. And where there wasn't paper, there were ferns: maidenhair, holly, sword, Boston, and several varieties I didn't recognize. They were bushy, beautiful, and in the way. The chaos explained much about the policeman. How he got anything done was beyond me. With no curtains, carpets, or paintings, the room's only other adornments consisted of two dirty coffee mugs, the tin watering can I had seen before, a framed photograph of twin towheaded boys and a petite woman wearing a black straw braid bonnet, a Wardian case containing an African violet with purple flowers, and a Crandall typewriter on the desk.

"I'll get us some coffee," Jackson said, leaving us alone in the room. Walter was clearing a space for us to sit and I was admiring his Crandall when he returned, carrying three steaming mugs.

"Hattie's a gardener too, Ben," Walter said, indicating the Boston fern he had placed on the floor at our feet.

"Really?" He sounded enthusiastic for the first time since I'd met him.

"I'm actually more of a specimen collector," I said. "I don't have much luck with live plants. But I wish I had; your ferns are lovely." It was difficult to watch the exuberance drain from his face and any respect I might've gained disappear.

"What was it you wanted again?" he said.

I told him about the conversation I'd overheard between Mary and George.

"I'll have someone secure that jail cell window tomorrow," he said. "Letter openers, huh?"

"And if you need to speak with Cordelia Anglewood," I said, "you should know that she's no longer staying at the Arcadia. She moved to the Hotel Byron late last night."

"You came down here this late to tell me a lady changed addresses and my prisoner refused a letter opener?" I ignored the policeman's sardonic tone. After what I had endured this past week, it would take more than that to discourage me.

"Colonel Walker, John Martin's father-in-law, left this morning," I said, "and he gave me this. I thought you should see it." I pulled the envelope out of my bag and told Jackson about its contents. He scowled, then read through the articles, shaking his head.

Several times he muttered something under his breath, "dead woman's daughter," "Mascavarti," "alias," and then, pushing it all aside, stared out the window.

"I read your report," Jackson offered after we had sat for several minutes in awkward silence, sipping our coffee. "If nothing else, Miss Davish, I have to admit you're thorough. What type of plants do you collect?"

I was taken aback by the question, but answered happily enough. "Everything I can find and collect personally. With my new specimens from Eureka Springs, I now have 1,854 plants pressed and identified."

"Impressive."

"Thank you." I hesitated before getting back to the matter at hand. "There was something not in my report that I want to show you." I reached into my bag and pulled out the gin-soaked handkerchief I'd found in Mrs. Trevelyan's room.

"A handkerchief?" Chief Jackson said, reaching across his desk and taking it from my hand. "What do I want with a handkerchief?"

"Give it a whiff," Walter suggested.

"The scent's very faint," I said. "I can't smell it anymore, but Walter said he could."

"You sure about this, Doc?" The policeman held it to his nose. "I don't smell anything." He crinkled the fabric between his fingers. "Hold on, do I smell . . . gin? Where did you get this?"

"In Mrs. Trevelyan's room," I said.

"When?"

"The day she died. It was tucked into a nightstand drawer. There's more." I retrieved the gin bottle from the bag.

Walter whistled. Chief Jackson furrowed his eyebrows. "So you did find concrete evidence," Walter said.

"A gin bottle, evidence?" the policeman said.

"This bottle was hidden behind towels and handkerchiefs like this one, in Mrs. Trevelyan's washroom. I found it this afternoon."

"Ben, you should compare this bottle with the pieces I extracted from the dead woman's scalp and with those found in the trunk," Walter said. "It's probably from the same case." Chief Jackson examined the bottle. "You treated her the night before she died, Doc. Did the temperance woman smell of gin?"

"Of course, gin and smoke and whiskey and ale. She had, after all, been smashing kegs and bottles with her ax and trying to burn down a barroom."

The policeman was silent for a moment or two. "You had no right searching the victim's rooms and tampering with evidence, Miss Davish. But I have to admit . . ."

"That it's worth investigating other possible suspects? John Martin had the strongest motive," I suggested. Chief Jackson sighed.

"If you think you're better than trained professionals, Miss Davish, maybe you can solve a little mystery of my own." He pulled a glass container with filmy brown splotches covering one side from a drawer in his desk. "We found this in the Grotto Spring cave."

"My specimen jar," I exclaimed, reaching for the jar. "I left it in the cave this morning." I looked closely at the splotches, surprised that mold or some other form of life had already started to colonize the jar. I blanched when I realized what they were.

"Blood, Miss Davish. It must've gotten on the glass when you dropped it near the body. Well, that's one mystery solved. But what about this?" He tossed a folded piece of paper across his desk. "What can you tell me about it?"

A simple sheet of white paper. *Give to secretary* was scrawled across the front. I unfolded the note. *I may be a drunk, but I'm no killer* was handwritten inside. It was signed *J.M.*

I was stunned. "I've never seen this before. Where did you find it?" I asked.

"Just like your jar. In the Grotto Spring cave, when we were investigating John Martin's death. It was in a pile of leaves with some other trash. Any ideas how it got there?"

"None, though John Martin was most certainly its author," I said.

"So you can't help me, then, with this simple mystery? The note's even addressed to you." The policeman sat back, folded his arms across his chest, and smirked. "I think I've proven my point. Time to go back to your typewriter, Miss Davish, and leave the murders to us."

CHAPTER 26

With few words between us, Walter escorted me back to the lobby. What was left to say? We had given Chief Jackson every reason to continue investigating Mrs. Trevelyan's murder, and he had rebuked us again. As Walter retrieved the umbrella he'd forgotten in Chief Jackson's office, I braced myself against the frame of the open door and closed my eyes. It'd been a long day. Was it only this morning that I'd found John Martin's dead body? I felt numb.

At first I'd been baffled when the policeman waved the scrap of paper in front of me. How could I have misplaced it? I'd never done anything so careless in my life. But then where had the note come from? How did it get to Grotto Spring? Had someone stolen it from my room? Or maybe John Martin had never even sent the note. Maybe he never got the chance? I had mentioned this to Chief Jackson, but he had responded by reminding me, to my humiliation, that it was obviously addressed to me. I knew it wasn't addressed to me but to Mrs. Trevelyan, like John Martin's other message, but it didn't matter. They were both dead.

Now, leaning against the door frame, listening to the patter of the rain, I felt only resignation and defeat. Increasingly loud splashes and the whinnying of a horse jarred me out of my thoughts of self-pity. A rider stopped right in front of me. He leapt off his horse, flipped the reins onto the wooden rail, and scurried through the door.

"Hank," I exclaimed, "what are you doing here?" Officer Norris and Walter joined me.

"What's going on?" the officer said.

"Miss Hattie," the telegraph operator said, doubling over, hands on his hips. He was soaking wet.

"Hank, what's wrong?"

"This came for you." He panted as he pulled an envelope from inside his raincoat and held it out to me. My heart sank. Only bad news came this quickly by telegram.

"Oh my goodness, Hank," I said, with false bravado, "you didn't have to come out in this rain. Whatever it is, it could've waited."

"But you had marked it urgent."

"I had marked it urgent?"

Then it dawned on me. It was the response I'd been waiting for. I had forgotten all about it. The dread I'd felt a moment ago was instantly replaced by anxious excitement.

"Thank you, Hank. Thank you." I ripped open the envelope and quickly scanned the contents. My heart leapt in my chest. I'd been right about my suspicions about Cordelia Anglewood.

"What is it, Hattie?" Walter said.

"It's the response from Fayetteville," I said.

"It arrived earlier, but I've had a devil of a time tracking you down." Hank wrung his dripping hat on the threshold. "I wanted to deliver it personally."

"Thank you again, Hank." I waved the slip in my hand. "Walter, I need to show this to Chief Jackson."

"Sorry, Hattie, he's gone home for the night, slipped out the back door. Which is where we need to go—home. Whatever it is, it can wait until morning." Walter was right; I was exhausted.

"And, Mr. Floyd, if you'd like to ride back to the hotel, I'm sure Mr. Kimberling's stables could accommodate your horse for the night," Walter said. Hank eagerly agreed. "They have a telephone. Would you call for us, Norris? I'd like to get Miss Davish back as soon as possible."

"Of course, Dr. Grice."

The ride back was circuitous, though uneventful. Several roads flowed with mud or were too steep to be attempted in the rain. Walter deftly avoided getting stuck, most likely by traveling so fast. The wheels barely touched the ground. When we finally alighted before the Arcadia Hotel, the rain had stopped, the sky had begun to clear, and moonlight streamed between breaks in the clouds. It was a relief to be back. Hank bid us a good night, wide-eyed and slightly shaking. Although he was appreciative, I couldn't imagine him riding with Walter again. We watched him head for a cluster of cottages on the edge of the hotel grounds. We turned when the rattle of carriage wheels alerted us to a departing carriage.

"Busy night." Walter laughed, escorting me toward the hotel's front doors. "So what was in the telegram?"

I turned to reply when I caught a glimpse of a woman in the carriage. She ducked out of sight when she saw me. Another woman leaned over her to peer out.

"Cordelia Anglewood!" I said. "And Mrs. Piers is with her."

"Where?"

"In the Rockaway."

"What on earth?"

"Walter," I said, gripping his arm, "we have to follow them."

As if it heard me, the Rockaway carriage picked up speed

and disappeared down the ravine. I ran toward his phaeton, without wondering if Walter followed me. Without a question, he waved off the stable hand holding the reins of his horse, bounded in beside me, and sped after Cordelia Anglewood's carriage. For the first time, I was grateful for Walter's characteristic driving. Although I was shouting, *Faster, Faster,* in my head, I don't think we could've. We caught up and kept them in sight until they reached the train depot. We skidded to a halt beside the Rockaway as porters were unloading Cordelia Anglewood's trunks.

"Are you going somewhere, Mrs. Anglewood?" I said. Both women swirled around at my question.

"You," Cordelia Anglewood hissed. "What are you doing here?"

"I could ask the same of you, Mrs. Anglewood, Mrs. Piers."

"Ah, Miss Davish," the other woman said, "Sister Cordelia and I are going home. We're catching the 10:14 train."

"Oh, Josephine, the meeting is over," Cordelia said. "Stop calling me that."

"But I thought you planned to stay the winter?" I said.

"I don't have to answer to you, secretary. Come, Josephine." Cordelia moved away, down the deserted platform. I took a step toward her.

"Sister Cordelia has suffered." Mrs. Piers put her hand on my arm, stopping me. "Please let her go in peace."

"But you were specifically told by the police that no temperance club member was to leave town until the investigation was concluded," Walter said.

"The police have arrested the man from the saloon, Dr. Grice. We are no longer obligated to stay."

"What about the temperance cause, Mrs. Piers?" I said. "What about the coalition?"

"As Sister Cordelia explained, the meeting is over, Miss

Davish. Most members of the coalition are leaving or have already left. Not everyone winters here. We'll do our good works from our respective homes now." She too began to move away.

"Hattie." Walter dropped his voice to a whisper. "What's this all about?"

"What about your fallen leader? What about John Martin?" I shouted after the retreating women. "I know who killed Mrs. Trevelyan." Both women stopped as if stunned, then turned and rushed at me. Walter stepped in, blocking their approach.

"How dare you. I didn't kill anyone." Cordelia Anglewood tried to strike me with her handbag. Walter snatched it away in midair.

"Then why did you threaten Mrs. Trevelyan that morning?" I said.

"You don't have to tell them anything, Sister Cordelia," Josephine Piers said.

"You needed money, didn't you?" I said.

"You had no right to inquire into my private affairs," Cordelia said.

"Don't you know how rich Commodore Anglewood is, Miss Davish?" Mrs. Piers said.

"Yes, but I believe he's cut his wife off from that wealth," I said.

"That's outlandish, Miss Davish. Why would the commodore do such a thing?" Mrs. Piers said.

"I can only speculate as to why," I said. "But if you had access to your husband's riches, why the need to ask your friends for money or to sell your jewelry? Why, Mrs. Anglewood?" Cordelia Anglewood stared silently at the ground, refusing to meet my eyes. "That was a final refusal from your husband, wasn't it, that telegram that caused you visible distress at breakfast yesterday morning? Why else would you move to a budget hotel in the middle of the night, or leave Eureka Springs prematurely?"

"It's not possible, Miss Davish," Josephine said. "The commodore is a stanch supporter of our cause. Tell them, Sister . . . I mean, Cordelia. Tell them that Brother Gerald is our biggest contributor." She sounded slightly panicked. "What would we do without his support? Surely he would never deny our cause its due?"

"No, Josephine, it's true," Cordelia said, flashing me an angry glance. "Gerald cut off my allowance. My husband, a stanch Cleveland supporter, as you know, disapproved of my increased involvement with the AWTC. He thought I was an embarrassment. He wired me, after Cleveland was elected, that I was to come home immediately. When I refused, he cut off my allowance, as well as his promised support of the coalition. I was going to have to spend everything I had to pay for the rally. I was so relieved when Mr. Martin's unsolicited donation came through. A gift sent from God."

Walter and I looked at one another and then back at the two women.

"You didn't know it was blackmail money?" Walter said. "Paid to Mrs. Trevelyan to keep her silent about his involvement in her daughter's death?"

Cordelia's jaw tightened, her face reddened, and recognizing the expression on her countenance, both Josephine and I took a step back. "No," she seethed.

"And that he was a known alcoholic?" Walter said.

"That I knew." Her head snapped to one side in disgust. "I couldn't believe it."

"You found out at the rally, didn't you?" I said. "I saw you arguing."

"What a fool I must've looked." Cordelia threw clenched fists into the air. "He was a disgrace, staggering about the rally for all to see. And I had praised that drunkard, in front of the entire coalition, at Magnetic Spring, of all places. I thought at least the money was his penance. And now you tell me he's a blackmailer and a killer? It's bad enough I have to go groveling back to Gerald. Now I'll be the laughingstock. I'll lose my position. I'll . . ."

She wheeled around and slammed her fists into a pile of stacked luggage. The top two suitcases clattered to the platform floor. A porter approached but scurried away after one glaring look from Cordelia.

"Take solace that justice was done, Cordelia," Josephine said. "It was no accident that the man slipped and hit his head on that bench. John Martin was drunk, and God's will was at work."

"I don't ever want to hear that name again. For that matter, I don't want anything more to do with this godforsaken town either," Cordelia said. "We're holding the annual meeting in Hot Springs next year, Josephine."

"But Hot Springs is a town of gamblers and thieves. It's an ideal destination for saloon smashing, I grant you, but—"

"Shut up, Josephine. Let's go."

"Money is a strong motive for murder, Mrs. Anglewood," Walter said.

"I didn't kill Edwina," she said through clenched teeth.

"No, Mrs. Anglewood, your only crimes were ambition and pride." I pulled out the telegram that Hank had valiantly delivered. "This was wired from your jeweler today, confirming that you were in Fayetteville secretly selling your jewelry at the time Mrs. Trevelyan was killed."

The high-pitched whistle of steam releasing and a rush of wind ruffling our coats and hats heralded the 10:14 train.

"Then who did kill her?" Walter said.

Josephine Piers sprang around and ran.

"Catch her!" I cried.

For a brief moment, Cordelia and Walter stood there stunned, gaping after the fleeing figure. I lifted my skirts and sprinted down the platform. Walter, spurred by my action, outpaced me and caught Josephine by the wrist as she attempted to board the train. He shouted for a porter to telephone the police station. He was securing her wrists with his cravat when I reached them. Cordelia Anglewood, panting and breathless, had followed.

"Tell this girl she's wrong, tell her . . . Josephine, how could you?" Cordelia said.

"Oh, Cordelia, I didn't plan to," Josephine Piers said, her shoulders drooping. "It just happened."

"Nothing just happens."

"Cordelia, you don't understand. I went to speak with Mother Trevelyan that morning, to pray with her, to relish our shared victory, to celebrate our triumphant fight against the devil's rum and . . ." Her whole body trembled.

"And you saw her, drunk," I said.

"Yes, the woman I'd proudly stood by the night before was partaking of the very evil we fought against."

"You lie!" Cordelia sprang at the woman, trying to slap her face. Walter jumped between the two women, taking the first blow. Several porters rushed to his aid, one man restraining Josephine, three restraining Cordelia.

"I'm sorry, Mrs. Anglewood," I said. "It's true. I found the evidence myself. That's why she laughed off your threat to whip her. She'd already had some gin in her morning coffee."

Her body slackened and she shook off her restrainers. She looked at Josephine Piers and then took a long glaring look at me, her countenance full of recrimination. Without another word, she stomped away and boarded the train.

"So you grabbed the offending gin bottle you found her drinking from, didn't you, Mrs. Piers?" I said. "And smashed it over her head."

"Yes. Seeing our leader sitting there, infested with liquor . . . I simply reacted. It was like storming into the saloon, ignoring the cries and the protests and, hatchets held high, doing what needed to be done."

"You stuffed her into one of her trunks," I said. "Why?"

"She was dead. I had to hide the body. The temperance vote was the next day and the annual meeting was about to begin. I could only think of what it would do to the coalition for her, our president, to be found like that. I couldn't chance it."

"Like that, you mean intoxicated?" Walter said.

"Of course, it would've jeopardized everything. As it was, I barely finished cleaning up when Eleanor arrived." She paused and sighed. "And we lost the vote anyway. What a disappointment after all our hard work. But we can try again in two years. In that at least, the law is with us."

The clanking and creaking of the wheels on the departing train, as they labored to make the first few rotations, caused her to pause. "Sister Cordelia may never forgive me for disillusioning her about Mother Trevelyan," Josephine said. "I wish she never had to know. It's a burden I was willing to bear alone."

"But you killed a woman," I sputtered, incredulous. "Don't you think that's the more heinous act?"

"That's different. She'll forgive me for that, for what I did, I did for the good of the coalition. Cordelia knows I loved Mother Trevelyan and that it pained me greatly to have killed her. But we've worked too hard to free this nation from destruction and Godlessness to have it all ruined now. Cordelia would understand."

"I don't think Cordelia or any member of the coalition would understand murdering someone," I said.

"Yes, they would," she said. "We fight for what's right. We do God's work, even if it means killing the greatest among us. That bottle was a holy weapon meting out justice."

"She wasn't dead, Mrs. Piers," Walter interjected as Officer

Norris and the station security guards arrived. "The bottle didn't kill Mrs. Trevelyan."

"What?" Josephine said, alarm rising in her voice. "But I saw her head fall. I saw her bleed. She wasn't moving or breathing when I put her in the trunk. She was dead."

"No, the cause of death was suffocation from the clothes you piled on top of her, and not the head wound you inflicted with the bottle," Dr. Grice said. "It was your callousness and not any act of holy justice that killed Mrs. Trevelyan."

"Noooooo!" The woman's wail as she collapsed to the platform was something I'll never forget. She held her head in her hands, rocking back and forth against the wooden planks, muttering, "No, no, no, no." It was hard not to feel some pity for her.

"Oh, Mother Trevelyan," Josephine said, raising her eyes and bound hands to the sky in supplication. "If only I could've held my hand fast, I might've saved your soul."

"Take her away, Norris," Walter said to the policeman. "It's her own soul she needs to worry about now."

Chapter 27

"I still can't believe Josephine killed Edwina, dear," Miss Lizzie said as we sat on the hotel's second-story veranda, sipping coffee. She held a plate on her lap, collecting the toast crumbs on the tip of her finger. "She adored Edwina, was devoted to her."

"I'm afraid Josephine Piers was more devoted to her cause," I said.

"But how did you know it was Josephine, Davish?" Miss Lucy asked.

"It was John Martin's note, the one Chief Jackson showed me that said, *I may be a drunk, but I'm no killer.* At the time, only John Martin and Mrs. Trevelyan would've known that it pertained to the death of Mrs. Trevelyan's daughter. We all know that now. But Mrs. Trevelyan's killer, upon reading it, wouldn't have and thus might think the note referred to them. There were witnesses who said John Martin wasn't alone that night, that he was overheard talking to a woman. I'm guessing once she discovered the identity of J.M., Josephine confronted John

Martin with the note at Grotto Spring, after the rally. One of them must've dropped it."

"But that doesn't explain how you knew it was Josephine, dear," Miss Lizzie said.

"Yes, it does. The desk clerk had written *Give to secretary* on the note, so it was logical that it had been given to Mrs. Trevelyan's secretary. But I never received the letter, and it had bothered me at the time that I hadn't, so that left Josephine Piers, who everyone knows had once served as Mrs. Trevelyan's secretary. Once I suspected her, everything else fell into place."

"But John Martin's death was accidental, Davish," Miss Lucy said.

"That's the official verdict, yes," I said.

"But you think otherwise?"

"We'll never know, Miss Lucy," I said. "But either way, I think Mrs. Piers is culpable."

"How can you believe that, dear?" Miss Lizzie said. "Even if she met him at the spring, there's no evidence she was involved in any way."

"But there is, Miss Lizzie. Josephine Piers mentioned that he died by hitting his head on the bench. She wouldn't have known that unless she'd seen him fall. The police report hadn't been released to the public yet."

"Are you saying she might've pushed him herself, Davish?" Miss Lucy said, licking her lips. "Then it wouldn't be an accident at all, would it? It would be," she paused for effect, "a double murder." Miss Lucy sounded almost gleeful. I couldn't understand why.

"I'm saying that even if she didn't push him, Josephine Piers should still bear partial responsibility for his death. If you or I had seen John Martin fall, we would've cried out, sought help for the dying man. But she didn't. She left him to die. I'd wondered what would've happened had any of the coalition members discovered Mrs. Trevelyan's secret drinking habit," I said. "Now we know."

"None of us condone such violence, Davish," Miss Lucy snapped, suddenly annoyed.

"I knew nothing good would come of slashing up saloons," Miss Lizzie said, slowly shaking her head.

"Lizzie," her sister rebuked, "Josephine was an extremist. We all knew it, but no one could've foreseen this."

"But we should have, Lucy, dear. We should have. Shouldn't the AWTC strive for temperance in all things?" It wasn't my place to say, but I agreed completely with Miss Lizzie. An awkward silence followed.

"Ladies," Walter said from behind me as he stepped out onto the veranda.

"Walter, I'm so glad you're here." And I meant it. The growing tension was making me uncomfortable. The sisters had been kind to me. Whenever they began to disagree, I tried not to get caught in the middle. I rose from the rocking chair to meet him halfway. "I was hoping to see you before I left. Did the police tell you anything?" I whispered. He took my hand, and kissed it, though uncertainty showed in his face.

"Only that they contacted Colonel Walker, who provided an alibi for his son-in-law. Supposedly, John Martin, upon returning from his night in prison, received a disturbing telegram and stormed out of the hotel."

"The demand for more money from Mrs. Trevelyan," I said.

"Probably. Worried, the colonel followed him. The colonel swears John never left his sight all morning and that they never approached the Arcadia Hotel."

"Then where were they all that time?" I said.

"The little Catholic chapel on the outskirts of town," Walter said. "It's quite a hike from here. The colonel stood outside for over an hour listening while his son-in-law prayed, mumbling things about redemption and forgiveness over and over. He must've had renewed feelings of remorse over his first wife's death." I was having feelings of remorse of my own. I had all but accused John Martin of Mrs. Trevelyan's murder. I'd met John Martin at that little chapel. I'd seen Joseph Mascavarti's name in the chapel's petition book, dated that very day. I should've made the connection. I should've mentioned it earlier. I mentioned it now.

"But why didn't the colonel reveal this immediately?" I said.

"Chief Jackson speculates it's because the colonel was ashamed, first of his son-in-law's behavior, and then, after discovering the articles about Ruth Mascavarti's death, of his own culpability in exposing his own daughter to a drunken killer. That's probably why he gave you the articles and left town, instead of facing the police."

"I said, 'Good morning, Dr. Grice,' " Miss Lucy said. I had the feeling it wasn't the first time. "Are you now as deaf as a copper kettle? Or do you only have ears for Davish here? Will you two sit down?" We complied. Walter reached for my hand under the table. "We were interrogating Davish here on last night's adventures."

"Oh, really? Did she explain how she knew about Cordelia Anglewood's lack of funds?" Walter said.

"No, dear, you never did tell us," Miss Lizzie said.

"It was you, Miss Lizzie. I saw Cordelia Anglewood fiddle with her collar the same way you did after your stick pin broke. Then you mentioned taking the train on Monday to visit a jeweler in Fayetteville."

"That doesn't explain a thing, Davish," Miss Lucy said.

"When I first arrived, Cordelia wore exquisite jewelry, but of late had been wearing less expensive pieces or not wearing anything at all," I said. "You ladies even commented on it after the memorial service. Her moving to the Hotel Byron substantiated my suspicions. So when I discovered she had received a money wire, not from her husband, but from a jeweler in Fayetteville, I contacted them. She had taken the same train you mentioned, the day Mrs. Trevelyan died."

"The 9:15," Miss Lizzie said.

"Yes, the 9:15. Mrs. Trevelyan was still alive at 9:18, so Cordelia couldn't have killed her."

"Clever of you, Davish," Miss Lucy said. "Or should I start calling you Holmes? You've already got a Dr. Watson." Walter laughed.

"I'm afraid we've missed that train today, dear," Miss Lizzie said. "By the way, who are Holmes and Dr. Watson?"

"Oh, Lizzie," Miss Lucy said, "don't fret. We'll go to Fayetteville tomorrow and I'll read you a good detective story on the train. Oh, Diana, come join us."

Diana Halbert, the presumptive new AWTC president, approached and engaged us with an amusing story about Charlie the dog and last night's dessert course.

"And there he was, covered with whipping cream and cherries, lapping up the last of the chocolate sauce," Miss Halbert said. Miss Lucy laughed and slapped her knee. Miss Lizzie wiped tears from her eyes. Walter and I chuckled at their reaction. "Oh, I almost forgot to tell you the latest gossip, Miss Lucy. You know the saloonkeeper, the one that—"

"Yes, Diana, dear, we know all about Mr. Shulman," Miss Lizzie said.

"You do? Well, I should've known you'd be the first to know that he's getting married."

"Married?" Miss Lucy cried, almost spilling her coffee.

"Oh, good," Diana said, clapping her hands in delight, "you don't already know. Well, I spoke to Annie Butler at the *Daily Democrat* this morning, and she said the man came in after being released from jail, wanting the banns published in the paper."

"To whom?" Miss Lucy said. "Who would marry that brute?"

"A chambermaid from this hotel." Miss Halbert paused for effect. "The very one that cleaned for Mother Trevelyan. She quit her job this morning."

"Well, I never," Miss Lucy declared. I pictured my letter opener as I'd found it upon my return last night, and smiled. The blade had gleamed under the electric lights. I'd touched its edge lightly. It had recently been sharpened and polished.

"And now that he's Councilman Shulman, he's turning the saloon over to a cousin or some such relative. There's even a rumor that he never drank in the first place, and to prove it, has taken the temperance pledge!"

"No!" Beyond this exclamation, Miss Lucy was speechless. I thought she was going to fall out of her chair.

"Now that you've solved our mystery, Miss Davish," Miss Halbert said, satisfied with the effect her news had had on our companions, "what now? Thanksgiving with family, I presume?"

"No, I'm off to Illinois for a new engagement, for Sir Arthur Windom-Greene."

I couldn't keep the gratitude and excitement out of my voice and Walter released my hand. I could read the disappointment in his face and regretted it. But I had no choice but to take another position—that's who I am. And I could never refuse Sir Arthur anything. Nor would I doubt him again; he had given me the adventure of a lifetime and was indirectly responsible for my meeting Walter in the first place.

"When Sir Arthur received my news about Mrs. Piers's arrest this morning, he immediately wired back, requesting my services indefinitely," I said. "I'll be here a few more days yet, traveling back and forth between here and Pea Ridge, and then I'll go to Galena. I may be there well past the New Year. He's begun work on a new book."

"Well, that sounds exciting, Hattie," Walter said, attempting to sound enthusiastic. "But less eventful, I hope."

I had to admit, the thought of working with Sir Arthur again and getting caught up in his passion for Civil War history was thrilling. The idea of not spending Christmas alone, but in the presence of Sir Arthur's large and boisterous family, was also tremendously appealing. I was relieved Walter was at least attempting to understand.

"But you do mean Chicago, don't you, dear?" Miss Lizzie said. "I wired him there just a few days ago."

"No, Miss Lizzie," I said. "He's currently doing research on Civil War generals from Galena, including President Grant, so he's rented a house there."

"Now, there was a man in need of some temperance," Miss Lucy said, recovered from her shock over the gossip about George Shulman.

"I hope you mean General Grant, Lucy, dear, and not Arthur."

"Of course, I mean Grant, Lizzie. Arthur's one of us."

"Well, I think we shouldn't be hasty to judge anyone," Miss Lizzie said, "considering the shocking behavior we've witnessed this past week. I believe a pervasive lack of temperance exists, even among the best of us." For several moments, we sat in silence, each contemplating Miss Lizzie's insightful comment. "Well, Hattie, dear, give our best to Arthur. The holidays always remind me of him. I wonder . . ."

"Oh, no, Lizzie, we're not leaving the Springs," her sister said. "Look at this weather." Behind the rain had come a calm morning of blue skies and warm sunshine.

"But think of it, Lucy, Christmas in Illinois."

"Thanksgiving, maybe, but Christmas?" Miss Lucy said. "I'm not trudging through ten-foot snowdrifts, with wet boots that weigh like clothes irons, so you can sing carols through the night with Arthur Windom-Greene again."

Walter looked at me, eyebrows raised. "Again?" his lips read silently. I shrugged. I'd no idea what the sisters were talking about. I couldn't imagine Sir Arthur caroling in any weather. He hated being outdoors, preferring his pipe and a good book to fresh air and a hike.

"It has a romantic ring about it, don't you think, dear? Your dear Oliver loved Christmas at Arthur's that year, don't you remember?"

Miss Lucy glowered at her sister. "Of course, I remember. Those two fools were up all night singing Willis's 'Carol' over and over again. I don't think any of us got any sleep that night." Despite her complaints, a hint of a smile passed Miss Lucy's lips.

"Then we should do it again," Miss Lizzie said. "And it will give us a chance to see how Hattie is getting along. I think I'll write to Arthur this very evening."

"There you go butting in again, Lizzie. I thought we discussed that."

"That's all right, Miss Lucy," I said. "I don't mind."

Walter took my hand again. "Oh, Miss Davish, I think you've proven you don't need anyone checking up on you."

"Unless it's you administrating the checkup, eh, Dr. Grice?" Miss Lucy said.

"You're right about that, Miss Lucy," Walter said, roaring with laughter, and then he kissed me, to my astonishment and the satisfaction of our companions.